NO ONE BUT
Madison
DOREEN ORSINI

ELLORA'S CAVE
ROMANTICA PUBLISHING

What the critics are saying...

❦

"Ms. Orsini's *No One but Madison* is a cautionary tale about the dangerousness of the BDSM world. This story makes me pant in anticipation for Ms. Orsini's next story." ~ *TwoLips Reviews*

"Doreen Orsini's NO ONE BUT MADISON is a thrilling joyride into the wonders of BDSM—both the good and bad sides of the lifestyle. […] I loved every second of this book and hope to see many more like it from Ms. Orsini." ~ *Romance Junkies*

"*No One but Madison* took my breath away and consumed me at the same time. In-your-face intense with the right amount of tenderness, this book set me aflame." ~ *Joyfully Reviewed*

An Ellora's Cave Romantica Publication

www.ellorascave.com

No One But Madison

ISBN 9781419958946
ALL RIGHTS RESERVED.
No One But Madison Copyright © 2008 Doreen Orsini
Edited by Briana St. James.
Cover art by Syneca.

This book printed in the U.S.A. by Jasmine-Jade Enterprises, LLC.

Electronic book Publication November 2008
Trade paperback Publication February 2009

With the exception of quotes used in reviews, this book may not be reproduced or used in whole or in part by any means existing without written permission from the publisher, Ellora's Cave Publishing, Inc.® 1056 Home Avenue, Akron OH 44310-3502.

Warning: The unauthorized reproduction or distribution of this copyrighted work is illegal. Criminal copyright infringement, including infringement without monetary gain, is investigated by the FBI and is punishable by up to 5 years in federal prison and a fine of $250,000. (http://www.fbi.gov/ipr/)

This book is a work of fiction and any resemblance to persons, living or dead, or places, events or locales is purely coincidental. The characters are productions of the author's imagination and used fictitiously.

NO ONE BUT MADISON
ಐ

Dedication

ೞ

To Dora, who lived when women had to hide their erotica in the attic.

Acknowledgements

ೞ

I'd like to thank the wonderful people I met at Paddles NYC and at LILNR for welcoming me, teaching me, and giving me an understanding few possess about the love and trust in true D/s relationships.

Trademarks Acknowledgement

ೞ

The author acknowledges the trademarked status and trademark owners of the following wordmarks mentioned in this work of fiction:

Barbie: Mattel, Inc.

Calgon: Calgon Corporation

Jack Rabbit: California Exotic Novelties LLC

Jacuzzi: Jacuzzi Inc. Corporation

Lucite: Lucite International, Inc.

Lysol: Reckitt Benckiser, Inc.

Macy's Thanksgiving Day Parade: Federated Department Stores, Inc.

National Enquirer: American Media Operations, Inc.

The Oprah Winfrey Show: Harpo, Inc.

Chapter One

ಬ

"You really had me going there, Rob." Madison Garrett peeled off her wig and slapped it down on top of her cousin's gleaming desk.

She swallowed the giggle that tickled her throat when dust billowed out of the matted, gray strands. Sunlight reflected off the Empire State Building and streamed through Rob's office window, casting each dancing mote in a shimmering spotlight.

Ignoring her cousin's scowl, she tilted her head back and twisted it from side to side until a loud crack eased the tension gripping her neck. One more night on a park bench and she'd have to call her chiropractor for some heavy-duty adjustments. Then again, a psychologist would probably be more in order.

Ever since she had entered her cousin's office, she'd avoided the eyes of the man sitting beside her. He hadn't risen, hadn't even acknowledged her presence. But she sure felt his and found herself tensely awaiting, anxiously anticipating this man's attention. Thankfully Rob was too busy swatting away dust particles to notice. Like most, he knew her as a woman who would rather wear a pink, ruffled dress than give any man the upper hand.

While the new VP of *Exposed* continued to ignore her, her gaze darted to his long legs, then to his equally long fingers tapping the arm of his chair. Out of the corner of her eyes, she watched him shift, then cross his legs at the ankles. His shoes creaked as if calling to her, telling her to look. To see that he had big feet. Sneaking a peek at his lap, she accepted that the old "big feet, big dick" saying was true, at least in his case. She led her covert inspection higher, past a chest that could easily engulf any woman, up to a profile that revealed a straight nose, full lips and endless black lashes. Thick, raven hair hung a few inches past the black rawhide thong securing it at the nape of his neck. She always had a weak spot for men with long hair and her fingers itched to untie the rawhide and set that hair free. The tension in her neck returned with a vengeance. The spacious office suddenly felt too small. Too damn hot.

She propped her size-thirteen work boots on the edge of the desk. "So, what's the real assignment? And it better be good. I gave up a comfortable bench to be here. Those bums believe in squatters' rights."

Rob pressed the intercom. "Sandy, get in here with some wipes."

Covering his nose and mouth with a tissue, he grasped the wig between his thumb and index finger. Sandy, Rob's secretary, scurried into the office. Madison watched as the young woman held out a box of anti-bacterial pre-treated towelettes and a shoebox. After Rob whipped out a few of the moist towelettes and dropped the wig in the shoebox, Sandy cast Madison a furtive grin, then scurried out.

"We're not kidding, Maddy," Rob said the moment the door closed. "This story could knock *People* right off the racks! And no one goes undercover better than you."

"True. But the answer's still no." Madison dropped her head back and closed her eyes. Peeking out, she watched Rob's face turn red. It was too damned easy to ruffle his perfectly coifed feathers. She waited while he polished the rich mahogany surface of his desk until it gleamed, returned everything he had removed back to its assigned position, then laid out the contents of a folder exactly as before.

When he finally glanced up, she raised her head. "Since when is it news that I won't fuck for a story?"

Rob glared at her, then turned to the new VP and let out a long, weary sigh. "You'll have to excuse my cousin, Drake. It always takes her awhile to remember her manners whenever she comes in from a job. Apparently she's been hanging out with bums too long."

"Yeah, it takes a few days for the roaches to crawl out from under my lily-white skin." She turned to the man sitting beside her and smirked.

Drake Williams stretched out those long legs and peered at her as if he were trying to see beneath the dirt and grime smeared across her face.

Eyes the color of the midnight blue sky she spent hours staring up at during her endless nights huddled on a park bench held her spellbound.

"I'm telling you, Drake, she works magic when she takes on a role." Rob slapped the desk, but the other man didn't flinch or break eye contact with her.

Her smirk dissolved. "Are you both blind? Look at me."

Both men stared.

She stood up, grabbed the sides of her XXL, stain-covered chinos, pulled them out and slowly spun around. "Mr. Will—"

"Drake," a deep, velvet voice cut in, a voice that made her heart flutter in the strangest way.

Madison swallowed. "Sure. Drake." She cleared her throat and started to back away from the desk. "Ah, listen...I'd love to help out, but I do bums and bag ladies. Once, just once, I tried a waitress in a strip club and—I humbly admit—failed. I don't do sexy. I don't do feminine. And—hello!—I certainly don't do sub!"

"Or slave?"

Halfway to the door, to escaping this ridiculous meeting, she halted. Again, her train of thoughts fragmented at the sound of his voice. "Excuse me?"

"He's chosen a few subs, but mostly he's targeting slaves." Drake's eyes lowered to the eight-by-ten in his hands. "Ones whose Masters failed to protect them."

An image of willowy, meek women in strips of cloth and chains flashed before her eyes. "You're kidding, right? Me? A slave girl? Shit, they'd never let me near Train Me, Chain Me." Out of the corner of her eye, she saw Rob blanch and quickly added, "That is the name. Right?"

Everyone in their family knew how much Rob hated that his mother was Head Mistress of Train Me, Chain Me. The man practically foamed at the mouth if word of Aunt Louisa or her club entered any conversation. Madison and her brothers had constantly ribbed him about it when they were kids and still did when they had him alone. But never in public. Never in front of strangers or his small group of friends.

His mention of the club when he had called her in for this meeting had shocked her. When he added the tantalizing fact that Drake Williams would be present at the meeting, she couldn't refuse. For weeks, Rob had been complaining that the secretaries spent more time ogling the new VP than working. She would never admit it, but she had been dying to meet this so-called hunk. Well, no longer so-called in her book. Rob should consider himself lucky the secretaries only ogled.

She turned to Drake. "How's it abuse if those girls went to Train Me, Chain Me because they like getting beat up?"

Drake rose with a sigh and circled her, his eyes languidly focusing on every inch of her face and body. Her cheeks flushed with heat. Something brushed across her hair. From over her shoulder, that delicious voice slid like warm honey into the ear she could swear she felt lips caressing.

"They go there to surrender themselves to their desires, Miss Garrett. They allow their Masters to bind them and, yes, even punish them because they trust their Masters. Do you know what happens when they are bound and no longer in control? When their morals and insecurities have no hold over them, Miss Garrett?"

"Well…n-no…I…" Madison cleared her throat. She could barely think with the man's breath sweeping over her neck and the heat of his body seeping through the layers of her clothes. Forget the images flashing before her eyes. The petite, willowy slave girls in her previous vision transformed into tall, muscular women who all looked a little too much like her.

"They enter a world of pleasure most people only dream about." His voice lowered and grew huskier with every word. "They have orgasms so powerful they scream or cry, completely losing control of their bodies and minds. And sometimes, Miss Garrett, sometimes the pleasure is so intense…"

Madison felt every word vibrate through her body and converge to that long neglected place between her legs. Seconds passed. She held her breath and wondered how one unfinished sentence could hold her captive, could leave her speechless. Finally she heard him draw in a breath.

"They faint."

Other than some heavy moaning, she had never lost complete control with man or toy. Scream? Cry? Faint? Before she could envy the women he described, before she dropped to her knees and begged him to show her the way to such an orgasm, she reminded herself that these women were merely slaves, pawns at the mercy of depraved men.

"You left out the pain." Her voice, nearly as deep as his, sounded alien to her ears.

"Pain, when administered properly, begets pleasure. A slap might sting for a few seconds, but then heat flares across the skin. Another slap, more heat. Another and a fire erupts."

As if he had slapped her with each word, heat fanned out over her butt. Tempted to ask him to repeat himself, Madison clenched her teeth.

His lips moved closer to her ear. Realizing that the heat on her butt came from his thigh's touch, she told herself to move, but her body insisted on staying put. When he spoke again, he whispered so softly, she had to strain to hear.

"Imagine, Miss Garrett, that fire burning your most sensitive skin."

Her legs trembled beneath the weight of his words. She locked her knees—locked every damn muscle—and held on for dear life. Shit, the man had a way with words. One sentence and she could see herself strapped to a bed while some man—namely the hunky one behind her—had his way with her body. Yeah, she wouldn't mind a few light smacks to her butt. That thought and the images he had branded into her mind made her body ache.

"Imagine your Master soothing that burn with his mouth, his hands."

Her breasts felt as if they would burst through the cloth binding them. Moisture tickled the sensitive skin his words and voice had set aflame. She nearly leaned back into him. Nearly begged him to demonstrate. His next words, said in a voice ice cold with an edge of steel, saved her from that embarrassing move.

"Now, imagine being bound and reaching that line separating pleasurable pain from true pain...you trust the Dom in charge to see it and stop...but he crosses that line, Madison."

Tensing as if they were truly living the fantasy he had unfurled in her mind, Madison drew in a hissing breath.

Drake's voice snatched her from the nightmare that seemed all too real. "Imagine unbearable pain slicing into you over and over until you're hoarse from screaming. And still he goes on. Now the burn is real, Miss Garrett. Now it comes from the whip cutting through your skin, from a cigarette stabbed out in your flesh. Do you think these women asked for that kind of pain? For scars that never fade?"

Madison tried to come up with an answer, but the ice-cold fear encasing her body that only moments ago burned with desire snatched the words from her mind.

He continued his inspection, then ended directly in front of her. For the first time, she felt petite. At five feet nine inches, she rarely had to tilt her head quite so far back to meet a man's gaze.

But his eyes were focused on her body. She inwardly groaned, saw herself through his eyes. Filthy, oversized shirt and pants, men's shoes and haphazardly pinned hair. She closed her eyes and cursed Rob for calling her in on such short notice.

"I'm sorry," Drake murmured. His finger traced the jagged scar on her cheek. "I imagine you understand more than either Rob or me just what those women went through."

"Well, actually," she hesitated, touching the dollar-store scar, amazed that it felt so real, that she could still feel the heat of his touch, "it's not—"

He leaned forward slightly, scattering her thoughts.

Sniffed.

Wrinkled his nose.

"Sorry if I smell." She spilled every ounce of sarcasm she could into her voice. "Unlike your cozy, air-conditioned office, it's ninety degrees outside."

"She's right, Rob. We'll have to find someone else."

"Like hell." Rob scowled at her.

Madison scowled right back. "What is this, Rob? Payback for screwing with your head when we were kids? Or for being a bigger man than you, then and now?"

"Listen to her." Drake shook his head and folded his arms across his chest. "She's got too big a mouth."

Big mouth? Snorting, she wondered if he actually thought he was the first to tell her that. She opened her mouth, her usual witty retort prepared long ago. Memorized. Said too many times to too many men.

Forgotten the moment his eyes raked her from head to toe.

"No offense, Miss Garrett, but we need someone hot enough to seduce the Masters of Train Me, Chain Me."

His words hurt more than they should have, considering she knew he had no idea what lay beneath her disguise. She crossed her arms over her bound breasts and gave him the once over. As she took in the sweet sight before her, she had to remind herself that this counter inspection had to insult him the way he had insulted her.

She met his gaze. Again those midnight blue eyes captured her, held her prisoner. Pinching the side of her thigh, she broke free. With a snort, she raised her chin and stared down her nose at him. "Like the Mistresses would want you?"

"Take off the guise, Maddy." Rob demanded, rising from his chair. "Now."

"It won't make a damn difference, Rob. I'm not sub or slave material."

Her body trembled. Sweat trickled down between her breasts when she thought of baring herself in front of some strange man who loved to take charge. It may have fed a few late-night fantasies, but she doubted she had the personality or guts to do it in reality. Not even for a story that might catapult her to Geraldo Rivera status. How could she bare her butt and let some man slap it until she screamed? Or worse...came.

She suddenly saw herself draped over Drake Williams' lap and moaning with pleasure as he spanked her. Blood rose to her cheeks.

Recalling the young, sexy reporter they had just hired, she snapped her fingers. "Call in Sherry Thornton. Now there's a sex slave. Shit, even Rob drools when he sees her!"

Rob's face scrunched up the way it did when they were kids and she would try to goad him into joining her at the top of the cherry tree in their grandfather's yard. "Sherry Thornton? The woman looks like a Barbie doll. Probably has less brains than one."

She barely knew Sherry, yet she felt she had to defend her, defend all those bimbos who made the likes of her look like men in drag. "Hey, it takes brains to get into those fashion shows. And didn't she pose as a model and uncover that some designer, LePulcen or something, used polyester in his gowns?"

"Dammit, Maddy." Rob slapped the desktop.

"No, really, Rob." Her heart beat at a frightening rate. She couldn't do this. It was too frightening. Too damn enticing. "Take Sherry off that ridiculous 'Bra Slasher' story. No man can resist her." She turned to Drake. "I'm telling you. That Master won't know what hit him."

"Well, she has the look, but," Drake chuckled, "the woman freaks if a man so much as bumps into her."

"She does?" Madison grinned, walking back to the desk. "Well, maybe this is just what she needs." Feeling comfortable for the first time since she had entered Rob's office, she leaned her hip against the edge of the desk. "So we have to find someone with the look and the guts."

"For Chrissakes, Maddy!" Rob leaned forward and pushed her away from his desk. "Why do you think I called you in?"

Drake cleared his throat. "We need the look, Rob."

Rob glared at her. "Cousin or not, I'll fire you in a New York minute if you don't take off that goddamn, filthy disguise."

"Fine." Cursing under her breath, she kicked off her shoes, then dragged her shirt over her head and slammed it down onto his desk.

Eight by ten glossies flew off it. Rob crawled around on his hands and knees and blew dust off each picture he retrieved. Her pants, padded leggings and tunic, one dingy sock and a pair of boxers followed. More pictures rose up, then floated down around her cousin. Gritting her teeth against the curses flitting through her mind, she rested her hands on her hips.

"Son of a bitch," Drake whispered, backing up a few steps.

Madison didn't move as his eyes took in every curve her leotard hugged then moved on to explore every inch of exposed skin on her slender arms and legs.

He returned to the chair beside Rob's desk, his gaze fixed on her face. "I'm still not convinced she's got what it takes to bait our abuser."

"You haven't seen enough. Maddy, you know damn well I meant the whole disguise."

Turning the burning insult of Drake's words on her cousin, she yelled, "Get your rocks off with one of your boyfriends, Rob, before I send the three bears after you."

"Three bears?" Drake asked, his lips quirking up for a second.

Rob turned toward Drake. "Her sick brothers," he answered, then narrowed his eyes at Madison. "Don't forget, Maddy, legally they have to stay at least five-hundred feet away from me."

"Since when does anyone in our family follow the law?" She hated reminding Rob of his humiliating beating at the hands of her overprotective brothers when he had sent her undercover and some druggie sent her to the hospital, but she wanted out of the office and out of Drake William's line of vision.

The man's muscles strained against his suit and Madison hadn't touched a man in, well, she couldn't even remember how long. Spending weeks at a time in a park dressed as a bum or bag lady had a way of throwing a wrench in a gal's social life. She had thought her trusty vibrators had fulfilled her. Obviously—judging by the way her mind kept imagining how Drake's muscles would feel covered with nothing but skin—her toy collection had failed to satisfy her need for a living, breathing, hot-blooded male.

She stared Rob down, praying he would see the plea in her eyes. She didn't want this job. Something about it intrigued her so much, it scared her.

"The rest, Mad. Get in the bathroom and clean up." Rob shuffled the pile of pictures on his desk until they all lined up perfectly. He pressed the intercom. "Sandy. More wipes. Sandy! Where the hell is she?"

Madison reached up to touch the fake scar. "Dammit, this makeup took two hours to apply. Why can't you just find someone else for this job?"

In a way only she would understand, Rob tapped the name of the club scrawled across the folder. "No one else will do it and for some reason—one I'm hoping you'll uncover—the cops are turning a blind eye. You either take the job, Maddy, or you're out."

"Some cousin. Why don't you just sell me to an Asian slave trader?"

As she slammed the door, she couldn't help but smile when she heard him mutter, "I would, if I thought they had a chance in hell of subduing you long enough to get you out of the country."

When she returned a half hour later with the white strip of cloth that had bound her breasts twined between her fingers and her waist-length red hair brushed to a lustrous shine, she knew she looked good enough to catch even a Master's eye. Her brown contacts no longer hid her green eyes. She had removed the fake scar and scrubbed her face clean of all blemishes, revealing a creamy complexion her friends envied.

Giving in to the feminine side she usually ignored, she had even applied a little mascara and lip gloss. She felt downright smug watching Drake Williams shift uncomfortably in his chair as he gaped at her face.

Turning away, he stated in a voice that brooked no argument, "She'll never pull it off."

"W-w-what?" She sputtered like a fool.

Flabbergasted and more than a little offended, she drew in a deep breath to argue, then grinned when his eyes widened at the sight of her more than ample breasts rising up and out in his direction. She sucked in more air, then let it out with an exaggerated sigh, aware that her nipples stretched the thin spandex of her leotard. Crossing her arms under her breasts so her already impressive cleavage rose even higher and nearly spilled over the neckline, she tilted her head down to catch his eye and purred, "Oh, I think I can seduce the Masters in Train Me, don't you, Drake?"

Drake glanced up at her face. His lips parted as if he was going to speak, but then his gaze lowered and remained fixed on her chest.

Needing to get some of her pride and power back, she rolled her eyes and muttered, "Oh, please. Now get your eyes off my breasts and find someone else for this job."

He blinked, then glanced up and held her captive with a predatory stare. His eyes narrowed. His lips thinned. He rose from his chair and crossed the room in two long strides.

"Apologize."

Madison stiffened. "Excuse me?"

Drake took a step closer. "Apologize. Now."

"Or what?" She drew up her shoulders. "You can't fire me. My aunt owns this magazine and—"

He stepped closer. Looming over her, his face taut, he repeated his demand through clenched teeth. "Apologize. Now."

Her heart stuttered, shocking her almost as much as his order. Her reputation as a hard-ass always preceded her at the magazine and, while it killed the prospect of ever dating a fellow employee, it kept the men from pulling this chauvinistic crap. They usually scattered like scared sheep in the path of a wolf when she stepped off the elevator.

He whispered in a voice filled with menace, "Apologize."

Every muscle in Madison's body trembled with the need to escape, but she held her ground. "Back off, Williams, before I crush the family jewels."

"Maddy!" Rob stood up. "What the hell has gotten into you?"

"And that, my sweet, is why you'll never pull this off." He grasped her chin between his fingers and tilted her face up until his breath flowed over her lips. His expression softened. Smiling, he murmured, "You're too damn tough to pass for a sub, much less a sweet slave."

Yanking her chin free, she poked her finger into his chest. "You're damn right I'm tough. But I'm also the best investigative reporter you've got." She tossed her head, rolled her shoulders, took a deep breath, then blew it out into his face. "Okay, now I'm ready. Try me, again."

Drake transformed. His eyes hardened. His lips thinned. "Apologize, *slave*."

"Oh, now he adds slave," she muttered before lowering her head. She whispered in a contrite voice that usually had her three burly brothers falling all over themselves to please her, "I'm sorry."

"I'm sorry, *Master*. And look at me when you say it."

Everything in her revolted against the domineering tone of his voice, but she tilted her face up and repeated his words. "I'm sorry, *Master*."

"You just failed, my sweet slave."

"What?" Madison cringed at the husky tone of her voice. After all the wimps she had dated, facing a man with Drake's power sent her hormones into overdrive. Giving in to him and calling him Master only succeeded in reawakening the image of him spanking her bare butt. Sweet slave should have sent another curse to her lips. Instead, she felt her nipples harden until they hurt.

"Oh, you used the right words, but your eyes were filled with defiance. No sub defies her Master. It's through his pleasure in her submission that she gets her own."

"Really? And you would know this because?"

He answered with the slightest smile. "Why don't *you* tell me how I would know?"

Trapped in his gaze, she struggled to grasp what he obviously thought she already knew. When his meaning hit home, it hit her right between the legs.

"Yeah, right. You moonlight as a Master." Her voice sounded deeper than she had ever recalled hearing it and bore none of the mockery she had intended.

Drake, a Master? Drake spanking the bare butt of some woman, making her scream? Making her faint? Madison blinked. Swallowed what little saliva remained in her mouth.

"You're a lot smarter than you act," he whispered, so low she doubted Rob heard his admission.

She had no idea how long they stood staring at each other, him invading her space while she trembled deep within from the wicked images filling her overheated mind. When his gaze lowered to her mouth, she moistened the lips too many hot days spent on the park bench had chapped. He glanced up. She watched pupils flare in eyes that now burned with unhidden desire.

She slid her tongue back into her mouth. With every breath he took, his suit skimmed her nipples. Instead of hunching her shoulders and drawing her chest away, she could not stop herself from leaning forward until Rob's voice broke the spell ensnaring her.

"Ahem, well, we'd better come up with something. It won't be long before someone else reveals that a Master there is ignoring safe words."

Drake frowned down at Madison a moment before turning on his heel and striding to Rob's desk. He gathered up the pictures and tossed them into the garbage. "Forget it. This assignment is off the table. She won't work."

Madison balled her fists. Every foul name she knew rose to her lips, but when she moved closer, her heart lurched.

Rage twisted Drake Williams' face as he leaned over Rob's desk. "You're sick, Rob. How can you even consider putting your own cousin in that place?" He glanced over his shoulder at her, his gaze landing on her fists. "Look at her, goddamit. Someone in that club is sending women who know how to act to the hospital. He'll have a field day beating that superior attitude out of her. She'll never survive. We'll just have to wait until one of the injured women comes forward."

Rob retrieved the pictures from the garbage and held them up. "And admits to the world that she even goes to that place? That she asked to be whipped? If it wasn't for the nurse in the emergency room tipping me off, we never would have known about it until he went too far and killed one. Be real, Drake, getting Maddy in there is our only chance."

"This meeting is over." Drake strode to the door.

"Maddy, please." Rob shoved the pictures toward her. "If one of those girls gets killed, all the news stations and papers will be in on this."

An unspoken plea in his statement, one she didn't miss, filled her with guilt. Revealing and exposing an abusive Master in *Exposed* might get Mistress Louisa's name in the news, but it would end there. Connect an unsolved murder to her club and name? The journalists would be falling all over each other in an attempt to uncover more and more about the club and its owner. She knew what Rob feared. The son of Madam Louisa exposed.

She took the pictures from his trembling hand, looked down at the first one. Bile filled her mouth. Blood dripped from slashes covering a young woman's buttocks. She flipped to the next. Cigarette burns pockmarked bruised breasts. Dropping it on the floor, she looked at the next and gasped. Bleeding welts covered a woman's back, buttocks and thighs. The next few revealed faces so swollen, she couldn't even tell they belonged to women.

So much blood.

So much pain.

Tears blurred her vision, but she saw their eyes. Eyes filled with shock, confusion and shame. Before she could think too much about it, before she even knew what her words would entail, she blurted out, "Train me."

* * * * *

Ten minutes later, trapped in the elevator with her, Drake understood just how Madison Garrett had managed to succeed where other reporters had failed. The woman didn't know the meaning of the word "no". While he couldn't help but admire her determination, she was the type of woman he normally steered clear of. The need to dominate her, to seduce her into his world, would eventually grow beyond his control.

The beauty of owning a slave—a strong, willful slave—came from her surrendering her power willingly to her Master. The more power she had to offer, the larger the gift. Drake had a vision of Madison purring as she relinquished her power to him, like a she-cat dropping to her knees for the male mounting her.

According to Rob, Madison courted danger and shunned any man who thought she couldn't take care of herself. Drake's place in the world of domination stemmed from a need to protect women, one forged too many years ago to ignore. Madison might purr as he mounted her, but she would claw and bite at any restraints meant to keep her safe. "Ten minutes ago, you didn't even want this assignment."

She stood with her fists on her hips, making those luscious breasts taunt him. "Ten minutes ago, you said I couldn't do it. No one tells me what I can or cannot do."

The desire to silence that big mouth with a kiss that would convince her he was the man capable of doing just that—at least when it came to sex—hit him so fast and hard he realized he had to end this argument before it was too late, before he put her over his knee. Before he found himself facing a sexual harassment charge. "Look, I wasn't putting you down. You don't have to prove anything to your cousin or me."

"I could give a flying fuck what you or Rob think of me. I'm doing this for those girls. I want to plaster the face of this sick bastard and his victims' wounds all over the cover of *Exposed*." Madison's eyes flashed with anger.

"You go in there and you can add your picture to that file." She was tall, tough and used to succeeding, but he knew she would fail. And failing this assignment could wipe that fire from her eyes, a fire he found way too appealing.

"All I need is a little training. God, do you think I go into these assignments blind? I research and train, then research and train some more until I can't even tell the difference between me and my role."

Every time she said "train", he saw her bound to his bed, his crossbar, his spanking bench. "For the last time, forget it. You're untrainable."

"You don't think I'm sexy enough." She pressed her fingers over his mouth before he could respond to such a ridiculous claim. "I'll give you every name of every guy I've slept with. Call them and ask how I handled them in bed. They begged me for more!"

Drake wrapped his hand around her wrist and drew her fingers away from his mouth before he gave in to temptation and tasted them. He would have preferred wrapping both his hands around the necks of the men stupid enough to beg this spitfire. She deserved a man who left *her* begging, then returned and took her sweet body again and again, until she had not an ounce of energy left to do anything more than breathe.

She needed a Master.

A Master who would sate her but still manage to leave the she-cat that dwelt within her alive.

A Master who would enslave her body but not her soul.

A Master like him.

"Forget it. I'm not training you and this assignment stays off the table." He stepped around her and waited for the elevator to reach his floor. As soon as he could, he would hire a private investigator, one he could trust to be discreet. Too many people at Train Me, Chain Me would have their lives ruined if word of their involvement there hit the news.

"Mistress Louisa has a beginner's night at her private club."

Her soft voice saying those words wrapped around his cock and squeezed. He blinked until the image of her body spread-eagled on Mistress Louisa's new St. Andrews Cross vanished. Turning to face her, he studied the flushed, determined woman. "Not many people know Mistress Louisa's private club exists."

"Apparently you do." She angled her chin at him.

"Yes, I do. And I also know she's very picky about who she allows into her training sessions."

"She'll let *me* in." Madison's mouth curved into a lopsided grin.

"And why would she do that, if you don't mind me asking?" Drake watched in shock as Madison leaned across him and slammed the emergency stop button just before the doors opened.

She leaned back against the panel, a defiant look on her face.

He arched a brow.

Madison snorted, crossed her arms over her chest and smirked. "That, Mr. Williams, is none of your business. One phone call and she'll get one of her Masters to train me. Her best."

His cock came to attention. Mistress Louisa owed him quite a few favors. The idea of Madison dressed in nothing but his collar and following his every command slammed into him, giving him an erection more painful than any of his nights with one of Mistress Louisa's subs had inspired.

But the image of her pleading for mercy while some nut took pleasure in whipping her until she passed out succeeded in shrinking him down faster than an ice cold shower. Placing his hands on either side of her shoulders, he leaned in until her warm breath flowed into his mouth. "We're talking sex, Madison. Hardcore sex. Subs do anything their Masters want. You'll be expected to take the Master and any toy he picks any way and any*where* he desires. And if he so much as thinks you hesitate in following his commands—even if it's just in his mind—you'll be punished. Spanked. Whipped. Flogged."

When her eyes darkened and she stuck her chin up, he reached down and slid his hand between her thighs. Cupping her, he pressed his palm into the drenched crotch of her leotard. He steeled himself against the surge of blood that filled his engorged cock upon his discovery. Realizing what it revealed about Madison's desires, he added through clenched teeth, "Something tells me the Master at Louisa's will have you screaming when you come."

Not surprised when she held her ground and glared into his eyes, he gently slid his fingers back and forth over the slick outline of her crease and the nubbin that seemed to rise for his touch. Her eyes closed. A small whimper escaped through her parted lips.

"Oh, yes, you'll enjoy every minute, my sweet." He brought his lips to the whorl of her ear and whispered, "But step into Train Me, Chain Me, and you'll find yourself screaming until you're hoarse while another flays every inch of skin from your back."

Beneath his palm, those swollen, trembling lips flared. He thought he heard her purr. "You're definitely a she-cat worth taking," he added, bringing his damp palm to her cheek. Madison's face tilted forward. He spread her juices over her parted lips, then growled when her tongue darted out and flicked the tip of his finger. Reminding himself that he had meant to scare her off, he pressed his erection into her stomach. "Listen to me, dammit. This isn't some candy-assed assignment. This could kill you."

Slender hands with more strength than he expected shoved against his chest.

"Candy-assed? Is that what you think I go for? Candy-assed jobs?" She poked her finger into his chest with each word. "I walked into a shelter where they were killing bums and selling their identities to illegal aliens. I was bait for the teens setting fire to the bag ladies last summer. And I just spent the last five nights sleeping on a bench in the middle of Central Park. And pain?" Her eyes glittered with anger. "You try getting the crap kicked out of you by a bunch of drug addicts because you made the mistake of sleeping on their stoop. You try staying in your role and not screaming your head off while you feel every rib crack."

She slid her arms out of her leotard, then yanked it down. Drake drew in a sharp breath at the sight of her pale heaving breasts. Before he could react or swallow the saliva flooding his mouth, she shoved the leotard lower and revealed a three-inch scar beside her bellybutton.

"Who the hell did that?"

Madison drew her leotard up over her breasts then shoved her arms in the short sleeves. "Can you take a knife in the gut and lie in your own blood until it's safe to break cover and scream your head off?" She reached behind her back and yanked out the emergency stop button. "I'm doing this with or without the approval of the magazine or you, Mr. Williams."

The elevator stopped. Before she could rush through the doors, Drake grabbed her arm and spun her around. "Listen to me. With most subs, even while they're pulling against the ropes and crying their eyes out, we know if they managed to free themselves, they'd beg us to re-shackle them. But you'll go in there and no matter how much you train, no matter how meek you act, you'll reek of the power you feel you have over your Master. Do you have any idea how that will affect the one abusing subs? What he'll do?"

Before he could open his mouth to answer his own question, Madison had his balls clenched painfully in her fist.

"I'm perfectly capable of taking any man down, Mr. Williams."

"Grabbing a man by the balls proves nothing," he hissed between his teeth just before she brought him to his knees with one quick twist of her wrist.

"No?" She drew up her shoulders and smirked. "I think I've made my point, Mr. Williams. As you can see, I can take care of myself."

"Not if you're in chains." He struggled to catch a breath as she slipped through the doors a moment before they slammed shut.

Chapter Two

Madison drew in a deep breath as she followed Aunt Louisa down the steps into her private dungeon. Gothic torches lit with electricity lined flagstone walls. As much as she loved her aunt and accepted her, she had never entered Train Me, Chain Me or her private club, Sweet Submissions. "Cool, Aunt Louisa. I especially like the gilt-framed mirrors."

Aunt Louisa fluttered her fingers over her shoulder at the floor-to-ceiling mirrors. "It cost me a fortune. Train Me was decorated much like every other club. Drab concrete walls. Black leather and wood. Nothing sensual, nothing to soften the setting. I wanted Sweet Submissions to break the mold."

Used to seeing her aunt in sweats and sneakers, she couldn't stop staring at the long, slender legs peeking out from the black leather micro-mini or the luscious swells of her breasts rising above a studded bustier. It always amazed Madison that this woman and her mother once slept side by side in her grandmother's womb. Alike in every physical way, her mother and her aunt had nothing in common except their parents and looks.

Dropping her gaze to the five-inch, metal-tipped spike heels striking the marble floor before her, she bit her lip. While her stomach churned at the thought of her upcoming training session, she had to admit that part of her looked forward to exploring this new frontier. She glanced down at her body and wondered how she would look in leather and heels, doubted for the first time whether she could slide comfortably into a role and carry off the required disguise. Self-defense classes and a lifetime of wrestling with the three bears had left her more muscular than svelte.

Drake was right. She was as tough as they come. Growing up with three overbearing brothers, spending most of her youth with her head in their palms while she swung out at their massive bodies and hit nothing but air had hardened her body and soul. By the time she reached her teens, she had learned how to outfight, outsmart and outcurse not only them, but also any man stupid enough to think God had made him the master of their species.

Yet, deep down inside, she hated the kind of men she attracted. Too many of them allowed her to rule the relationship in and out of the bedroom. Her last boyfriend had put her up on that dreaded pedestal and bent over backward catering to her every whim, going so far as to ask her every few seconds exactly where she wanted his mouth and hands and what they should do and with how much pressure. As with all the others, she had grown bored and kicked him out on his soft ass. That had been a year ago and her battery budget to keep her Jack Rabbit buzzing had grown with each month.

Madison heard a yelp from behind one of the doors they passed and considered spinning on her heels and bolting. "Why did you open this place, Aunt Louisa? Why didn't you just set up a private area at Train Me, Chain Me?"

"I sold that place last year. The new owner is paying me a nice monthly stipend to keep my mouth shut and my name on the door."

The crack of a whip came from behind another door and sent a chill down Madison's spine. "Why did you sell? Because of Rob?"

"Rob? He doesn't even know I sold." Aunt Louisa halted so suddenly, Madison nearly slammed into her. "And he won't hear about it from you. What's said between Louisa and Madison stays between Louisa and Madison."

"As always." Madison grinned.

The day after she had lost her virginity, needing to vent about the disappointing encounter with her high school crush, Madison had gone straight to her favorite aunt. After bawling, drinking and then puking her brains out, she had been relieved to hear her aunt say those words. A bond had formed between them that night. A bond stronger than any she had with anyone, even her brothers. Never feeling close or comfortable with her mother, Madison had quickly fallen into the habit of running to Aunt Louisa for help, advice or just a relaxing night of wine and wicked confessions.

Aunt Louisa now had enough dirt on Madison to make her parents disown her. And if she spilled just a quarter of Madison's secrets, the three bears would be combing the city for the poor men whose teenage memories included their precious sister in numerous compromising positions. "My lips are sealed. But wouldn't the sale of Train Me please Rob?"

"Sweetheart, nothing I do will please that man. I swear the doctors switched babies in the hospital." She resumed the long trek down the hall. "The year before I sold Train Me, I was audited by the IRS, called in to Mayor Bloomberg's office nearly every month and investigated by the Board of Health. Thank the powers that be, I had at least a few clients working in those offices, or Train Me would have been shut down. I know Rob had a hand in it all. He's been trying to shut me down for years."

Madison touched her arm. "I didn't know. I mean, I knew how he felt, but I didn't know he'd been harassing you like that."

A flash of sadness crossed her aunt's face. "Imagine. My only son."

"Oh, Aunt Louisa, I'm so sorry."

Her aunt patted her hand. "Well, I got more money than I would have made before retiring. It's perfect, actually. Let Rob go after the new owner of Train Me. That man has more connections than I do." Her aunt winked. "Only a select few know about Sweet Submissions. Now, about your training.

You'll wear a collar—my Collar of Protection—and nothing more. And you'll have two Masters, so to speak, Master D and his..."

Madison wondered if the woman had somehow delved into her fantasy the night before. She had pictured herself tied spread-eagle to her bed with nothing on but a velvet choker while Drake Williams slammed the impressive cock she'd felt in the elevator deep into her. She had nearly broken her precious rabbit. When she had finally come and failed to utter so much as a whimper, much less scream or cry or faint, she had flung her favorite electric boyfriend across the room in disgust.

Suddenly she stopped in her tracks. "Excuse me? Did you just say two? As in men?"

Louisa stopped outside a door at the end of the hall. "Haven't you been listening, Maddy? This is a trainer's night."

"Well, yeah, but I thought it meant I would be trained by a Master. One Master."

Her aunt shook her head. "Maddy, I'm a Mistress. The best according to those who know. People may be born dominant, but they need training if they wish to become good Mistresses and Masters. So they come to me. Trainer's night is just that. I always have an experienced Master or Mistress train a new one."

Madison's stomach rolled. "Two."

Aunt Louisa chucked her under the chin. "Don't look so worried. The Master in charge tonight is well aware that you are also in training."

Swallowing the lump lodged in her throat, she said in a voice that sounded too whiney to be her own. "I thought you would train me."

"Madison, you need to learn from a man. While our lifestyles and expectations of our subs are similar, there are differences between Mistresses and their subs and Masters and their subs."

"B-but, I thought *you* would tell me how to act submissive, Aunt Louisa, before I met with a Master." Madison rubbed her damp palms up and down her jean-clad thighs. "I thought we'd talk first. Maybe you could let me peek in on some couples."

"Sweetie, you won't learn anything about submission from me. You read those emails I sent you, didn't you?"

"I thought we'd go over it all tonight."

Aunt Louisa arched her right eyebrow. That one raised eyebrow propelled Madison back to her youth. If Madison ever disappointed her aunt, if she ever disrespected her mother, that eyebrow would rise.

"I read a little. Maybe I should go back and read some more."

Aunt Louisa's eyebrow rose even higher.

Madison rubbed the back of her neck. "Isn't there some way to do this without, well, without my training under some strangers?"

"After what you told me is going on, I couldn't possibly send you into that place without the proper training. Your mother would kill me." Aunt Louisa opened the door and motioned her in.

"She'd kill you if she knew you even let me in here." Madison gasped as she entered the room. "Some dungeon!"

"Actually this is my special room. Master D insisted on it." Aunt Louisa beamed. "You, my dear niece, have not only the best room in Sweet Submissions, but also the most sought after Master in the city."

Madison didn't know about this Master D, but the room fulfilled her darkest fantasies. Red satin lined a long bench in front of one of the mirrored walls. A king-size four-poster bed covered with satin sheets that matched the bench took up a large portion of the room. Somewhere incense burned. She sniffed but couldn't figure out what sweet scent tickled the hairs inside her nose.

"It's not your usual dungeon. Definitely not for the harsher Doms or Dommes."

Madison nodded, taking note of the subtle touches that created an almost safe atmosphere. Beside another mirrored wall stood a black marble table that looked like a sacrificial altar.

Her fantasies screeched to a halt.

"Um...Aunt Louisa?"

Aunt Louisa continued from behind her. "And this is brand new. Your Masters will be the first to use it."

Apprehension trickled down Madison's spine and an edge of excitement fluttered between her legs when she turned and saw a large marble X in the center of the room. Velvet-lined black leather manacles hung from the four ends. She noticed similar manacles on the bedposts and hanging from the legs of the altar. Turning, she wondered how she hadn't noticed the sets of manacles on the bench, or hanging from gadgets protruding from the walls, the ceiling, the door and — dear God — inside a small cage in the corner. Her mouth went dry. "Two Masters. B-but you're the boss here. Couldn't you get *one* really nice guy to train me?"

"You'll be dealing with quite a few Masters at Train Me before you catch the abuser, Maddy." Walking toward the X, Aunt Louisa fondled the inside of one of the manacles. "And as for the Master in charge tonight, he's as strict as they come, but I've never had a complaint. Don't ask me how word got out that I had a non-submissive coming in to be trained — I certainly never said a word — but my Masters nearly killed each other to run this session. And being the good businesswoman that I am, when my most requested one demanded the right and offered twice as much as my highest bidder, I gave in."

"You let them bid on me?" Madison voice cracked. Knowing her aunt, she had let it slip that a newbie needed training.

"Oh, Maddy. Don't be so naïve. This is a business, after all." Aunt Louisa glanced at her slender diamond watch. "We're running late. Hair up."

Madison held her hair up while her aunt buckled a cold leather collar around her neck. Dropping her hair, she turned around and began to undress. "You could have tried being a good aunt and picked the meekest Master instead of the richest."

"Now, sweetie, you haven't been listening to your mother. I am definitely not a good aunt. Don't worry. I've known Master D for years and, to tell you the truth, I'd chosen him before he even requested the honor of being your Master. Believe me, Maddy, Master D's a pussycat compared to some of the Masters at Train Me."

"Master D. How original." Blushing uncontrollably, Madison reached for her thong. She may have bared her soul to her aunt, but never her body. "Must I take this off? I shave and, well, I feel a little, um, exposed." She peeked under the black satin. "Shit, I have nubs. I never thought you'd throw me to the lions so soon."

"Knowing Master D, if those nubs are too long, he'll call for a razor and my special edible shaving cream within the first five minutes of your session."

"Damn." Those words blinded her, blurred the room and her aunt. A tiny pulse fluttered against the crotch of her thong. Suddenly she saw herself sprawled on her back with her legs held apart by one leather-clad hunk while another slid a razor through the shaving cream covering her mound. She could almost feel the cool blades scraping over her skin. Her aunt's voice brought the room back into focus just as one of the hunks leaned in for a taste.

"Now, Master D left orders that you wear nothing but your collar. You mustn't do anything you don't want to, but I wouldn't advise starting the session out on the wrong foot." Aunt Louisa glanced meaningfully down at the thong.

Madison shifted uncomfortably. "But I can say no."

Her aunt sighed. "Since you're new to this scene, I negotiated the contract with Master D. I never thought you'd have a problem removing a slip of material that hardly hides anything anyway."

Madison crossed her arms over her chest. "You said I can say no."

Aunt Louisa raised her brow.

When Madison still didn't move to take off her thong, her aunt raised that brow higher. "Have it your way."

She led her to the center of the room and positioned her so that her hands were clasped behind her back. "Spread your legs."

Madison shifted her feet farther apart.

"More."

Following her aunt's prodding, she continued to shift her legs farther and farther apart until she felt as if she would topple over if someone so much as tapped her shoulder.

"Good. Now don't move. And head down. At least he'll find you in the proper position."

"This isn't *too* humiliating."

"It's supposed to be, dear." Aunt Louisa walked to the door.

Madison groaned. "Thank God Drake Williams didn't take me up on my request that he train me."

Aunt Louisa paused in the doorway. "What did you say?"

"Nothing. Just this arrogant jerk I work for supposedly does this sort of thing in his spare time." Madison rolled her shoulders. "Is this going to take long?"

Her aunt continued to frown at her, then shrugged and blew her a kiss. "Where tonight leads is entirely up to you, Maddy. Just pick a safe word and remember it. That's how subs control their Masters."

Before Madison could reply, her aunt swept out of the room. She stared at the closed door. Any second this Master D would walk in and see more of her than any stranger had a right to.

Seconds turned into minutes. Although the room had felt warm when she'd entered it, she could feel a cool draft caressing her skin. The sweet smell of the incense seemed stronger. Her nose itched, taunting her, tempting her to release her hands and scratch it. Her shoulders started to ache. Deciding she would have enough time to get back into position once she saw the doorknob turn, she dropped her arms to her side and brought her feet closer together. At first, she avoided looking at her reflection. Not easy, considering mirrors surrounded her on all sides. After a while, she scurried up to one and scrutinized every bare inch of her body.

Other than the pink scar beside her bellybutton and the one on her back, she looked, well, damned sexy. A diamond-shaped, silver tag with an "L" engraved in the middle hung from a metal ring in the center of her collar. When she moved, the cold tag tapped the hollow of her collarbone. "What the hell is this? A dog tag?"

Muffled voices from outside the door sent her running back to where Aunt Louisa had left her standing. Ticking off seconds with each pound of her heart, she stared at the door until her eyes stung.

No one entered. Bringing her feet close together again and crossing her arms over her breasts, she continued to wait in nothing more than her collar and her thong for what felt like hours.

By the time one of the mirrored panels beside the door opened, she was cold and ready to rip a hole in whoever had made her wait. Her anger died a sudden death when two gods stepped into the room. Black masks with holes for their eyes, nose and mouth hid their faces, but the black leather pants that someone had to have sewn them in enhanced their muscular legs and massive erections. Tearing her eyes away from those sweet ridges, she took in their bare torsos. Just looking at their broad, solid chests made her mouth water. Jack Rabbit move over, she just might enjoy this.

She watched the taller of the two whisper something to the other before sitting on the satin bench. Leaning down, he picked up a long, slender, stiff thingamajig she hadn't noticed. A leather band with a flat silver teardrop dangling from a loop encircled the biceps bulging on his right arm. As he pointed with the stick to her thong, the leather band creaked from the strain of his biceps flexing.

The other man nodded, then crossed his arms. "Master D wants you to take off your thong. You have already disobeyed him by not following his instructions and standing in the prescribed position. He will let that pass, but the thong must go and you will be punished for not removing it before his arrival."

"Listen, I'd really prefer to do this with my thong on." Madison turned to Master D. She vaguely wondered why the other Master chose that moment to bow. "Mistress Louisa said—hey!"

The bowing Master shoved his shoulder into her stomach and hoisted her up. Air whooshed out of her lungs, her face slammed into his back. Before she could catch a breath, he dropped her, stomach first, onto Master D's lap.

"Slaves do not talk unless they are asked a question. Before Master D carries out your punishment, you must pick a safe word," the Master with no name stated as if he were reciting the rules of a board game.

"Safe word?" Madison asked on a wheeze, still trying to recapture some of the air she had lost when she was tossed onto Master D's lap and her stomach hit his hard thighs.

"A word that will tell us you want the session to stop."

"Oh. Right."

She wondered if she could stop it now, but damn, the silent man pinning her to his lap with his hands on her back and butt would not stop rubbing her skin with his thumbs. Rough thumbs she imagined rubbing her in all the right places.

"Hmm. A safe word, huh? Tomato? No. Wait. How about fuck off?" Madison giggled, trying to ignore the hard ridge pressing into her stomach. Her giggle evolved into a yelp when a hand landed on her butt with stinging force. "Ow! What the hell?"

The sting of another slap, though slight, had a frightening effect. Wriggling against the arm holding her over the Master's lap and the pleasurable heat seeping under her skin where she had been spanked, she cried, "Fine! Tomato. Geez, you don't have to be so—"

Before she could say anything else, another smack resounded on her other cheek. Her butt really started to burn and tingle, now. She craned her head and watched in horror and anticipation as his hand swung down again. On impact, her legs flew up. The Master-in-training promptly brought them down and held them apart. Shame swept over her, heating her already burning skin when she imagined him staring at the sheer crotch of her thong.

Again that hand landed with a stinging blow, this time lower, grazing her pussy. Gritting her teeth against the pain and strange tingling of pleasure, she held her screams in. After only two more, she started groaning and moaning and begging him to stop.

"Your silence will end this sooner than your worthless pleas, slave," the trainee holding her flailing legs muttered.

Madison bit down on her lip. Each time she thought her punishment had finally come to an end, another exquisite slap sent heat flowing over her cheeks and down to her aching clit. By the time Master D stopped, she could feel her juices ooze down her thighs. Her face burned with shame when she felt his finger slide under her thong, trail down the crack of her butt, then skim across her wet flesh. The tightening grip and heavy breathing of the trainee reminded her that he was watching. Could he see her lips flutter? Could Master D feel them as they flared and swelled in silent acceptance of his touch? Although she hadn't thought it could possibly get any bigger, she felt his erection grow and press into her stomach.

His fingernail grazed over her skin.

She lost touch with the other man in the room, with her job, her training, her embarrassment. Every thought, every nerve centered on his finger as it found her clit and proceeded to torture it until she clenched her thighs and prepared to tumble into an orgasm.

When she thought her next breath would release that scream of ecstasy Drake had spoken of, Master D unceremoniously lifted her off his lap and stood her before him. Madison struggled to remain standing. Her legs trembled as she tried to regain some semblance of dignity and not beg him to finish what he had started.

"Now, take the thong off," the trainee ordered in a deep, demanding voice that made her wonder if he worked as a drill sergeant during the day.

She glanced at the trainee. He blatantly rubbed his erection, licked his lips and stared at her mound with eyes glittering with desire. The Master, on the other hand, acted totally unaffected as he stared at the offending cloth that had up until this point given her a small amount of control.

Anger cooled the simmering embers of her unresolved orgasm. She cursed Rob and vowed to really crush Drake's balls the next time she saw him. She grasped the thin straps of her thong, muttering, "Fucking men."

"You will respond to all orders with 'Yes, Master'," the trainee barked out.

Madison groaned and rolled her eyes. She tried but failed to keep the mirth out of her voice as she mumbled, "Yes, Master."

Stepping out of her thong, she balled it up and tossed it across the room before the trainee could discover just how much she enjoyed her spanking. Master D surged up from the bench, crossed the room on those magnificently long legs and scooped up her thong.

Over his shoulder, she watched his reflection in the mirrored wall. He raised her thong to his face and drew in a deep breath.

Madison groaned, embarrassed and inflamed at the same time. When he returned to the bench and she saw herself in the mirror with her nub-covered mound and enflamed clit, her face burned anew.

Someone knocked on the door.

Master D shoved her thong in his front pocket and strode to the door.

Madison ran to the bed. By the time the door squeaked open, she had slid completely under the cool sheets. A few minutes later, someone yanked them down from her face.

"This session will resume tomorrow night," the trainee muttered, then turned and walked toward the open door.

"What? Why?" She hopped off the bed. Yanking the sheet from the mattress, she wrapped it around her body and stumbled after him. "I'm on a schedule here, buddy. You get Master D and tell him to get his tight butt in here!"

"Master D was called away on urgent business."

The trainee halted in the doorway and glanced at her just as she stepped on the sheet and fell flat on her face. She let out a string of curses. The more she tried to stand, the more the slick, satin sheets entangled her.

Still struggling to rise, accomplishing nothing more than making a fool of herself, she barked, "A little help, if you don't mind?"

He chuckled. "I'll send Mistress Louisa in. It might work if you released that death grip on the sheet."

The door slammed shut. Crimson satin billowed out when she opened the fists she had held clenched between her breasts. The cool, slick material slid along her skin. She glanced at the door and growled. A little longer and she might have ended up on these sheets with two luscious men. Not something she'd normally do, but for the sake of justice, she would have suffered through it.

Grumbling to herself, she stood up and ran her fingers over the spot where Master D's erection had pressed into her belly. Yeah, for justice she'd come back for one more night of training.

One more night with Master D.

Chapter Three

At precisely ten o'clock, Drake sat in his office and watched Madison charge through his door. Wearing cut-off sweat shorts and a tight, little tank top, she looked good enough to eat. His cock sprang to life when she pierced him with a scathing glare.

"What the hell kind of message is 'In my office at nine'?" she asked, mimicking his voice.

"The kind I expect you to obey."

"Obey?" She leaned over his desk, giving him a nice view of her lace-clad breasts. "Excuse me? Who the hell do you think you are?"

His mouth watered. The foolish woman leaned closer, making the neckline gape even more. "Do I have to remind you that I'm your boss? And as much as I'm enjoying this, ah…little show." He forced himself to look up at her face. "I think you'd better sit down before you say something you'll regret."

Slapping her hand over her shirt, she opened her mouth.

"Careful," he murmured, then grinned when she cursed under her breath and dropped into the chair. "I had a very good reason for leaving that voicemail. One I would have explained if you'd answered your phone this morning."

Dropping her head, she picked at a thread dangling from the edge of her shorts. "I was out."

"At six in the morning?" Seconds ticked by. Drake waited. Wondered for the hundredth time that morning where she could possibly have been. He recalled how wet her pussy had felt. Last night, he'd primed her, then left. An odd stab of jealousy had him wondering if she'd left Sweet Submissions and found someone to finish what *he* had started. "At six in the morning?"

She wrapped the thread around her finger and, with a sharp tug, snapped it off. "I was eating breakfast...with a friend."

"A friend?" His mind painted a decadent picture, one that, for some strange reason, made his own breakfast churn in his stomach. "I see."

Madison's head snapped up. "No. You don't see. He's a bum. A very nice, very informative bum. I've met him every morning for the last three weeks. He's sweet, but he's manic depressive."

"You didn't want to just up and disappear." Drake's stomach calmed.

"Well, he is a bit of a worry wart." Her eyes softened.

"Would you like me to send in another journalist to keep him company? Just to make sure he's okay?"

A relieved smile transformed her face. Her concern revealed a side of her he couldn't help but like. "Our abuser got another slave last night."

Her eyes widened. Her smile vanished. "Oh no. How did you find out?"

"Rob and I left our numbers with the ER nurse who tipped him off about the others. When she couldn't reach Rob last night, she called my cell. The creep nearly killed this one. Messed her face up so bad, she'll never look the same." His voice shook, his hands curled into fists. Recalling Kitten's beauty and the sweet, innocent nature that prevailed even as she succumbed to his every command, Drake couldn't stem the tears burning his eyes. He looked down at the papers lying on his desk.

"You know her," Madison said in a stunned voice.

Pushing to his feet, Drake walked to the window and stared out at the skyline. "Everyone calls her Kitten."

"Kitten?"

Drake didn't want to discuss Kitten with Madison or anyone. The memory of Kitten lying in that hospital bed ate away at him.

"Drake?"

Somehow, Madison's soft, hesitant voice soothed him. "She was a little thing." He stared down at the people crowding the sidewalk below. "Sweet. Meek as they come. Playful. Like a kitten."

Madison's hand on his shoulder shocked him. He hadn't even heard her move.

Her hand slid to his shoulder blade. "She's your girl, I mean, sub?"

Shocked by the passion one touch from this woman stirred, he shook his head. "No. But I've done a few scenes with her."

"Scenes?"

"In public rooms. A temporary Master, so to speak." He turned and stared down into eyes shimmering with compassion. "She enjoys scenes where her Master shares her with others. When she was an especially good slave, her Master would reward her with one." He hesitated, thrown by a subtle flaring of Madison's pupils. When her breathing grew shallow, his groin ached at the thought that this spitfire might find such a scene arousing. "Kitten was a very good slave. Her Master loved her and rewarded her nearly every week."

Madison's eyes darkened. "He...he...allowed other men to screw her?"

"No. To punish her...in a good way."

Her breath hitched. Her tongue darted out to moisten her lips. Drake wanted to take those lips and draw her breath deep into his lungs. He knew she would succumb, press those luscious breasts into him and let him savor her taste as he explored every corner of her mouth. Yes. She would succumb. For a moment or two before she kneed him in the balls.

Tearing his gaze from hers, he went back to his desk. "Kitten lost her Master to cancer. She went unfettered last night after mourning for nearly a year."

"If I hadn't wasted time training last night, I could have—"

"Enough!" He slammed his fist on the desk, seeing Kitten's battered face, imagining Madison's looking as bad or worse. "It's time we let the cops handle this."

"She gave them a description?"

"What do you think? They couldn't even get her to admit she'd been beaten." He dropped his chin to his chest. "The little fool told them she'd fallen down her basement steps."

"I'll get who did this to your friend, Drake." She grabbed his arm. "I'll make the bastard—"

"Forget it."

"Look, I already told you. I'm going in, with or without your approval." She stepped up to him. Her breasts pressed against his arm, singeing him through his shirt. "Now, tell me all you know about this BDSM shit so at least I can go in armed."

Impressed with her courage, painfully aware of her hard nipples poking into his arm, he nodded and sat down. "What do you want to know?"

As she made her way back to her chair, she shocked him with her first question. "First help me understand why these women embrace slavery. Why they give up their freedom to these overbearing men."

"I thought you trained last night."

A blush stained Madison's cheeks. She avoided his eyes. "It was cut short."

He wondered how she would react if she knew her thong rested in his pants pocket. If she had any idea that even now the memory of her removing it made his cock harden and grow. "Tell me something, Madison. Have you ever yearned to do something, but couldn't because you were told it wasn't proper or moral?"

She shoved a wisp of hair from her face. "Sure. Hasn't everyone?"

"Give me two examples."

He watched her squirm in her seat and gaze around the office as if she would find the answer amongst his filing cabinets or bookshelves.

"Think, Madison. Something decadent. Something you doubt you'll ever do."

The mischievous grin that splashed across her face surprised him. He had expected her to balk.

"Well." She closed her eyes, giggled.

He waited, watched her breasts rise and fall as she sucked in one deep breath after another.

"Once, when I was a kid, we went camping in Yellowstone Park. We found this great clearing, right near a pond." She gazed at some point over his head.

"And?" His balls tightened in anticipation.

"I stumbled upon my brothers skinny dipping. When they came out, they wrestled and rolled around in the grass. So, in my innocence, I figured I could join in." She laughed. "I mean, why not? I stripped and did. They freaked! I never even got to feel the grass on my skin before Lex wrapped me in his shirt and carried me to my mother. I couldn't sit for days."

"So you want to roll around naked in the grass. Not very decadent, Madison. Dig deeper," he coaxed, his voice husky from the image of this beauty naked and wrestling with him in the grass.

She hung her head back and groaned. "Off the record and never to be mentioned in public?" When he nodded, she draped her arms over her eyes and continued in a low whisper that grew deeper with each word. "I've always wanted to know what it felt like to give someone a lap dance."

Drake almost winced aloud from the sudden surge of blood to his cock. "What stopped you?"

"Hello? I'm not exactly lap-dance material. And anyway, only...only..." she dropped her arms and smirked at him, "damn, how do I say this?"

"Only a whore would straddle a stranger in nothing but a thong and tease him senseless by gliding her body over his?"

Her chest heaved as her breathing deepened.

When she nodded, he continued, "And only a whore would enjoy rubbing her skin over his clothed body until she and he came?"

Madison leapt up. The chair crashed behind her. "Well, it's true," she snapped, righting the chair.

"Why, Madison?" He kept his voice calm, soothing. "Because your mother said so?"

"Did you talk to Rob about my mother?" She paced in front of his desk. "That creep."

"Actually Rob never mentioned your mother. But if she's like most—"

Madison laughed a sad, bitter laugh. "My mother is a puritanical, born again Virgin Mary. She thinks that if a woman never marries, she should die a virgin, an untouched anywhere on her body virgin. So, yes, she has something to do with my take on lap dancers. But in that respect, so do a lot of normal people."

The swells of her breasts quivered beneath her tank top with every breath she took. Every ounce of blood in his body headed south, leaving him lightheaded and in exquisite pain. "Calm down."

Madison stopped, drew in a deep breath. "I'm fine." She started pacing again. "I just don't see what this has to do with slaves."

"Sit down, Madison. You're giving me a headache."

She scowled but did as she was told.

A good sign.

A start.

He moved on to step two of enslaving Madison Garrett. "Close your eyes."

As he'd expected, she glared at him.

"Go on. Trust me."

"This is ridiculous," she muttered but closed her eyes.

"Imagine you're a slave. You have no say when your Master takes charge. No control. He knows your every desire. Your every wicked thought because when he asks you to reveal one, you must answer."

"Yada yada yada. Is there a point to this?" She peeked out from one eye. When he stood up, she closed her eye and let out a long, loud sigh. "Fine, go on."

Drake walked around the desk. He had seen the way her legs quivered slightly as he spoke. The way her nipples hardened and pushed against the fabric of her shirt.

"Imagine I'm your Master."

Madison snorted. "Like that's ever going to happen."

"Just work with me here." He leaned over until his face hovered inches from hers. "Knowing what I do, I take you to a park and order you to strip and roll around in the long, sun-warmed grass."

"And I tell you to go to hell," she muttered, but her eyes remained closed and a soft smile tilted her lips.

"Then I whip you. And you know that I'll only order you to do it, then whip you when you refuse again…and again. What happens then, Madison?"

"I obey?" she asked, in a deeper, less defiant voice.

"You have no other choice. After a while, I call you over…" He sucked in her warm breath, imagined how good it would feel flowing over his aching cock. "I sit on a bench and order my sweet slave to give me a lap dance."

Her smile faltered. Drake brought his lips closer to hers. "In the park, Madison. Where anyone might happen upon us and see me sitting there...clothed...while my beautiful slave entices me with her naked body."

"I'd never do it." Her voice held none of the conviction he imagined she had intended.

"Then I'd toss you over my lap and spank your bare butt until it's pink." When she shifted in her seat, he continued, "I spank you until you're so close to reaching an orgasm, you beg me to let you come."

He waited, gave her time absorb his words, imagine his hand on her bare skin. Her lips parted. He moved closer. His knee glanced along her thigh.

When she sucked in a hissing breath, as he knew she would, he murmured. "You know, even before I speak, that I'll withhold my permission to come unless you do as I ordered. Do you know what you do next, my sweet slave?"

Madison's tongue darted out to moisten her lips. "I...I..."

"You give your Master a lap dance."

Drake hesitated, could almost see the scene unravel in her mind. Her knees drew together. Her blush turned into a telltale flush.

"Do you see it, Madison? Me watching as you do something you've always longed to do, something you never would have had the nerve to experience...without me? Now imagine me forcing you to bring *all* of your secret fantasies to life."

Her face relaxed. A soft smiled played on her lips.

"Have you lost your freedom? Or won it back?"

"I see, but—"

Drake took possession of her mouth before she could reply. She gasped. Her hand flew to his crotch and started to squeeze.

Stilled.

He didn't know for sure if her fingers relaxed because his tongue plunged into her sweet mouth. The reason her grip now felt more like a lover's caress didn't matter. Her soft moan mattered. Her palm pressing into the ridge of his cock mattered. And when he finally released her, the flush sweeping down her neck to the swell of her breasts mattered.

"Don't do that ever again, Williams," she warned in a voice filled with anger and lust. She rubbed her hand on her sweats.

When Madison left his office awhile later, Drake knew he'd succeeded in planting the seeds that would soon, with careful nurturing, sprout a willing slave. One he intended to own.

* * * * *

Madison waited for Master D in nothing but Aunt Louisa's collar as ordered. Her body still strummed with need from her visit with Drake. All day she had failed to shake the memory of his lips on hers, of the hard, hot ridge of his cock burning her palm. She closed her eyes and saw them on that park bench. In her mind, he wore coarse jeans and no shirt. She could almost feel them scraping her sensitized skin while she gave him a lap dance, could almost feel the cool breeze reminding her that they were outside, in public. The creak of the mirrored panel opening snatched her from her daydream.

When the two men entered the room, Master D took his position on the bench. Cleanly shaven, damp from her erotic visions involving Drake, she cringed when the trainee slid his fingers over her mound and announced in a disappointed voice, "No need to shave. She's smooth."

Master D reached down as he crooked his finger at her. Holding her tongue against the snide remark tickling her lips, she moved forward, then resumed her wide stance not two feet in front of his leather-clad legs. A deep, gnawing pain filled her womb. The silence in the room only amplified the tension riddling her body.

When he raised his hand, revealing what he held, she thought her legs would give out. They quivered uncontrollably when he slid the long, slender Lucite pole between her legs. Gliding it over her pussy until she moaned, he then held the wet end up to his mouth and licked it clean.

Watching his tongue gather up the evidence of her arousal, she barely felt the trainee take her limp arms and draw them behind her. Something cold wrapped around her wrists. When she heard the clink of metal, she realized she had been handcuffed. Breathing in short quick gulps, she watched Master D rise and slowly make his way to her.

The man oozed masculinity and power. Muscles flexed and rippled everywhere as he moved. Dark crinkly hair dusted his chest. Her eyes followed it down, down to the soft hairs smoothing over his taut stomach, down to the waistband of his pants and that bulge that never seemed to stop growing. She should have looked away, should never have let her greedy gaze linger. Like Drake, the damned man was built like a horse. Actually, she only saw a pony with a boner on the Discovery Channel. Master D definitely brought back the wicked thoughts that had gone through her mind when she had imagined something that big ramming into her.

Although she knew she was safe in her aunt's club, Drake's warnings that she would be helpless had her trembling uncontrollably as the Master knelt before her, and the trainee held her in place. She had no choice when Master D grabbed her ankles and pushed, she widened her stance until she felt her nether lips open, felt his warm breath coat her inner flesh. The trainee held her chin up, thwarting her attempts to look down.

Which was fine by her. She knew exactly what would happen next and had no qualms about closing her eyes and waiting for the first touch of those sexy lips. Her eyes flew open when cold metal embraced her ankles. This time when she heard the clinks, she groaned. A groan that soon turned into a humiliating whimper when she caught sight in the mirror of the long bar holding her legs apart.

Drake's warnings hit home. These men could do anything and she would have no way to stop them. The safe word tickled her tongue until she pictured Drake's smug face.

"These are training devices," the Master-in-training explained. "You will wear them for only a while. When they are removed, you will maintain this posture whenever in your Master's presence. This way, with your breasts jutting out and your legs spread wide, he can take his pleasure whenever he wants. A good sub's body is always ready for her Master's pleasure. A good sub never denies her Master what he rightfully owns. Her body. Do you understand?"

Madison nodded, too focused on the Master's head moving forward to speak. She no longer gave a damn about Drake's challenge. This god in front of her had breath that scorched. She could only imagine how his tongue would feel. Listening, like every good body should, her hips jutted out to meet his mouth halfway.

His head stilled.

"Do you understand?" repeated the man she wished would leave her and this Adonis at her feet alone. "And answer like a proper sub!"

"Y-yes, Master." Madison cringed. Fear of punishment hadn't rushed the words from her mouth. No. She spoke because she would do anything for the tongue that licked those fine lips peeking out of the mask.

Obviously she spoke too late. She watched Master D stand and walk over to the black marble table. He opened a drawer and returned with a long, slender, silver chain. Again, Drake's warning rang in her ears. Would they chain her? The idea excited and terrified her. Judging by the little spasms deep in her pussy, her body didn't hear the alarms ringing in her head. She barely breathed when his head moved toward one of her breasts, stopped altogether when he suckled each one until her lungs burned for air and someone—certainly not her—growled.

He nibbled on one hard peak. When she yelped on a particularly sharp bite, he sucked it into his hot mouth and soothed away the pain with the most exquisite, unbelievably hot tongue. After he tortured her other nipple and turned her into a quivering mass of desire, she closed her eyes. The door to whatever dignity she had left slammed shut. She allowed all her weight to rest on the hands the trainee had under her arms and arched her back. Master D's mouth released its hold with a loud pop. She remained motionless and wondered where he would pleasure her next. Being a sub definitely had its benefits.

Her eyes snapped open when she felt something cold wrap around her nipple, then immediately, before she could focus, cinch until it stung. She hesitated, shocked that a trill of pleasure raced through her breast directly to her clit. In that moment, her other nipple was ensnared in the same manner.

While this Master of pleasure dropped back down to his knees, she craned her neck and checked out the gold loops lassoing her breasts. The cool metal felt exquisite against her fevered skin. Her nipples bulged and began to pulse in time with her erratic heart. "Is this safe?"

In reply, Master D cinched the loops tighter. She drew in a sharp breath. Her head swam. Something warm slid down her inner thigh.

Master D's head moved lower. She shrank away and sucked in her stomach when his tongue touched her scar. Satin lips swept over the puckered skin, sucked it into his hot moist mouth, then kissed it almost reverently. Minutes passed and still he made sweet love with his mouth to the one flaw she always tried to hide. Her pussy wept, sending more of her juices down her leg. When she relaxed and sighed, he moved on to the rest of her body.

He nipped her stomach, licked away the sting, nipped her hip and soothed her once again. Madison thought she would die from the pulsing ache in her nipples and the nerves that tingled long after he moved on to the few inches of body he had yet to explore. She lost herself in the sensations until she felt his finger sliding up her inner thigh along the evidence of her arousal. Embarrassed, she jerked her leg away.

"She doesn't learn, does she, Master D?" The trainee sounded more pleased than annoyed.

Madison glanced over her shoulder and gave him a scathing glare for reminding her that someone else infringed on her fun with her Master.

Her Master?

No. No man would ever be Madison Garrett's Master. She knocked the three bears from that throne years ago. This guy was small potatoes compared to them.

"If you like what the Master does, you must say 'Thank you, Master.' If you do not, he will stop. Do you understand?"

"Yes, Master." Madison stared at the top of Master D's head. He didn't move an inch. Just knelt there, waiting. It irked her that he never spoke, that only the trainee gave her commands.

"What will you say so the pleasure continues?"

"Thank you, Master. I get it." She wriggled her hips forward. "Now, can we get back on track here?"

The trainee's fingers raked through her hair.

Master D's shoulders shook.

"Are you laughing at me?"

Just as Madison was about to ask again, the hand in her hair yanked her head back.

"Slaves do not speak unless they have permission," the trainee growled in her ear, "Understand?"

"Yes, Master."

Loosening his grip on her hair, he yelled into her ear, "When your mind begins to shatter and you lose yourself, what will you say?"

"Thank you, Master." Bit by bit, she tilted her head back down so she could once again watch Master D.

"You don't say it, he stops. You're lucky he pleasures you."

She almost laughed, almost told him she knew damn well how lucky she was. Never had she felt so aroused, so needy.

"You want him to continue, so you say what?" Again, he yanked her head up by her hair.

Madison swallowed a sassy retort and murmured, "Thank you, Master."

"Don't forget, slave. Master D wants to please his little novice. It will feel so good, but you must not forget your manners. 'Thank you, Master' brings pleasure. Forget and you will be punished. Understand?"

Madison nodded, wondering when she graduated to slave.

A resounding slap to the tender flesh between her legs sent a cry to her lips. She bit down on her lower lip when her clit tingled in response.

The trainee forced her head down in time to see the Master's hand fly up between her legs for another slap. "Understand?"

"Yes, Master!"

The sting, the surge of heat flowing over her nether lips and her hunger were too much to bear. Tears burned her eyes.

Master D grabbed her hips in a steely grip and pulled her toward him.

"And remember, slave," the trainee softly said beside her ear. "If Master D punishes you, it is only to help you learn how to be a good slave. And what do we say when someone helps us learn?"

"Thank you?" At this point, she'd cry uncle if he'd just shut up.

"Very good, slave. You learn fast. Do you want your reward?"

She bit her tongue on any wayward remarks. One pussy spanking was enough. "Yes, Master."

Once again Master D's mouth on her clit wiped all thought from her fevered mind. No mouth had ever felt so good, no tongue so hot. Just when she realized she forgot to thank him as she had been taught, fingers dug into her hips and shoved her away. Then one of the hands released her and flew up to deliver another piercing smack to her aching, dripping pussy.

Her mind shut down. It hurt like hell. So why did she want to thank him? Another and her labia and clit were on fire. After two more, Madison fought against the restraining bar to close her legs. To open them so the fire could delve deeper into her with the next slap. To close them when fear won out over desire.

"Thank you, Master!" she yelled, then sighed when instead of another stinging blow, she was rewarded with that amazing mouth. Muscles she never knew existed clenched as he sucked her clit into that wet heat, rasping his tongue over it until she heard someone pleading for release, someone saying 'Thank you, Master' over and over again.

This time, when she hovered at that precipice of release, he slid his finger into her and—oh, God—immediately found and stroked her elusive G-spot, immediately taught her the true meaning of the word shatter. Madison screamed and bucked against his face. His guttural moans as he lapped up her juices resonated through her body and sent her plummeting into another orgasm.

Too weak to stand, she leaned back against the trainee's chest, uncaring of the fact that his hands were kneading her breasts. Fingers slid into her mouth, fingers covered with her juices.

It took all the energy she had left, but she opened her eyes, thinking the session would now end, prepared to thank the man still kneeling before her for a truly enlightening training session.

She glanced down and discovered she had no idea just how far this submissive role could go. Sometime during her orgasm, her clit had been lassoed and now slender silver chains in the shape of a "Y" connected it to her nipples. The cold metal and the pull from the chains sent a tremor through her body. Master D's head moved forward.

Stopped.

"Please, Master," Madison begged him on a breath before she could stop herself. Her humiliation earned only one flick of his hot, moist tongue. Madison moaned from the hunger and need driving her hips forward for more. It didn't make sense. She came. Twice. Both were better than any she had ever experienced before. So why did she feel like she needed more? Why was the ache, the hunger worse than before?

"What are you?" the trainee whispered against her ear.

Sweat trickled down her temples from the inferno coursing through her veins. She would say anything, do anything. "A slave," she whispered.

"Who do you belong to, slave?" the trainee asked, pulling her hips away from the scorching breath she could feel flowing over her throbbing clit.

"Master D." She struggled to move her hips forward, but the trainee held her in place. "Please, Master…please!"

Master D raised his face and rewarded her with her first glimpse of the only feature not hidden by his mask. The erection of the trainee pressed against her back, but he no longer mattered. The Master kneeling before her held her complete attention. The Master with midnight blue eyes.

Chapter Four

ଚ

"You bastard!" Madison twisted free of the trainee. Her knees buckled. The trainee caught her before she crumpled to the floor. Wrenching out of his hands, she locked her knees and glared down.

Drake Williams grinned up at her with that arrogant, smug smile. His hand shot out and hooked the chains draped over her stomach then gently pulled her toward him before she had time to react. Gasping from the jolt of pain and pleasure triggered by the tension, she gritted her teeth.

Say something, her mind screamed, but she couldn't think straight. He rubbed his thumb over the silver links. Still holding the chain, he sat back on his heels and motioned to the trainee.

They whispered a moment then the trainer straightened and stated, with an edge of anger, "Master D wishes to be alone with you. But first you must tell him what you are."

Just as she opened her mouth to tell him she was his worst nightmare, Drake twisted the chain around his finger, increasing the pain and pleasure. Holding her gaze with eyes that burned with desire, he leaned forward and ran his tongue over the loops cinching her nipples. A whimper tickled her throat, but she bit down on her lower lip until she tasted blood and swallowed the telling sound.

Still ensnaring her with that smoldering gaze, he rasped his tongue over the throbbing peaks while his long fingers continued to play with her chains.

A slight tug down. She felt the inner chain binding her breasts to her core snap taut in response.

A slight tug up. The sweetest stab of pleasure-pain shot through her stomach and down her legs.

"What are you?" he asked, the rich timbre of his voice releasing the whimper she had worked so hard to restrain.

She wouldn't answer him, couldn't until she regained some control over her body. Her legs quivered. Her clit pulsed.

His lips thinned. With a jarring yank on the chains, he nipped his way down her stomach. Wondering how she made it through life without discovering just how many erotic zones dwelt along this route, praying she only imagined her hips surging up and forward, she thrashed her head from side to side in a panicked attempt to forestall the climax threatening to overtake her.

His hot mouth covered her clit and sucked gently while he tortured her with the chains. Pain stabbed muscles she refused to release as she tried not to come. The chains tugged and yanked. His teeth grazed her clit.

"What are you?"

She ground her teeth together but knew she was losing the battle before she felt something slide into her and rub her G-spot.

"You're tighter than I expected. Can you take two, I wonder. Three?"

"I can take anything you dish out, you bast—"

Her lungs seized. It felt like he plunged all his fingers into her.

"What are you, Madison?" He fluttered his fingers until she trembled uncontrollably. Without removing his fingers, he scraped his teeth over her clit. Madison screamed and came apart in his hands. Rising up on her toes, she once again bucked uncontrollably against his face. His fingers dug into her hips. A growl rumbled through her pussy while he sucked and squeezed her hips as if that would release one more drop. Why did that growl, that thought make her orgasm spiral back out of control?

Why did she long to send him out of control?

To quench his thirst?

When she could finally speak, she straightened her shoulders and narrowed her eyes. Hoping her anger would burn him with shame, she spat out, "I am your slave, Master D." She leaned forward. "I'll go through with this session, but when it's over, you'll be sorry you entered this room."

Arms snaked around her waist from behind and lifted her. Madison panicked. Could she have been wrong? Did she only imagine Drake's eyes and voice because she had fantasized about him training her? She struggled as the trainee put her on the cold marble table and flipped her onto her stomach as if she weighed no more than a child. They worked together, quickly and efficiently removing her handcuffs and bar then binding her to the table. Her arms and legs hung over the sides. She tugged at the manacles. The edge of the table dug into her mound. Never had she felt so exposed, so vulnerable.

Her heart pounded in her ears. She wondered if this job was out of her league, if the man meeting her wary gaze was indeed a stranger, albeit one with very familiar eyes. When he nodded toward the door, the trainee silently left the room.

"Has anyone ever taken you in the ass, slave?" he asked in a silken tone.

Her eyes flew open. "No!"

He slapped her butt. "Answer your Master properly."

"No, Master." Madison watched wide-eyed in the mirror as the Master opened a drawer and held up something she recognized from browsing the web and never, in a million years, imagined she would encounter.

"Then I will be the first. How sweet."

Nausea tickled her stomach but she had no choice. She had to be prepared for anything the Master at Train Me, Chain Me might do before revealing his penchant for inflicting real pain. Either way, she'd be damned if she let Drake Williams see her back down.

In the mirror, she saw him standing at the end of the table and staring at her open pussy for a moment before reaching out and sliding his finger into it. He withdrew it and spread the evidence of her arousal over her anus. She glanced at his face in the mirror and prayed he could read the plea in her eyes. Prayed he couldn't, wouldn't see how anything involving her anus terrified her and excited her at the same time.

As he continued to lubricate her tight virgin rim, burrowing his fingertip further in with each visit, her pussy lips pulsed and her inner muscles clenched, squeezing out more hot juice than she ever thought possible. She felt tears of shame come to her eyes over her body's betrayal and tried not to blink so none would fall. To her chagrin, one escaped and came to rest on the corner of her mouth.

"You can always use your safe word, my sweet slave. Say it and the night ends—the training ends."

She could tell from the way Drake's words seemed to rip from his throat that he was aroused nearly beyond control. One word would end her lesson. Simple.

But part of her—the entire physical part—wanted this. And, dammit, she still wanted to prove she could handle any job. Drawing in a deep breath, she rested her cheek against the cool marble and closed her eyes.

"Very well. I'll tell you what I'm going to do, my sweet slave. Then, I think you'll change your mind."

"I can handle anything you dish out, Master Dickhead." She spit the last word out, refusing to give him any satisfaction in this game.

A stinging slap to one of her cheeks shocked her and sent a fresh wave of lubricant onto the fingers she felt resting on her clit. His fingers moved. Concentrating on their slick journey, she stilled. When she felt one delve into her anus,

Madison struggled against her bonds and tried to shrink away from the invasion. She ground her teeth to stop from yelling out her safe word.

"I'm going to take you, slave. I'm going to take you every way a man can possibly take a woman. Do you understand?"

Madison swallowed. "Yes, Master."

"But it won't be me taking you when you go elsewhere, will it?"

Madison craned her neck, surprised by the rage lacing his words. "No, Master, it won't."

She gasped when his finger slid out. Something cold and hard landed on her anus. She felt something else ooze out onto her skin. Craning her neck, she peered at the mirror and caught sight of a tube rising up from between the swells of her butt.

"This will ease your muscles and lubricate you, slave. Thank your Master for being so kind."

Madison snorted and smirked until he delivered a particularly sharp slap to her already tender butt. "Thank you, Master."

Drake's finger massaged the gel into her skin in a slow, exotic dance that aroused her and calmed her fears. The cold nozzle delved deeper. Drake squeezed some of the gel into her then added more and more around her anus until it slid down the crease of her pussy. The cool tip of what she guessed was the butt plug pressed gently into her anus for a second then retreated.

"And you're still determined to bare yourself like this to another?"

Inwardly she screamed no, but she whispered, "Yes, Master."

The door slammed. She scanned the mirrors.

He left! Tugging on her restraints, she realized that she was trapped. She thought of her aunt finding her splayed out on this sacrificial alter or one of the other Masters taking over or—God, help her—a police raid and pictures in the *National Enquirer*. The three bears would undoubtedly end up in jail for murdering Drake, Aunt Louisa and every cop unfortunate enough to be in on the raid. And if by some chance, the trainee bragged about his part in her humiliation, he would discover just how like bears her brothers really were when it came to their sister.

A few minutes later, Drake flung open the door and led the trainee back into the room, back to Madison. She nearly begged him to send the trainee out when she saw him hand the butt plug and tube of lubricant over. She couldn't bear the thought of Drake watching as a stranger breached her tight anus.

And what if she cried, begged and pleaded for him to stop?

Or worse, go on?

"You will call my trainee "sir". He will prepare you for me."

Madison's struggles against the velvet manacles increased when he tied a blindfold around her eyes.

He whispered in her ear. "You can end this now, Madison. You already impressed me more than you can imagine. God, you're a she-cat, and you're helpless. Even I'm finding it impossible to keep in control. Abusers thrive on breaking women like you. Say the safe word. Give up this assignment."

She stilled. She barely knew Drake. They had no relationship, no commitment, yet his voice possessed her in a way no other man had, and she heard in his words the anguish she herself felt at the thought of another man touching her. It made no sense to her. She wondered if this stemmed from the fact that he had beenthe Master of this training session from the beginning. Refusing to admit defeat, she shook her head.

"Have it your way," he ground out. "Proceed with the preparation."

Trapped in darkness, Madison couldn't tell if Drake's or the trainee's fingers smeared more lubricant over then into her anus. The tip of the plug nudged in. She squeezed her eyes closed.

"Relax, slave," the trainee said in a soothing voice. "Tensing will only make this harder on you. Take a deep breath and hold it until I tell you that you may release it."

She dragged in so much air her head swam. Her lungs started to burn. When she thought she would pass out, the trainee finally spoke.

"Blow!"

Madison blew. The plug started to stretch her, gliding in inch by inch, leaving a subtle trail of fire. She couldn't control the groans accompanying each gulping breath she took, each lungful of air she blew out. The plug burned as it slid over her virgin flesh, arousing and terrifying her at the same time.

It had to be Drake pushing it in. Oh, *God, let it be Drake*, she silently prayed.

"Relax, Madison. It will burn for just a few seconds. If you feel real pain, let me know immediately."

Drake's voice beside her ear as the plug continued its invasion startled her and filled her with shame, shame that a total stranger had invaded her in such a way, shame that Drake watched. Tears rolled down her cheeks when lips gently brushed against hers, when someone tenderly smoothed her hair off her face.

Drake soothing her, her mind screamed.

Drake too far away to be the one pushing the plug deeper and deeper.

Just when she thought the flared base would rip her in two, her outer muscles clenched around the narrow neck and drew the flat bottom snuggly against her anus.

"That's my good slave. All done." Drake caressed her back as he spoke then planted a soft kiss to her cheek. His hand slid down her spine to the edge of the plug. She felt it burrow deeper, felt his lips skim across her cheek. Realized he could reach it while his voice still spoke in her ear. "Did I hurt my sweet slave? Do not forget how a slave answers her Master."

Tears of relief soaked the blindfold. Wetting her dry lips, she whispered, "No, Master, it didn't hurt...much. Was it you?" A sob choked her words. "Please, tell me."

"Did you really think I'd let another?"

The plug turned. She gasped.

"I *will* be the first to take you here, slave. Remember that. Whether you continue with your lessons or not, this ass is mine." His fingers traced the edge of the flat base then slid into her slick pussy. "The thought of me taking your virgin ass makes your body weep with joy, doesn't it, slave?"

"Yes, Master." Madison cringed when the trainee coughed.

God, any man she passed on the street after this could be him, and he would remember her like this. Heat seared her from head to toe.

"When you discover the joys of pleasuring me, you will never want your freedom back, sweet Madison." He slid his finger over her clit and squeezed it while his palm kept nudging the plug. "A taste, my slave, just a taste of what it will feel like when I take your ass with my cock."

The pressure of the nudges grew. He pushed faster as he pinched her clit again and again. She fought the heat rippling through her. Fought and lost.

Needing it deeper, faster, harder, she raised her hips and begged, "Please, Master, please!"

Drake slid the plug out then thrust it back. Flames licked her sensitive flesh.

"Again, my sweet?" he asked, his voice so wickedly deep. "Answer properly."

"Yes, Master. Please," she sobbed.

Drake complied once, twice. Muscles she did not know existed burst to life as spasms rippled exquisitely around the plug. At the same time, Drake shoved his thumb into her and pressed her G-spot while he tweaked her clit. Orgasms shook her simultaneously from her ass, her clit and deep within her pussy. She screamed from the intensity of each one.

When she started to float back down to earth, Drake whispered, "It's not enough. You need more."

Her heart slammed into her ribs.

He started all over again, catapulted her into another orgasm.

Whispered as she began her descent, "It's not enough. You need more."

Another assault on her anus.

"It's not enough."

Another orgasm.

"You need more."

The plug moved deeper.

"It's not enough, is it, my sweet Madison?"

She sobbed, too exhausted to answer.

"Your body will always want more. From me. Say it."

This time, she shattered after only one nudge of the plug. "It's not enough. I need more," she cried, then groaned when she felt the plug move, screamed when his fingers brought on another orgasm that took hold of her entire lower region.

"Say it," he demanded in a steel-laden voice.

"It's not enough. I need more." Losing touch with reality, Madison focused all her senses on Drake and the next orgasm.

"Why, Madison? Why aren't you satisfied?" His teeth scraped both cheeks of her butt.

"Because…because…" The plug turned then stopped. "It's not enough. I need more. More."

She could barely breathe. The orgasms continued. Her chanting started before one even ended. It was true. She would never have enough. Not until Drake's long hard cock replaced the plug. Not until he possessed her like no other ever had.

"It's not enough," she sobbed. "I need you. It's not enough!"

The plug stilled. She cried out in disappointment. Drenched in sweat, she writhed on the table. Her mind focused on the ache deep within her for one more orgasm, for Drake.

He leaned over and whispered, "That was nothing, my sweet slave. Nothing but a taste. Serve me well, and I'll reward this ass with my cock."

A groan ripped through her raw throat. Her hips ground painfully into the table. "Please," she whimpered, horrified at the plea she could not hold in. "Now, Drake. Please."

"Soon, my slave, when you and I are alone. When no one hears your screams but me. Are you addicted to my touch?"

She had totally forgotten that they were not alone. Heat flared over Madison's cheeks, but she couldn't stop herself from nodding then after a smack to her butt whispering, "Yes, Master."

He ran his moist fingers over her lips then kissed her and licked them clean. "Good, because I'm addicted to your taste, slave."

He removed the blindfold. Too ashamed to chance finding a smug smile curving his lips, she kept her eyes closed. Shame over the way she had acted overwhelmed her. When he freed her arms and legs, she curled up into the fetal position and softly sobbed.

She couldn't do this. No one had to tell her what would follow. That plug, that tiny plug that had felt so huge was nothing compared to the erection that strained against Drake's pants.

Again, the door slammed. Her breath caught. She peeked out through her tears and lashes. Scanning the room, she found only Drake sitting on the bench with his mask clenched in his hands. Sweat dripped down his chest, drenching the hair covering it. His hands trembled.

"We're alone. You're free to go, Madison." He dropped the mask to the floor then rubbed his hands over his face.

She opened her mouth to speak...closed it without uttering a word. How could she explain that she didn't want to go, that a part of her she had never known existed craved his domination of her body?

Drake raised his head and met her gaze with those dark, burning eyes. "Don't you want to go?"

She slowly shook her head, a blush creeping over her cheeks.

He stood up and walked to the table. "After all this, you still want to train for the job?"

Realizing she had forgotten this was only training for her next role, Madison met his gaze, then closed her eyes and nodded.

"Damn you! This isn't a game. You could end up beaten. Raped!"

"I have to do this. For them." Her voice shook. Tremors ripped through her body as if she stood naked in the snow. She opened her eyes, stared at Drake's hand gripping the edge of the table beside her face, the white knuckles trembling from the force of that grip. She covered his hand with hers and looked up into eyes so dark they looked black. "Th-this is w-what I do, Drake. I t-take on the role of someone being victimized. I l-live and breathe that role, no matter what it is, until I get it right and then I go in and get the bastards."

"This one's too dangerous, Madison." His hand wrapped around hers and squeezed.

"A-all my assignments are d-dangerous. Please, Drake. Do th-this for me. F-for those girls. Why can't I stop sh-shaking?"

"Your body's in shock. I went further than I should have so early in your training."

He lifted her into his arms and carried her over to the bench. When he sat and cradled her in his arms, Madison snuggled closer. The heat of his body, the soft brush of his damp chest hair against her skin and the firm support of his arms calmed her. As if he knew exactly what she needed, Drake tightened his embrace.

The shudders ripping through her body ebbed. "The shock made me cry. I never cry. Never."

"I know."

Nuzzling his neck while he softly chuckled and spoke in a deep, tender voice, she thought no man had ever smelled so good. The scent of her juices mingled with the musk and sweat rising off his neck tempted her. She skimmed the tip of her tongue over his Adam's apple and burrowed closer as his salty taste flooded her mouth.

He kissed the top of her head and drew in a ragged breath. "I should never have become involved with your training. As your boss, I should have ensured you trained with a stranger and shielded your identity. But I'm afraid that to train properly, even masked and with a stranger, your dignity will suffer. With you, Madison, any Master will find himself living his dream of controlling a woman born to dominate. Of becoming the only man she'll succumb to completely."

He hooked her chin with his finger and forced her to meet his gaze. "Making her his slave. His willing slave."

Madison stilled. Did Drake want that? Could he want to make her *his* slave? Heat pooled between her legs. Dear God, why did that thought actually turn her on?

"Do you want me to get someone else to continue your training? Someone you won't have to face outside this room?"

His hands caressed her back and legs, soothing yet reawakening her body. His eyes burned with hunger, with a silent plea she found she couldn't refuse.

"No."

"You can't learn how to be a sub in one session. Each night will be worse than the previous one. I'll punish and please you in ways you never imagined...take you higher and lower than you thought possible. At times, I'll try to humiliate or frighten you into backing out of the assignment. At times, I'll just lose myself in your submission. Like tonight." He grinned, but his eyes still burned into hers. "I'll taunt you just to bring out the she-cat who grabbed my balls, so I can punish you and watch you writhe and purr under my strap."

Although it felt like someone ran a cold finger down her spine, heat streaked through her lower stomach. Drawing in short breaths, unable to expand her lungs to take more, she feared she would hyperventilate and really humiliate herself. Taking what he dished out tonight would be nothing to admitting she couldn't handle just talking about it.

"Do you like being my slave?"

She didn't answer. Couldn't. But, judging by the increasing swell beneath her, he understood.

He grasped the flat end of the plug and gently tugged. "And you'll wear my plug, for as long as I say it takes to prepare your virgin ass for my cock?"

Closing her eyes, Madison nodded.

He reached between them and released his cock from the confines of his pants. He was so big and thick she couldn't imagine it fitting completely in her vagina, much less her ass.

"Straddle me, slave," he ordered with a voice filled with power.

Madison did as she was told. Swinging her legs over his, she planted her feet on the floor. Her legs gave out, but Drake's warm hands grabbed her hips and held her until she could stand on her own. She grabbed his shoulders and waited, unsure if she should wait for his okay or continue and slide down onto his cock.

"Don't forget your manners, slave."

Madison nodded and waited.

He held her gaze as he tugged on her chains and suckled her nipples. Arching her back, she embraced the tension building in her core. She whispered, "Thank you, Master," over and over until she cried, "Please, Master. I need…"

"What do you need, slave? You simply have to ask, and I will give it to you."

"I need…"

He nipped her tender peak.

"I want you to…to…"

"Say it!"

Unable to bring herself to say the words, she decided to show him and started to lower herself until she felt his thick head nudge between her labia. Seeing the disapproval in Drake's eyes, she froze.

Drake grabbed her by the waist and in one swift movement, stood and flung her over his shoulder.

"What the hell?" She pummeled his back. "You bastard! Put me down!"

When he did, she screamed at the cold touch of marble against her skin. Goose bumps erupted up and down her legs. His body pressed against her back, blanketing her in heat, pinning her to the marble X as he manacled her wrists and ankles. She couldn't believe how quickly and efficiently he trapped her. Before she even had a chance to respond, to struggle, escape was no longer an option. "Let me off this damn X!"

"St. Andrew's Cross, slave. You must acquaint yourself with the equipment for the assignment. Must get to know and love them all personally."

Feeling his hand slide between their bodies and rest on her lower back, she wriggled closer to the ridge of his cock. When she heard his zipper then still felt his pants separating her from the silken skin she craved, she whined, "Oh, come on, Drake. You want me! I'm willing." She arched and pushed back against that rod of joy. "Stop punishing both of us and whip it out!"

"You seem to enjoy punishment, slave. Is that why you insist on leaving out Master when you address me? Why you moved to take what is mine to give? Maybe you just like Mistress Louisa's manacles. So soft, so forgiving to your tender flesh."

She shivered when he brushed her hair aside and nibbled at her neck. The marble absorbed her body heat. She relaxed, melted against it. He had stumbled on her Achilles' heel. Any man could do what he pleased after just a few minutes of kissing her neck. Drake, it seemed, had discovered every sensitive inch of a woman's neck and knew exactly what to do once there. Tilting her head, offering more to his wicked mouth, she writhed and purred like a contented cat.

"Would you like to know how the Master you seek bound his victims?" he asked, his voice once again reflecting the anger and frustration she thought stemmed from his fear for her safety.

He grabbed fistfuls of her hair. Her scalp tingled when he tugged her head back. Rock hard muscles flanked her back.

"Please, Drake, don't—"

"Master, slave. Get it right. Did you look closely at those pictures, slave? Did you see the marks on some of the girls' wrists? The tiny cuts encircling them?" He kissed the back of her neck. "Do you like chains, slave? Chains strong enough to hold you yet so thin they'll slice into your skin if you struggle. But you can't stop yourself from struggling, Madison. The terror, the pain of his assault is too much and you pull on those chains until only your bones stop them from severing your hands."

Madison stilled. She imagined herself at Train Me, Chain Me, could almost feel the chains slicing into her like a knife. Helpless, she would be at the abuser's mercy. Flayed until her back dripped with blood.

Her heart broke. She couldn't do it. She dropped her forehead to the marble. "Okay, Drake. You can let me go. You made your point."

"No, slave. I don't think I have."

Her lungs seized. "I'll drop the assignment. Get me off this thing."

Something whooshed through the air a second before a sharp crack brought her head up and her body to attention, but nothing struck her. Yet.

Sweat broke out on her back as she twisted her head and looked in the mirror. She could see herself spread-eagled across the St. Andrew's Cross, could see Drake. His eyes darkened as he stared at the small, puckered scar beneath her shoulder blade from another knifing she'd suffered while undercover, the scar that had remained hidden under her hair all night. His hand clutched a bullwhip.

"What do you have, Madison, a death wish? Do you think the pain of a couple of stabbings will prepare you for a real flaying?" The knuckles of the hand holding the whip turned white. "What the fuck do I have to do to convince you to stay the hell out of there?" he asked in a desperate tone. The bullwhip struck the floor with a loud crack.

"Oh, shit, Drake. Tomato. Tomato!"

Drake just smirked. "This is training, slave. If you're going in that place, you can't play the role of a sub. You have to *be* a sub. And I hate to burst your bubble, sweetheart, but the Master abusing those girls doesn't hear safe words. So for the sake of training you properly, neither will I."

"What? I said I wouldn't go!" She tugged against her manacles, twisting her hands, refusing to admit she couldn't free herself.

He dropped the whip then turned and left the room. Not caring what led to his sudden exit, she slumped in relief against the cool marble. Madison wondered why part of her desperately wanted Drake to walk back through that door. Her body trembled with fear, but she yearned for his touch, his kiss.

And just one more orgasm.

As the minutes passed, her arms started to ache, and her need for him grew unbearable. Without him heating her body, the cool breeze from the air-conditioner chilled her sweat-covered skin. Doubting he'd return, she prayed he would have the sense to send her aunt in to release her.

She stood spread over the marble for so long that she started to doze just as the door opened. Drake closed the door behind him and stood staring at her.

His eyes pierced her with desire. In place of the anger twisting his face earlier, his brows slightly furrowed, and his mouth thinned in grim determination. "I think you would do anything to get out of here just so you could charge into that club and save the day. Even lie to your Master." Letting out a weary sigh, he added, "You leave me no choice, slave."

"Snap out of it, Conan!" Her eyes widened, and her struggles grew more frenzied as she watched him take a step forward and raise the whip.

"What are you?" His voice rumbled with power.

"I'm the one who's going to make you sterile the minute I get out of here, you bastard."

"Count out loud, slave. And be sure to thank your Master." Drake swung down. The silver teardrop resting on his biceps flashed.

Madison tensed then rammed her hips into the marble when the whip wrapped around her hips. The slight burning sting across her buttocks brought a cry to her lips then sent an electric jolt of heat straight to the nerves lining her vagina. Her inner flesh quivered. Her clit pulsed.

"Do not tempt a harsher punishment by defying me, slave. Count!"

"One! Thank you, Master." Sweat stung her eyes as she spat the words over her shoulder then flinched and hid her face against the marble for the next blow.

All her senses concentrated on the lashes that followed. Each stung on contact and wrenched a cry and the appropriate words from her lips, each burned long after, covering her back with heat, but the pain wasn't nearly as bad as she'd expected. She watched the reflection in the mirror of Drake's muscles flexing each time he brought his arm down, heard the whoosh of each lash. She smelled her arousal swirling around her, tasted her blood as she bit her lip to still her moans.

After ten lashes, she thrashed her head against the desire engulfing her. A part of her revolted, insisted sick, deranged people derived pleasure from this much pain. Another part drowned it out and looked forward to the next and the next. After fifteen, Drake's voice slid over her shoulder like warm honey.

"Your skin is so pretty, my sweet slave." He planted kisses where the whip had struck. "All red and hot for me. You handled your punishment well. You forgot to thank me for the last few, but I saw it in your eyes. In the way you thrust you sweet ass out for each strike. Would you like your reward, here?"

A strangled yelp escaped when she felt the cool leather whip and his warm knuckles touch her dripping pussy. He gently slid the entire length of the whip along her swollen lips, increasing the pressure until the last few inches delved between them. The knotted tip bumped over her clit.

A shudder rippled down her body. Heat flowed over her face when she couldn't stop herself from struggling to spread her legs farther apart.

"Now do you understand the sweet agony of total submission? Watch how you answer me, slave."

Madison fought to remain silent, but he continued to rub her with the whip. "Whatever. Just fuck me, will you?" She ground out the words between the tremors racking her body.

When the whip slid free, she couldn't stop the cry of dismay at its loss. She waited. And waited.

"You still don't understand, slave. When I fuck you, it will be when I want and for my pleasure. Only when I know that your pleasure stems from mine will I set you free."

He tortured her senses with the whip, inciting her to the brink of orgasm then stopping before it overtook her. Unable to take anymore, she sobbed uncontrollably and begged for his cock. He released her from the manacles, grabbed her wrists and shackled them in one massive hand behind her back. Too overcome to stand, Madison dropped to her knees and watched as he released his hair and used the rawhide to tie her hands together. His thick, black hair flowed over his shoulders. A lock fell over one eye. Drake swept it back, but it only slid back down when he lowered his head. Her fingers itched to delve into his hair and discover if it felt as soft as it looked.

"Look at me. See what you do to me." His voice trembled while his eyes seared her with the intensity of his hunger.

Too needy to deny him anything if there was some chance her compliance might give her what she so desperately craved, she drew in a ragged breath and lowered her gaze. Her pussy lips fluttered. Sweat covered the tense muscles rippling across his chest, highlighting each one. She watched his hands move to the snap of his pants.

Never, not in her wildest dreams, would she have pictured herself kneeling before a man, ready to beg him, if necessary, to take off his pants. He must have read her desire in her eyes because when she looked up, he grinned down at her. Sliding his finger along her jaw, he hooked her chin.

"What do you want, my sweet slave?" he asked in that rich timbre she would never get enough of.

Madison swallowed the lump in her throat and her pride. "I want to see you, Master."

"Then look. See how you affect me. No one has made me burn so. No one but you, Madison."

He stepped out of his pants. She drank in the sight of him. Never had she seen such a perfectly proportioned body. Her gaze trailed down his broad chest, over his flat belly and narrow hips. His cock jutted out from the soft black hair nestling it, as if trying to reach her lips. Imagining the feel of him sliding in her mouth, she ran her tongue over her lips. She gasped when his cock visibly jerked and a drop of pre-cum appeared on the tip. She leaned over, glanced up and waited until Drake nodded, then with a flick of her tongue brought that sweet glistening drop into her mouth.

Drake growled low in his throat and tossed his head back. The tendons on his neck bulged. His body shook. She realized he was fighting for control with every rasping breath. A sense of power engulfed her.

He grabbed her hair and knotted it around his fist. "When I punished you, I eased your pain with pleasure. You punish me and fill me with pain merely by your presence. Ease my pain, my sweet slave."

Madison allowed him to pull her forward. There was no way she would chance missing this by taking before he gave. She'd walk the walk. For now.

His hands trembled. Moaning from the hot, satin skin caressing her lips, she took as much of his thick length in her mouth as she could. He tugged on her hair until her head tilted enough for her eyes to meet his.

"Do not take your eyes off my face, slave." He frowned then smirked. "And get that damned look of power out of your eyes, Madison. Your goal is to please your Master, not prove you can take the throne."

Softly chuckling as she continued to suckle him, drawing him deeper with each stroke, she gazed up into his eyes and watched his face evolve into a beautiful sculpture of untold ecstasy. His eyes dilated, glazed over. The white teeth that had tortured her clit earlier snagged his lower lip. She swirled her tongue around the head of his cock. A drop of blood slid down his lip. She did it again. He twisted her hair.

Madison couldn't tell when the change in her occurred, when her concentration centered on how much pleasure she gave him instead of focusing on her own. She only knew that the more his fist tightened on her hair as he tensed in his battle to maintain control, the more her internal muscles clenched and throbbed and quivered. Soon, she felt subjugated by his power, his control.

"That's right. That's the look they'll expect." He closed his eyes. "Enough."

She cried out in disappointment when he pulled away.

He drew in one deep breath after another, staring at her in shock. "I could get away with imprisoning you. One minute with your mouth, and any judge would accept my plea of insanity."

His words brought a smile to her lips. God, how she longed to rip his control to shreds.

She sat back on her heels, stunned by the knowledge that he had been right, that by submitting to his every whim and allowing him to dominate her, she had the ultimate power over his pleasure. Her smile turned into a knowing smirk. She could rule him. Completely.

Drake scowled. "This session is over. I want you to keep that plug in you until tomorrow."

Madison nearly choked. She opened her mouth to ask why, to beg him to take her this instant and fill the painful void gnawing at her core. His fingers on her lips stilled her words. Kneeling before him, her body dripping with sweat and need, Madison Garrett, the toughest girl in her school, the kick-ass investigative reporter who made grown men cower, looked forward to his next command.

"I'll pick you up at noon. Before I arrive, you will shower and shave." His fingers brushed against her lips. "If you must take out the plug, you will immediately put it back. Do you understand, my sweet slave?"

Feeling so infinitely depraved, Madison whispered, "Yes, Master."

"And you will keep my chains on you to remind you that you are *my* slave."

"Yes, Master."

He reached down and loosened the loops slightly. "You will wear no bra, no underwear. Just my sign of ownership."

The woman she had been before she entered this room fought to return. His next statement silenced her.

"Do this and I promise, Madison, I will have you screaming like you never have with any man before."

Madison smirked. "More than I do with my Jack Rabbit?"

"You have my word." Drake laughed and dropped to his knees. He slid his fingers into her and grinned when her muscles tightened around them. "Throw all your vibrators out. You no longer need them. I have toys you will grow addicted to, my sweet. And do not touch yourself tonight, my sweet, sweet Madison. I'll know if you do."

He kissed her, his lips gentle, his tongue caressing hers with such tenderness, that Madison thought she would faint for the first time in her life. Calling her by name, saying it in a soft, endearing tone brought her under his command more than anything else he had done during the evening.

As his lips wreaked havoc on her mouth, his warm fingers slid under her collar. When he removed it, she breathed a sigh of relief into his mouth. At least she wouldn't have to prance around with that wrapped around her neck.

Her relief was short lived. Out of the corner of her eye, she watched him remove the leather band around his bulging biceps. Still drowning her in his kiss, he wrapped it around her neck. The warmth it had absorbed from his body seeped into her skin, branding her.

He raised his mouth from hers and gazed into her eyes with such a triumphant look, she thought she would bounce right back to her old self and wrench that look from his face by grabbing him by the balls.

Tracing the edge of the collar with his finger, he murmured, "As long as you wear my collar, you are mine to cherish. Mine to care for and protect. Mine to do with as I please. Forget any responsibilities you had before. Pleasing me is now the only one you need bear."

Something deep inside, some hard knot she had carried all these years slipped loose. She felt the cool silver teardrop resting on her skin.

"One more thing, slave. Stand." He helped her to her feet. Reaching behind her, he untied the rawhide that had bound her hands together. He kissed the red lines encircling her wrists then placed her hands behind her back, wrist over wrist. "Assume the position of slave."

Madison spread her legs and kept her hands resting on the small of her back. She held her breath, savoring the sight of his tight butt as he walked back to the table and rummaged through the drawer.

When he returned, he held out a tiny bell and knelt before her. Her lungs seized, her eyes widened and she nearly came when she felt a tug on the loop around her sensitive clit. Drake stood and turned her around so she faced the mirror. He ran his hands over her chains, causing them to pull at her nipples and clit until she gasped. She found herself neither surprised nor angry when he stilled, denying her release.

"Look, Madison." Meeting her gaze in the mirror, he flicked the bell, releasing a barely audible tinkle. "This will remind you, with every step, every move you make, even as you move in your sleep, that you belong to me. The bell has an inscription. Do you want to know what it says?"

"Ding dong?" She raised an eyebrow and grinned.

"It says what this says." He flicked the silver teardrop on her collar. "Property of Master D."

She met his gaze in the mirror. "God, Drake, this is sick."

He slid his fingers deep into her and groaned. "Hush, before I catch you in a lie. Your body weeps with the pleasure of wearing it, of doing as I demand."

And, as much as she hated to admit it, he was right. "But others, Drake."

She felt his erection grind into her butt.

"They'll hear it, but only you and I will know where it's coming from and what it means." Turning her to face him, he grasped her chin and kissed her until her body shook and the bell chimed. Grinning against her lips a moment before releasing her, he added, "Every time you hear it, Madison, remember…you belong to me." He flicked the bell. "What is it saying?"

She brushed up against his body. His skin felt so hot against hers. "It's saying that I belong to you," she purred. "Now, why don't you prove it and take me?"

He kissed her nose and laughed. "You are such a horny slave. Tomorrow, I'll teach you to be patient."

Madison watched him open a mirrored panel and remove a pale yellow sundress. Buttons ran down the front. "I'm really not into dresses, Drake."

Ignoring her, he stated, "You will wear this for me on your way home tonight…and tomorrow."

He slid it over her head. As it slithered down her body, the soft cotton caressed her skin. Standing still, allowing him to dress her and press a kiss of farewell to each inch of skin before he secured each button felt so right it frightened her. How had he managed to turn her into his willing slave?

This man was her boss in the real world. Someone she would have to face. From now on, no matter how tough she acted, he would see this meek, horny woman when he looked at her. He would see her dressed the way he preferred.

The neckline of the dress plunged nearly to her areola. The way her swollen nipples and the outline of the chains showed against the thin material had her shaking her head and frowning up at him.

Trailing her finger along the hem, discovering that it hovered precariously close to the bottom of her butt, she shook her head again. "You're asking too much of me, Drake."

"I'm not asking, slave." His lips thinned. "I will carry this," he grabbed her hand and pressed it against his rock-hard erection, "for everyone to see. And when they see you, when they see how beautiful you are and how I grow more pained with each minute in your presence, they will know that you own me just as much as I own you."

Beautiful. He called her beautiful. Assumed all saw her as beautiful. She glanced at her reflection in the mirror. For the first time, she did feel beautiful. Maybe it was the dress. Maybe the afterglow of countless orgasms. And maybe, maybe it was the way Drake spoke of her beauty, as if it were common knowledge. Madison leaned forward, enjoying how the chains pulled as she brushed against him. "You're a depraved man, Drake Williams. Wanting to completely own women, wanting to parade them around with your chains and bells."

"No one but you, Madison Garrett. I have finally found someone I desire to own completely. Someone who realizes her chains enslave me, as well. Someone who will parade around in those chains and ring that bell because she wants to bring me to my knees."

Madison rose onto her toes until she felt his hot cock slide over her mound. When the bell rang, she rubbed her cheek against his shoulder and purred. "Somehow, I can't imagine anyone bringing you to your knees."

"Up until now, if you don't count our little encounter in the elevator, no one has." He cupped her chin and tilted her face up. Staring into her eyes, he whispered, "But I think you just might succeed."

Chapter Five

☙

The next day exactly at noon, her intercom buzzed. Madison stood in the middle of her living room and waited for her heart to start beating again. Clad in the dress Drake had chosen and painfully aware that she still wore the collar, chains, bell and nothing else beneath it, she suddenly doubted she could step outside. No matter how much she hunched, how much she loosened the nooses engorging her nipples, the dress clung to them and the chains. As if that was not enough to keep her locked in her apartment, the damn bell rang all night. By morning, its volume seemed to have grown to deafening proportions.

How could she go out like this?

She jumped when the intercom buzzed again. As she strode to the window, the bell and tug of the chains amplified the hunger she had struggled to ignore all night. Every time she had drifted off to sleep, her erotic dreams had her waking with cries of frustration. She must have skimmed her hands down her stomach ten times, determined to ease the constant ache in her core. Each time, she pulled back. Drake's promise of an orgasm stronger she had never known if she followed his instructions left her an obedient, if at times enraged, slave.

Opening her window, she leaned out and grinned. Drake paced the length of her stoop then stopped. Untying the rawhide holding his hair, he glanced in the window of a parked car and re-did it. When he turned with an erection his jeans failed to conceal, then looked up and caught her watching, he scowled. The shadows under his eyes and tense set of his face shocked her. She had thought he would find his game easier to handle.

"Get out here, Madison, before I climb up the damn fire escape."

The idea tempted her, sent her temperature soaring, made her body strum in so many spots she thought she might come if she so much as moved an inch. Suddenly she longed to feel the breeze on her bare pussy. No, if she taunted him into charging up the fire escape, the fire, passion and hunger holding them both captive would explode.

Then what? No more chains? No more teasing and torturing? Would her training end?

Gritting her teeth against the sensations the chains set off with every movement, she grabbed her bag and rushed from her apartment. The bell tinkled as she hopped down the stairs to the foyer. Madison giggled and wondered what it would sound like if he had attached similar bells to her nipples.

Opening the door and stepping out onto the stoop, she fought to control just how much the sight of him affected her. His eyes seemed to brand every inch of her body, raising goose bumps on her skin. The muscles along his jaw rippled.

Trying to regain her composure, she smirked. "You look terrible."

"I couldn't sleep."

When she giggled, he grunted, took her hand and led her down the steps toward the gate.

"And you look beautiful, my sweet slave. You're handling your training better than me."

Madison spun in front of him just as he reached the gate and pushed him back into the tiny garden. Blushing from the constant ringing of the bell, she pressed her chest against his. She wrapped her arms around his waist. "I spent the entire night tossing and turning. Your chains turned me on all night. And your damn bell kept chanting that you and only you could make me scream." She pressed her stomach into his erection. "Let's go back to my place. You know you want to. Make me scream, Drake."

Grasping her under her arms, Drake slid her body up until her mouth was level with his. "I'm not done with you," he whispered into her mouth then swallowed her retort in a brief, tender kiss. "God, you smell good."

"How long is this going to go on? I'm dying here." She nipped his lip then licked it.

"No less than I am, Madison." He lowered her to the ground. "Now, where would you like to eat?"

"You mean I, a worthless slave, get to pick?"

"You are far from worthless. And I am quite aware that in the real world, you are no slave, Madison."

"Drake, I'm wearing your chains and bell in the real world." Taking his hand, she slid it between their bodies and let him feel the chains through her dress. She pushed his hand lower until his palm skimmed over the bell and her knuckles brushed over the hard ridge of his erection. "I'd say you want the world to know I'm your slave," she murmured in a husky voice.

"You just touched without asking. A word of advice, my sweet slave. Pick a restaurant you don't usually frequent. One you doubt you'll ever go to again."

He didn't have to say anything more. Madison understood that Drake would now punish her. Publicly. The thought excited her and frightened her at the same time. She chose an Irish pub uptown she had last eaten in years ago.

When they arrived, Drake held the door for her. He rested his hand on the small of her back and led her into the dark interior.

"It's awfully dark in here." He slid his hand up her back and clasped her shoulder.

"Did you think I'd pick someplace where people could see my chains?" Madison bumped her hip against his. "You'll have to work a lot harder to put one over on me, Drake."

Drake gave her butt a light smack. "Oh, Madison, you have no faith in me."

She chose a booth in the darkest corner. Drake ignored the place setting on the opposite side of the booth and slid in next to her, trapping her between his body and the wall. The steady hum of chatter calmed her nerves. No one would see her chains or hear the bell.

Drake stared ahead and strummed his fingers on the table. Each tap reminded her how they had felt fluttering deep inside her the previous night. By the time the waiter approached, she had to blink away the decadent images swirling before her eyes.

Drake asked for a candle. "Gotta have some light in here. Right, honey?" He grinned up at the young man and slammed his hip into hers.

Thankfully the bell rested too snugly between her thighs to ring, but Madison knew that Drake had only just begun her punishment. As the waiter left, she wondered what would happen when he returned.

Drake surprised her by pouncing immediately. He reached under the table and tugged on her chains, tightening the nooses around her nipples until she whimpered. Glancing down at her chest, she cringed at the way they protruded. He slid his arm behind her back, forcing her to push her chest out just as the waiter returned and set a small votive candle in the center of the table.

As they gave their order, the young man's eyes strayed to her chest so many times that Madison doubted he would bring the right food. As if that were not bad enough, when he brought their beers and she gulped down hers, Drake reached across to grab a napkin and bumped her elbow. Beer poured down her neck and soaked the front of her dress, making it transparent. Spewing apologies for his clumsiness, he proceeded to wipe the napkin across her breasts.

She watched her pink areolas and darker nipples appear as if nothing covered them. The loops ensnaring her throbbing buds were also apparent. Her eyes flew up to the waiter. He stood transfixed, watching that napkin brush across the chains hanging from her nipples, chains she was sure he could clearly make out through the wet material.

Her cheeks burned, even as the feel of Drake's other hand creeping up her thigh sent liquid heat seeping onto the bench. She knew what he intended, could almost hear her wayward pussy opening in welcome.

"A little privacy here, pal," she snapped.

The waiter blinked, looked at her flushed face. Her bell softly tinkled. When the waiter's eyes fixed on Drake's other hand buried between her thighs, he spun around and nearly knocked over a waitress in his haste to leave.

"Damn you, Drake. Why did you do that?" she whispered.

"You tried to thwart my plans. I told you I wanted to show you off. That, my sweet," he flicked her bell again, "sweet, slave was your punishment."

Rage and humiliation engulfed her. She had never agreed to carry on their lessons outside of Sweet Submissions. Had she? Struggling to ignore the desire coursing through her body, she shoved his hand away and tried to push him out of the booth. "Fuck you. I'm out of here."

"You just failed a test. When I humiliate you, you may cry and even beg, but you may not mouth off or attack." Drake glowered at her. "And, *slave*, you will *never* stop me from touching you, again. You lost the rights to your body last night when you insisted on pursuing this crazy idea about going into that club and catching that creep."

His hand delved between her thighs before she recovered from the shock of his reprimand. When at least three of his fingers slid between her lips, she drew in a hissing breath. His thumb nudged the base of the plug. Vibrations strummed her tender flesh. "Drake, please. Don't do this. I told you last night, I won't go in that place."

"I know you. You'll find some way to sneak in there without anyone's knowledge. Without the proper training." He leaned over and nuzzled her neck. "I can't chance that."

"Why? What do you care? You hardly know me." Goose bumps tickled her skin when she felt him languidly lick the sensitive spot below her ear.

"I'll be damned if I know, Madison. You're mouthy, too smart for your own good and far too brave for your own safety or that of anyone foolish enough to get involved with you." His lips brushed her ear as he spoke. His fingers picked up speed, the vibrations followed suit making her wonder if there was some dial on the base or a remote in his pocket. "A sensible man would walk away. A sensible man would break your will to protect you."

She gripped the edge of the bench and fought to remain in control even though his fingers pumping in and out of her had her legs trembling. "You'll never break me."

"I never said I was a sensible man."

"Oh God, stop that." She grabbed his arm, felt his muscles flex beneath her fingers as he continued to torture her.

"What?" He sucked her skin between his teeth.

"Saying all the right things," she gasped, digging her nails into his skin.

"Don't fight it, Madison. Don't fight me,"

"Why," she asked through clenched teeth, "You'll stop before I come."

He increased the pace, his thumb alternately nudging the plug and her clit. Madison felt sweat trickle down her neck, between her breasts.

"If you promise to do as I say, I'll let you come. Right here, right now."

She closed her eyes and drew in a deep breath through her nose.

"Open your eyes," he demanded.

Her eyes flew open.

Grasping her chin, he forced her to face him and brought his lips up to hers. Holding her gaze with those eyes she just couldn't get enough of, he said in a harsh voice, "Since the minute you took off that damned bum disguise, I've been in fucking agony from wanting you. Giving you release last night and today while I suffer, goes against everything I believe in. But I will…if you promise to stop fighting me."

"How long?"

His fingers stilled. "What?"

"I'm agreeing to obey you for how long?" she asked, not leaving anything to chance.

He shoved against the plug. Madison yelped from the pleasure-pain of the intrusion.

Bringing his lips to the whorl of her ear, he whispered, "One week. You'll be my sweet sex slave for one week."

Her mouth dropped. "Go to hell."

"One week, Madison. You do everything I ask for one week. Every decadent command." He shoved his fingers so deep she felt his knuckles press the bell into her flesh. "You're so close, Madison. Say yes. I can feel your muscles. They're so tight, so painfully tight around my fingers."

She tried to hide her face in the crook of his neck, but he backed away, refusing to release her from his gaze. She closed her eyes in defiance.

"Last chance, Madison. Say you'll be my slave for one week, or I pull out, right now."

Madison opened her eyes and glared at him.

Drake nibbled on her lips. "Say the words, Madison. Then close your eyes and let go."

She held her ground. Felt his fingers start to slide out. "Okay! I'll be your slave for one week." Her body tingled at the thought of what the coming week would entail. She closed her eyes and added, "Then I'm going to fucking kill you."

His magic fingers slid out.

"Son of a bitch, you prom—"

Drake's fingers wrapped around her wrist. A sharp pain shot through her arm.

"Ouch! What the hell is wrong with you?"

Drake smiled into the dark interior of the pub. The waiter approached, carrying their lunch.

"Thanks," she mumbled, wrenching her wrist from his grip. "But you owe me."

The moment the waiter left, Drake slid his hand between her thighs. Shielding her with his body, he dragged her leg over his lap. Madison gasped when he shoved what felt like four fingers into her tight channel. His thumb snagged her bell and tugged on it with each thrust of his hand. Lost to the stab of pleasure and pain it wrought, she ground her teeth to keep from releasing the loud moans shooting up her throat. They came out sounding like a growl, which only incited her even more.

"Remember, Madison. Do not come without permission." He wet his thumb with her juices then tortured her clit some more.

She spread her legs wider, aware that he shielded her completely with his body. Her head fell back with a soft thump against the wall. It took all her will to hold off her orgasm.

"I won't lie to you," he stated, his voice filled with desire. "And I'll never break my promises. I expect the same in return. What are you?"

"Your slave," she gasped out. "Please, I can't wait."

"And how long will you be my slave?"

"O-one week."

He raised his brow.

"Master," she hissed.

"Come for me, slave."

His fingers fluttered against her G-spot and sent her right over the edge. Drake covered her mouth with his and muffled her cries. Her body convulsed in his arms. Every nerve exploded with sensation, every muscle unfurled. Tears of relief from the hours upon hours that she had craved this flowed down her cheeks and seeped between their lips. As she came back to earth, he gently kissed her lids, nose and cheeks, taking her tears in his mouth.

"God, you're beautiful when you come," he whispered, pressing his lips to her temple. "Such a good, beautiful slave. Shh, don't cry. You did well."

They stayed like that, with her wrapped in his embrace while he smoothed her hair until her breathing calmed, and her aftershocks subsided. Madison drew in his musky scent mingled with that of her release. Another tear slid down her face. She swatted it away. Never one to reveal any weakness, she couldn't remember the last time she had shed one tear in front of a man. Last night and today, she had actually wept in front of Drake. How could she control tears she couldn't even understand?

Drake's fingers skimmed up the side of her neck. Nudging her chin up with his thumb, he smiled down at her. "Was it worth a week of your freedom?"

"I'll tell you at the end of the week. Right before I kill you." Her voice held none of the anger she intended.

After they left the pub, Drake insisted on stopping in *Banana Republic*.

"Try this on." He held up a calf-length, cream-colored sweater.

"You're joking, right? In case you haven't noticed, we're in the midst of a heat wave."

"Trust me."

A half hour later, sweating profusely in the sweater Drake insisted she wear and missing the bell he had discretely removed in the store, Madison followed him through the editorial department of *Exposed*. Passing men who had never seen her wearing anything more feminine than jeans and a tank top, she silently thanked her new Master. Once inside his office, she untied the sash. "Thanks, Dra—"

"Leave it on." He grabbed the sash from her hands and retied it. "I'll be done in an hour. Lift the back." When she hesitated, he barked, "Now!"

Her compliance led to a sweet kiss. He lifted her and carried her over to the window beside the door then plopped her bare butt down onto the vent lining the sill. She bit her tongue and watched him cross the room to his desk.

"Stay." He sat behind the desk and opened a folder. "I always liked this office. No one else wanted it. For some reason, they all want their windows behind their desk. Like Rob. Do you know why I like this office?"

Squirming against the stream of ice-cold air chilling her moist skin and the thin bars of the vent digging into her flesh, Madison opened her mouth to answer.

He cut her off. "The view. When I'm working, I look up and see Manhattan in all her glory. Now open your legs."

Her heart lurched. Her clit tingled. "Here?"

"I'll take that sweater and parade you through every office if you question me again. Open your legs."

Enjoying this much more than the daughter of a puritan should, she spread her legs.

"Wider!" he barked. When she spread them as far as they would go, he nodded then lowered his head to work, muttering, "You have my permission to close them if someone comes in."

"Well, that's a relief." Madison snorted and silently told her pussy to stop acting like such a pussy. The damn thing wouldn't stop blushing and weeping.

Drake raised a brow.

"What?"

His brow furrowed.

"What? What'd I do?"

"Manners, slave. Or do I—"

"Thank you, Master, sir!" Madison saluted and wriggled her hips.

Smirking, Drake slid a piece of paper into his shredder. "You're lucky you look so adorable sitting there with your wet pussy exposed. If you didn't, that little act would have led to your next punishment."

Madison dropped her hand to her lap. "You're taking this week of slavery awfully seriously."

"That's right." Rising, he carried the folder over to her.

She watched his approach, expecting him to use her or make her come again.

"What do you make of this?" Opening the folder, he explained the office politics surrounding the enclosed story and asked her advice on his decision. The hour turned into two as they discussed one story after another. They argued heatedly over some, agreed about others. If not for her widespread legs and the growing annoyance of the vent, she might have forgotten her enslavement.

Drake set her straight as soon as they entered the elevator. Promptly re-attaching her bell he murmured, "You were such a good slave."

He rewarded her with dinner and a stroll through Greenwich Village. The warm night air crept up her dress, a constant reminder that she wore no underwear. Her bell tinkled relentlessly that she belonged to Drake. The chains draping down her stomach grew heavier by the minute. And the collar hugging her neck never let her forget her loss of freedom.

Drake acted as if they were a normal couple on a date. He talked about his family and asked about hers.

"So your brothers made fun of you for being a...what'd they call you?"

"Sissy girl. And if you ever tell a soul, I'll reintroduce myself to your balls!"

Drake laughed. "Honey, nobody will ever call you a sissy."

"Yeah, well," she slumped, "I made sure of that. From the time I was five, I lived to prove them wrong. Played football, wrestled and fought with them. I never shed a tear. And believe me, I had bruises everywhere."

"They weren't gentle?"

"The three bears? They fret over me like mother hens, but they haven't a clue how to be gentle." She chuckled. "Did you ever see a movie where some brute slaps a guy on the back in a greeting and sends the guy flying then hugs the guy and practically breaks his bones?"

Drake nodded.

"Well, I have three brutes. I've been seeing a chiropractor since I was twelve."

He reached over and tucked a stray hair behind her ear. "When I meet them, remind me to thank them."

"For what?"

"For my she-cat."

Madison stared up at him. Her heart fluttered in the strangest way.

Drake stopped on the corner of Bleeker and Seventh. "You've walked long enough in those shoes."

"Drake?" Madison glanced down at their clasped hands as he hailed a cab.

"Yeah?"

A cab swerved out of traffic and came their way.

She hesitated at the curb after he opened the door. "Why are you being so nice?"

"You say that like I'm not a nice guy."

"You know what I mean."

"I may own you this week, but," he nodded toward the cab, "you're my slave only when it comes to sex, Madison. Otherwise, you and I are equal…in all ways."

She slid in and pressed her hand over the butterflies taking flight in her chest.

"Tenth and University," he slammed the door and frowned. "Get over here, she-cat."

Smoothly, effortlessly, which considering her size was quite a feat, he lifted her onto his lap.

Rubbing his knuckles over her crimson cheeks, he whispered, "I'm not a bad guy, Madison. And you'll soon discover that I'm not a bad Master, either."

"Where are we going?" Her breathless voice sounded alien to her ears.

"Where I keep all my possessions. Home."

"Possessions? Home? Listen, I never agreed…"

Satin lips silenced her. His tongue delved into her mouth, caressed and explored in a way that left her gasping, that broke down all her defenses, that declared he owned her, all of her. Madison had no doubt, this kiss branded her his. If she had any thoughts of escape, of refuting his claim, Drake had wiped them from her mind with one, brief, possessive kiss.

His hand slid under her sweater and meandered up her inner thigh. "Ready to learn about freedom through slavery?"

Screw the lesson. If she had one, Madison would wave a white flag and offer her body up as the spoils of war. That kiss had set her aflame. She could almost hear every nerve ending screaming for one touch of his raspy tongue. As she raised her head to nod, the clicking of a blinker snatched her out of the erotic web of desire he had woven around her. She tried to push his hand away as she nodded toward the driver.

"This is out of your control, slave," he whispered against her lips. "Now, close your eyes like a good slave and let go."

Madison peeked at the back of the driver's head. Drake touched her cheek with his finger and turned her face to his.

"Close your eyes, baby."

Feeling powerless, already addicted to his touch, she snagged her lower lip between her teeth and squeezed her eyes shut. "Drake, please—"

"Maybe I'll shield you from his eyes... Maybe I won't," he whispered, capturing her imprisoned lip with the pad of his thumb and pulling it free.

If she had ever gone to a therapist and revealed all her fantasies, Madison would have some case against him for breaching doctor patient confidentiality. She could swear someone had told Drake each and every wicked dream she ever had.

She prayed he would shield her, fantasized he would expose her to this stranger's hungry gaze. The hem of her dress slid up her thighs. Fingers caressed her skin, slid under her knee. She felt Drake shift under her and tried to focus on the direction they faced, but his tongue plunged into her mouth and scattered her thoughts.

Like a drowning victim bursting out of the water before sinking back under, she managed to break free of the effects of his kiss just long enough to realize her legs splayed open while his fingers slid up her inner thigh, his nails scraping just enough for her to feel the subtle trail. She gasped from the touch of his fingertips against the sensitive skin of her nether lips. His hand retreated down her leg, his nails digging deeper as they made their way back down the trail, creating a more intense burn.

Wriggling, she whispered on a breathy sigh, "Free me."

When he failed to respond, she knew what he wanted but couldn't bring herself to say the words with the driver close enough to hear. Drake's nails started to move again but only in a small circle on the inside of her knees. The circle grew and grew until she thought that he would finally give her what she so desperately wanted, needed. Madison spread her legs wider. His hand stilled. Quivering head to toe, she admitted defeat. Screw the lesson. Screw the driver. Screw her damn pride. "Please…Master."

She felt his lips smiling as they slid down her neck to her collarbone. Her dress slid higher. His hand delved between her legs, but he only stoked the fires raging through her body. Every touch, every kiss promised completion then stilled if she so much as shifted in response.

If she even thought of opening her eyes, he somehow sensed it and whispered a harsh warning in her ear. If she allowed a moan to escape each time he denied her, he gave her lips a sharp nip, a reminder that he held the reins, and she did not even have the right to moan in retaliation. He tortured her senseless until the cab came to a halt and the driver coughed. Madison opened her eyes, dazed and unsure where she was for a minute.

Drake met her gaze, his eyes burning with an intensity that stole her breath away.

A wink from the cabby sent a wave of heat over her cheeks. She moved to lower her dress but found it and the sweater covering her legs. As she stepped out of the cab, Madison took in Drake's neighborhood. Stately brownstones lined both sides of the street. A few doors down, classical music filtered out from open ornate French windows and calmed her pounding heart.

As the cab pulled away, Drake swept her into his arms. A woman passing as she followed two toddlers on trikes giggled when he bumped the gate to his brownstone open and carried Madison to the door.

Inside, Madison barely had time to notice the antique mahogany furniture filling the rooms he sped by before bounding up the stairs two at a time. Setting her on her feet outside a door, he frowned down into her face. When she leaned in for another kiss, he held her back.

"What game are you playing with me, Madison?" Passion still darkened his eyes, but now suspicion lurked beside it.

"This is your game, Drake. Your game, your rules."

He fingered the neckline of her dress. "Take off your dress."

"Here? In the hall?" She peered around his shoulders down the dimly lit hall.

"We're alone, Maddy. Now take off your dress. And remember, you promised me a week."

Recalling how easily he had overpowered her in the cab, she stepped back. "Yeah, about that."

He grabbed the front of her dress and ripped it open. Buttons fell and scattered across the hardwood the floor. After shoving the dress off her shoulders, he turned her around, opened the door and pushed her into the room. Ready to fight if he tried to force himself on her, Madison spun around. Stunned, she watched Drake leave, slamming the door shut.

She grabbed the doorknob but quickly released it. Leaving now would only prove she didn't have what it took to handle Train Me, Chain Me.

Calling him every name she could think of, she checked out her prison cell. It looked as though Drake had planned for her arrival. Manacles hung from the headboard and footboard of a massive four-poster bed. Several kinds of whips, paddles and leather straps covered a round nightstand. Her legs quivered when she imagined her introduction to each one. A bar suspended from the ceiling hung in front of the only window in the room. Her mouth went dry. In the far corner stood a large wooden St. Andrew's Cross.

Light glinted off something on the bed. She took a tentative step toward it. What looked like a leash, what she prayed was not a leash, rested beside a note on the red satin sheets. Lifting up the note, she started to read a list of instructions. Halfway through her hands shook.

"I've handed myself over to a madman," she muttered, "a control freak." Cursing under her breath, she removed her chains and plug then tossed them on the floor.

She yanked the red satin sheet off the bed and wrapped it around her body. After peeking out the door, she crept down the long corridor. She had grown used to wearing the plug and chains and felt naked without them. Mentally smacking herself in the head, she pushed the thought aside and concentrated on her plan. It was simple. She would find some clothes, her bag and cell phone then get the hell out of Drake Williams' prison.

He intended to break her will, subject her to such degradation that she would never stand up for herself again. Why?

She recalled his explanation that she had to *be* a slave, not just play a slave to succeed. His instructions ended with the declaration that at the end of the week, she would no longer have to act out the part.

"In your dreams, buddy."

Halfway to the stairs she heard Drake's muffled voice coming from behind a door. Her stomach leapt to her throat. Bunching up the sheet, she prepared to run.

Then giving in to curiosity, she tossed her hair over her shoulder and leaned her ear against the door.

"There's no fucking way she's going in there!"

Madison flinched when something struck the other side of the door directly where her ear rested.

"This isn't some game. God, he'll break her. She'll never be the same, Rob. No more fire and brimstone, no more shooting sparks from those eyes, no more snappy comebacks."

Drake liked her? The real her?

Her eyes burned. This time she welcomed the tears, smiled as they blurred her vision. Nearly screamed when his voice broke the silence.

"Fuck you, she's not going in! I'll burn the place down first."

Madison backed away from the door when she heard the phone slam down. Turning, she ran back to her room and quietly shut the door behind her. She leaned against it and stared at the slip of paper on the floor. The blare of a horn from outside startled her. Clutching the sheet, she gritted her teeth and pushed away from the door.

After replacing her chains and bell, she hooked the leash to her collar. She stepped into the bathroom, Drake's instructions clutched in her hand. Numbered and underlined, they set the stage for her first night of slavery.

She filled the tub with hot water, sprinkled in the Epsom salt, tied her hair up into a high ponytail and washed off all her make-up. She swiped away a tear then fastened the leather cuffs around her wrists and ankles. Each bore three silver D-rings. Telling herself she was doing this for those subs and slaves in the pictures, she returned to the bedroom. She lifted the paddle Drake described, slapped it against her palm until her hand stung, then put it on the windowsill. Focusing on the lingering sting as instructed, she checked the time and considered her choices for the allotted five minutes.

She could leave and give up the assignment or stay and give up her freedom. The minutes ticked by.

Her hand stung.

In her mind, she flipped through the pictures Rob had of those girls. Before the five minutes passed, she raised the instructions and read what to do next.

Standing beneath the suspended bar, she bent over and attached the spreader bar Drake had left on the floor to her ankles. She had to rise up onto her toes to grasp the bar hanging above her, but she managed not to fall. As instructed, she pushed the D-rings into the side of the metal loops attached to the bar. When the side of each loop snapped open then shut, locking her to the bar, her heart lodged in her throat.

She could hear the traffic below, feel a hundred eyes staring at her bare back and buttocks from the buildings across the street. Lowering her head, as instructed, she awaited her Master's return.

The door opened. She held her breath and wondered if she should have escaped when she had the chance.

Chapter Six

Drake returned to his bedroom and found his she-cat properly restrained. His body hardened to the point of pain. Her toes danced across the floor as she struggled for balance. Deep down inside, he had hoped he would find the room empty and Madison long gone, prayed he would find her waiting with fists clenched, ready to fight him the minute he entered the room. Every time he thought he had figured her out, she shocked him.

"Madison?"

She raised her head and met his gaze. Her eyes burned with challenge. "Get into character, Drake, before I change my mind." Her lips twitched up into a smile before she lowered her head. "Can we get moving here, before I get the female equivalent of blue balls?"

Muscles tense from his phone conversation with Rob coiled painfully in anticipation. He slammed the door.

Madison flinched and lost her balance. While she swayed and skimmed her toes on the rug, he retrieved the paddle from the sill.

Other than counting and thanking him, she made no sound for the first three strikes. While her determination impressed him, her first yelp quickly followed by a husky 'Thank you, Master' burned him with desire. By the tenth, she sobbed, begged and jutted her sweet ass out for the next. It took all his strength to stay in control. He knelt behind her, kissed her pink skin until her sobs turned to moans.

"Now, I'll show you how a proper slave prepares for her Master."

When he released her from the bar, she slumped into his arms. Wishing he had removed his clothes so he could feel her damp skin against his, he held her for a few minutes, caressed every slick inch he could reach.

He removed the spreader bar and carried her to the bathroom then set her on her feet beside the tub. "You removed my plug."

"Shit!"

"Slaves do not curse when speaking to their Masters. Where is it?" He bent over and tested the water.

"I threw it in the garbage." Madison leaned over and whispered in his ear, "Your letter pissed me off."

"Excuse me?" He glanced over his shoulder, raising a brow.

Her eyes twinkled with mischief. "Oh, forgive me, Master. I took it out and forgot to put it back…Master."

Finding it hard not to smile, he deftly removed her chains and bell. "You will not forget again. Step into the tub. The salts will soothe you."

When she lowered herself into the warm water, Madison sighed.

"Feel good?" He knelt beside the tub.

"Oh, yes…Master."

He squirted some gel onto a loofah sponge and proceeded to wash her back. He smiled down at her when her sighs filled the silence. "Stand, slave. I wish to see you."

Water cascaded down her body. He leaned forward and licked her mound, then replaced the loofah with a net puff and scrubbed her entire body until her skin was pink and her legs trembled. The pain in his groin grew unbearable when he told her to put her foot on the edge of the tub and she complied without a moment's hesitation.

"I changed my mind. *I* will prepare you from now on. Understand?"

"Yes, Master," she murmured.

"I will bathe you, care for your every need." He reached for the feminine shaving cream he had bought earlier, then grinned and stood, deciding she would appreciate the cool burn of the menthol gel he kept in his room. "Stay."

When he returned with the gel, he smeared it over her mound and the lips of her pussy. He spread some more over her anus then slipped his finger slightly into each of her entries as he made his way to her clit. He exposed the swollen nub and coated it before watching it slip back into its sheath.

Seconds passed.

Madison drew in a hissing breath.

He picked up the razor and carefully shaved every sign of pubic hair from her tender mound and lips. When her legs and underarms were also completely free of cream and hair, he rinsed her with the showerhead, holding it between her legs so she could feel the hot water surge up into her.

She gasped, groaned. "Oh my God, why didn't they put this in the manual for the showerhead I bought?"

Drake controlled the urge to smile and turned off the water. "You must learn not to speak without permission. Out."

Madison grumbled, but when he brusquely toweled her dry, paying special attention to her nipples and pussy, she leaned into him and murmured, "May I speak, Master?"

"Yes, but make sure it's not some bratty remark."

She brought her lips up to his and smiled into his eyes. "I could get used to this, Master."

He grinned as he spread the towel on the floor. "On your back with your legs up and wide apart, slave."

She scowled but obeyed. The crimson blush spreading over her body as she complied incited him. "You might just be the one to kill me, slave."

"Oh, I'll kill you all right," she muttered, "Master."

Drake shaved her anus, giving in to temptation and playing with her open pussy while he worked. Blood surged to his cock when her juices cut a path through the foaming gel.

"Stay," he ordered as he rose and drenched a washrag with cold water. Well aware that the coarse washrag would cool the burn while it scraped over her irritated skin, he rinsed the remnants of the shaving cream. Her pink, swollen lips quivered. "Can you feel the menthol, slave? The cool burn on your hot nub and deep inside your pussy?"

She nodded, biting her lip.

"I buy this gel in a special store. It's stronger than most. Shall I always shave you with it?"

Her blush darkened, but she nodded.

He ran the tip of his finger over her anus. "Stay."

Madison felt like a puppy with her legs up in the air as she waited for her owner's touch. She kept her eyes on Drake, watched him return and squirt a glob of lubricant on the tip of his finger. The heat of the menthol still pulsed over her pussy and anus. The touch of the cold lubricant sent a gasp to her lips.

"Relax, baby. Just relax."

She felt the plug slide in. Drake kept his eyes on her face the entire time. When her unforgiving muscles pinched and she bit her lip to still her cry, he halted.

"This one is larger, my sweet slave. I'm thicker than most men. When I take you here," he said in a soothing tone as he resumed pushing the plug in, "I want to make sure you feel no real pain and enjoy every second. Tell me if you feel more than a slight pinch and I'll stop."

From the way he talked, you would think he was pulling out a splinter rather than sticking the odd-looking device up her ass. His tone and concerned expression managed to calm her, though, and take away the embarrassment that had swept over her when he started. She drew in a sharp breath when the last of it slid in and her body clamped around the narrow rim.

After replacing her chains and bell, he carried her to the bedroom. As Drake sat her on the edge of the bed, he handled her as if she were made of the most delicate glass. Still, the plug surged up into her, reminding her of its presence. Shame enflamed her cheeks, desire simmered in her veins, but something about the way he treated her made the scenario about so much more than sex. He blow dried her hair and brushed it until it shone. When he finished, he lifted her legs and slid her under the cool satin sheets. Madison nearly came when he yanked off his shirt.

She drank in the sight of him as inch by inch he exposed his magnificent body. A shudder ran through her when she imagined that massive shaft of heat plunging into her pussy. As he moved, the muscles on his legs flexed and rippled.

He stood staring down at her. She recalled his conversation with Rob.

"Do you like me?" she asked, meeting his gaze.

Instead of answering, he flicked off the light and climbed onto the bed. The mattress sank from the weight of his body causing her to tilt in toward him. Her bell softly chimed. She belonged to Drake. His sex slave. Her fingers slid down the length of her chains to the bell.

"Do not touch yourself without my permission." His voice sounded weary, as if he were reprimanding a child or puppy who could not seem to learn how to obey.

"But..." She stared into the darkness at the mirror over the bed. He stared back, his expression blank.

"Go to sleep, Madison." Remaining on his back, he pulled the sheets over them.

Sleep?

Her eyes burned. She turned onto her side with her back to him so he wouldn't see her tears. Staring at the glowing numbers on the alarm clock, she wondered what tomorrow would be like. A few minutes later she heard him shift and felt his body spoon hers. Heat blanketed her back, buttocks and legs. He wrapped his arm around her waist and pulled her closer. She kept her breathing even and stared into the darkness.

Nearly an hour passed, but his arm draped over her waist and his hard cock pressed into her buttocks defeated any attempts at sleep. She sniffed and burrowed her head into the pillow.

His whisper flowed over her cheek. "Like is too weak a word for what I'm feeling, Madison Garrett." He drew in a ragged breath. "And it kills me that by the end of this week, you'll probably hate the sight of me."

She wondered what he meant by that. Why he was so sure she would hate him.

Still, the fact that he cared about her brought a smile to her lips.

* * * * *

Drake opened his eyes and squinted into the shaft of sunlight spilling through his window. For one brief moment, he wondered why he had spent the night in the room he normally kept for scenes with the few subs he trusted with his identity. No one, not even Giselle, his short-lived affair of the heart, had earned the right to spend the night.

The image of Madison nuzzling his chest as she slept brought a smile to his face. Last night, he had watched her feign sleep. Convinced that she would flee the moment he dozed, he had stayed up most of the night. When his sweet slave finally started to snore then turned and snuggled into his arms, he had closed his eyes.

Now, he glanced down at the pillow cradled in his arms and cursed. Thinking she had learned enough to play a sub, the little she-cat must have snuck out and gone to the club.

Berating himself, he raced to his room and threw on some clothes. Halfway down the stairs the stench of burnt bacon broke through his fear. He waited in the hall until his heart beat a little slower then casually strode into the kitchen. The sight that greeted him sent his heart rate spiraling out of control.

Sunlight streamed through the windows over the sink highlighting the pans, dishes and splattered food covering every available surface. The sight of his once pristine kitchen in such complete disarray had little to do with his pulse racing.

Standing in a halo of light, Madison swayed naked before the stove. Humming softly to herself, she took the last egg from the carton and cracked it over the frying pan.

"Yes!" she cried, shoving her fist into the air. "You can do it." She did a little jig.

Drake held in the chuckle that tickled his throat.

Smoke billowed from another pan on the stove. A loud pop sent her leaping back with a cry. He rushed up to her and grabbed her as she started to step back up to the stove.

She swatted his hands away. "Go sit. I'm trying to cook you breakfast, like a good slave."

"You're only a slave to my sexual needs, Madison." He slid his hands over her hips and ground his erection into the cushion of her buttocks. "Something I seem to have every time I'm near you."

"Hmmm..." She spun around and handed him the spatula. "That's a relief. I thought we'd starve this week."

"God, what have you done to yourself?" He lifted her up and sat her on the only uncluttered spot on the island. Tiny red dots covered her stomach and breasts.

"Oh, those. No matter what I tried, the bacon wouldn't stop spitting at me." She peered up at his face with those big green eyes and shrugged. "It only burns a little. Well, this one's a killer."

Drake followed her gaze to a nasty blister next to the scar beside her belly button. "Stay."

He opened the drawer next to the sink and took out burn ointment.

Madison released a loud, weary sigh. "You know, you have to stop talking to me like I'm some puppy."

When he threw her a warning glance, she stuck out her tongue. Dabbing ointment over each dot, he shook his head. "You're lucky. Some Masters and Mistresses really do treat their slaves like dogs."

"The abusive ones?" she asked, brushing his hair off his forehead.

"No. They literally treat them like dogs. Cherished pets. Their subs eat and drink from bowls on the floor. Watch TV curled at their feet and sleep in a large dog bed on the floor." He kissed the red dots marring the pure white skin of her breasts. "They even take them for walks."

"No!" Madison cupped his cheeks and, drawing his face up to meet hers, glared into his eyes. "I do not squat and pee on command. Geez, I mean, think about it. Me?"

Drake tried to picture her doing just that. Laughing at the image of this jewel-crushing dynamo meekly squatting as he held her leash, he admitted, "It's too ridiculous to even consider." He flicked her nipple. "Then again, last night I do recall you getting into some positions I never imagined the Madison Garrett I first met would."

"I *thought* I was going to get laid. If I'd known you only had sleep on your mind...well, let's just say I might have reconsidered my actions." She stuck out her lower lip and slumped.

Drake laughed so hard at her attempt to look contrite that he dropped the tube of burn ointment. While he bent to pick it up, Madison slid the side of her foot up his thigh.

"You should do that more often, Drake."

"What," he asked, squeezing more ointment and smoothing it as gently as he could over another burn.

"Laugh." Her foot continued to caress his thigh. "With your whole body

He glanced up, her words cutting through him more than she could know. Sure, he laughed sometimes, but not like this, not where he felt that laugh inside as well as on the surface. It struck him that with Madison he had been doing that more and more often.

The smell of burning bacon forced him to turn away from her probing gaze. The egg she had been so pleased with stared up at him with blackened edges, and the offending bacon looked ready to burst into flames.

"I don't suppose there are anymore eggs or bacon in the house?" He flicked off the two burners.

"I burned them. I'm not that skilled in the kitchen."

"Really? I never would have noticed." He tossed the smoking pan into the sink. "I think that pan has lived its last day."

"You're angry." She moved to hop off the counter.

"Stay, puppy." He wedged himself between her legs. Had any other woman aroused him as easily? If so, he couldn't remember. "Is there coffee?"

"I made a wicked pot of coffee. Let me down and I'll pour you some." Her fingers tangled in his hair, sending chills down his spine.

"How about you go upstairs to your room, pick out a dress, then I take you out to breakfast."

She wiggled closer and ran her tongue over his lips. "Really?"

"Keep it up, and I'll change my mind and resume your training on an empty stomach."

"Drake?" She wrapped her legs around his waist and burrowed her moist pussy into his aching erection.

"You're pushing it." He ground himself into her.

"Just one question."

"Okay, shoot."

"You see, I've never," she stated in a husky voice as she shifted her hips forward, "*ever* had sex with a man unless he wore a condom and well, I, well, shit, how do I say this?"

"When was the last time I went without one?"

She nodded, her lip once again snagged between her teeth.

He could almost feel those teeth grazing down the length of his cock. "Not since I was a stupid fourteen-year-old."

"So that would be how long ago?"

"Just under twenty years."

"So we're both not a risk." She shimmied forward. "I say we skip breakfast."

"If I were intending to do that, you just blew it, slave. I say when. And where." He grasped her around the waist and picked her up. Placing her on her feet, he turned her around to face the hall and gave her butt a light smack. "Go, slave."

When she had disappeared up the stairs, he ground his teeth and tried to calm his painful erection. The thought of sliding into her hot pussy with nothing separating her flesh from his skin had him wincing as blood surged into his cock.

Only closing his eyes and picturing the burns she suffered from her attempts to make him breakfast stopped him from charging up those stairs after her and demanding she spread her legs. Instead, he set about cleaning the kitchen.

* * * * *

Standing in the midst of hundreds of tables, Madison wondered how she had managed to live here so long without once checking out the annual New York City Fetish Market. The vast size of it, the crush of people weaving their way between the tables stunned her. She never knew so many dabbled in lifestyles considered outside society's boundaries of normal or acceptable.

Long tables were laden with leather manacles, straps and belts. Others had stands to display whips and floggers in every color, slender sticks of cane and Lucite and frightening-looking knives of all shapes and sizes. Booths housed furnishings that either baffled her or sent a bevy of decadent fantasies running through her mind.

Fetish clothing she had never known existed caught her eye at every turn. Teddies that consisted of nothing but studded leather straps. Corsets in leather, latex and lace called to her. Shoes with heels that were too high to even consider and ankle straps that reminded her of the manacles she'd struggled against the previous night sent an apprehensive shudder down her spine when Drake held them up and winked.

Taking the shoes from his hands, she returned them to the table and smiled at the burly man sitting behind it. "Thanks, but we're not interested."

Retrieving the shoes, Drake scowled. "How much?"

"Drake," Madison grabbed his upper arm. "They'll kill me after two minutes."

"Keep forgetting your place, and you'll be wearing them for two hours." Turning, he nodded toward a low stool. "Sit."

"Listen, Conan, I'm not wearing them." Jamming her clenched fists on her hips, she watched him lean close. When his nubs scratched her cheek, she closed her eyes and ground her teeth. They were so sharp, so damn abrasive. She could almost feel them rubbing her nipples until they were raw. Deciding to turn the tables, to take his mind off the shoes, she rubbed her cheek against his and brought her mouth flush against his ear. "Damn, those nubs feel good. I can think of two or three places I'd like to feel them scratching."

"Sit, Madison, or I'll put you over my knee and show everyone here just how pretty your ass looks when it's all pink," he said in her ear, the rich timbre of his voice edged with that steeliness that always made her tingle.

"You wouldn't." Turning, she looked up into his eyes. Stark, unbridled desire held her prisoner.

"Can you see it, my sweet slave?"

The vision blindsided her. Heat pooled between her legs, pulsed and throbbed like a breathing, living beast that demanded he carry out his threat, that he drape her over his knee and show all those around them just how much she enjoyed the feel of his hands striking her butt. Had she closed the distance between them without realizing it? Clad all in black, Drake seemed taller, more powerful. His eyes, although darkened, appeared bluer.

Ten minutes later, Madison eyed the bag in Drake's hand. "I really don't want to wear them, Drake. I'll fall."

"Who said you'd be walking around in them?" Drake snaked his arm around her shoulder. "I was hoping you'd argue a little longer. You left me with a raging hard-on, my sweet."

Snorting, Madison glanced down. "Yeah, I can see that. But don't get all full of yourself. I only gave in because you had me so hot, another minute with you looking at me like that, and I would have knocked you down and raped you right there."

When he laughed, a rich, hearty laugh, her heart beat faster.

"Raped me?"

"That's right. I would have taken you down, whipped out that raging hard-on and rocked until I came." Giggling, she added, "For the sake of propriety, I'd come within seconds. You, on the other hand, would have had to wait until we got back to your place."

He halted so suddenly, she almost toppled back from the pull of his arm on her shoulder. "What are you? A dominatrix in disguise?"

Brushing her chest up against his, she leered, "Maybe I am. Would you let me tie you up and tease and torture you, Master?"

He shocked her by cupping her face in his palms. Staring intently into her eyes, he leaned in and licked her lower lip. "It'll never happen, slave. I don't switch."

"Switch?" How did he do it, she wondered. How did he manage to turn her legs to mush with a simple glance? A swipe of his tongue?

"When a Dom switches with his sub and becomes the sub."

Licking where his tongue had licked moments before, Madison nodded solemnly. "Oh, I could never imagine you on your knees wiggling that tight ass up for a spanking. It would scar me for life."

Wincing, he tightened his hold on her. "Well, that took care of my hard on."

"Bet I can get it back up with two words."

Someone bumped into Drake's shoulder. He didn't move, didn't take his eyes from hers. "Two?"

She smiled, "Just two."

"What do I get if you don't?" His eyes crinkled as he dazzled her with his smile.

"I will, so whatever you want."

"Shoot."

Madison licked her lips. "I'm dripping."

Drake's fingertips dug into her hair. "Dripping?" His voice cracked.

"Literally dripping. As in down my legs." God, she loved bringing this man to his knees, even if just mentally. "So? Did it work?"

In reply, Drake crushed her lips in a jarring kiss. She felt him grind his rock-hard erection into her stomach, wondered how he managed to draw her in until her entire torso met his hard body while he still held her face in his hands. Lost in his kiss, wishing she could open her mouth more, take in more of his sweet taste, she saw them as those around them did. Her rising up on her toes so his tongue could delve deeper and the ridge of his cock could burrow against the bell hanging from her clit. She heard it ring that she belonged to the Drake. Could others? Did they know what it meant?

And why didn't she care?

Wearing the dress Drake had laid out for her that day and only her chains beneath it, she found she felt neither concern nor shame that she wore a collar, that her nipples strained against the thin fabric, or that the crease where her thighs met her butt smiled at all who passed behind her. Women and men with collars and leashes, some with shirts bearing slogans such as "Spank Me, It's My Birthday" ran their fingers reverently over various items of punishment. Others wearing jeans and tee shirts chatted and laughed with those holding up skimpy latex dresses and jumpsuits.

The scents of exotic aphrodisiac oils and leather mingled, swirled around them. Candles burned at one table, but when Madison lifted them to sniff then frowned up at Drake after uncovering no scent, both Drake and the vendor laughed at some secret joke. Another glance behind the table, and she understood. A tall, bald man with tattoos emblazoned on his arms, chest and back tilted one of the candles until liquid wax poured onto the palm of a tall, muscular woman. The equally muscular man beside her adjusted the leather collar around his neck then held his hand, palm down, beneath the stream of wax.

"That looks dangerous," she muttered.

Tugging a lock of her hair, Drake led her away from the vendor's table. "It is, if the person holding the candle doesn't know what he's doing."

"I take it, you do?" Hooking her arm in his, they squeezed into a tightly crowded lane. She struggled to ignore the twinges of pain and ensuing tingles of pleasure from the arms and elbows brushing against her chains.

Drake halted in front of a table dripping with silver-chained and bejeweled clamps. "I am considered a Master of most of the arts."

She snorted. "Arts. Gimme a break!"

Steering her away from the table, he brought her to the back of a crowd milling around one of the vendors. "Watch."

Even at her height, all she could see was the broad back in front of her. "Watch what? This guy's back?"

Sighing, Drake grabbed her by the waist and hoisted her up onto his shoulders. "That better?"

Better? Madison couldn't answer. At first, she tumbled back to her youth so swiftly, she thought she'd fall off Drake's shoulders. She was five again, sitting atop her father's shoulders as she watched the Macy's Thanksgiving Day Parade pass. Drake's hairs tickling her bare pussy, snatched her from the past and brought her attention to the scene that had caught the attention of so many. A man clad in tight leather pants and a matching studded vest raised a long whip high above his head. With a flick of his wrist the whip shot out and knocked a thorn from the long-stemmed rose in tall bud vase.

"Shit! Did you see that?" Leaning down to the side, Madison glanced at Drake. "The vase didn't move!"

Another whack brought her attention back to the demonstration. Another thorn. Wriggling on Drake's shoulders, she watched in awe until the last thorn dropped onto the table. Peering over the heads below, she caught sight of another crowd.

"Oh, Drake! Over there!" She leaned down and gazed into smiling eyes. "Corsets!"

Later, in the makeshift dressing room with Drake, Madison regretted her decision. "Okay, okay, that's tight enough."

Madison gasped as Drake tugged on the ribbon lacing the back of the corset. "What are you trying to do? Kill me?"

Another sharp tug sent any air remaining in her lungs whooshing out. "You're forgetting your manners, slave," he murmured. The soft rustle of ribbon and a glance over her shoulder revealed that he'd tied the ribbon into a bow.

Telling her weeping pussy to quit crying at the worst times, she spun around. "Da...rake. I can't breathe."

A loud, stinging smack to her butt and gruff "Master" sent a yelp to her lips and heat to her face. She had no doubt all on the other side of the curtain heard.

"All right, Master," she whispered, "please. I'm dying here."

Stepping to the side, he revealed her reflection in the mirror. Her waist looked so small, she wondered if Drake's long fingers would meet wrapped around it. Her breasts spilled over the top. Nipples, clamps and all, were bared. Her chains draped in front of the leather corset appeared starker and more decadent. Oh her pussy sobbed at the sight. She could barely inhale, barely move.

Drake smirked. "Well?"

Madison looked in the mirror. "I can't wear it to work." Then with a wink, she laughed, "Oh, right! I can. I'm working now!"

Dipping his head, Drake lapped at a swollen nipple. "I think these loops need to be loosened."

Grateful, enjoying the feel of his rough tongue abrading the over-sensitized, puckered bud, she jutted her chest toward him. His tongue stilled.

"Oh, God, don't stop now!"

Drake released a long, weary-sounding sigh.

Realizing what she had forgotten, what he now waited for, she took a deep breath and yelled, "Thank you, Master!"

Applause from outside the dressing room filtered into her mind a moment before darkness engulfed her. When she opened her eyes from what felt like a mere blink, she found herself cradled on Drake's lap. Midnight blue eyes beneath a furrowed brow and filled with concern met hers.

"Are you all right?" He pressed a brief tender kiss to her lips before she could reply.

Madison smiled up at him. "That must have been some orgasm. I don't even remember having it."

Drake grinned. "I think it had more to do with me getting carried away with the corset."

She felt his arm shift over her breasts. Sitting up, she held his gaze and licked his lips. "Well, don't let a little fainting spell stop you. Back to work, my masterful Master of orgasms."

"Ah, Madison I—"

"Oh, come on. I said Master!" Madison tried to shove his arm away from her breasts, but Drake held firm.

"Madison."

"Please, Master. Okay? I said it again." Taking a deep breath, she noticed she no longer felt the death grip of the corset. At the same time, she heard a soft chuckle behind her, saw the empty dressing room a few feet behind Drake, noticed her corset lying on the floor. "We're not alone, are we?" she whispered.

Drake shook his head. "Say it again."

She stared into his eyes, knew exactly what he meant. "Or?"

"Or I move my arm."

Silence loomed from whoever stood listening. "Um...just out of curiosity. How many people are behind me?"

An evil glint in his eyes made her stomach sink.

"Do you want just the five or six who watched me and the vendor cut you out of the corset, or should I start counting heads in the crowd that has gathered since I carried you out here?"

"Can I keep the corset?" She licked her lips and leaned in close to his chest.

"Say it, slave. They all heard you yell it, so saying it won't make a difference now." White teeth flashed as he laughed.

Wrapping her arms around his neck, she brought her lips to his ear. "Master, Master, Master."

Drake leaned back and peered at her. "Is that sarcastic?"

Kissing his lips, she rubbed her cheek into his nubs and sighed. "Not at all, my sweet Master."

"Really?" He raised a brow. "I will expose you if you disobey me. You have to learn how to act like a proper slave."

Madison rebelled against Drake's domination, yet, some part of her embraced her role as his submissive so fully that it terrified her. As he carried her back into the dressing room, she breathed in his scent. "Drake?"

He closed the curtain then lowered her to her feet. "Yes?"

"I...I...need a couple of hours to...to bring my cat to my neighbor for the week and check my mail."

"Spread your legs."

Spreading her legs, she watched him drop to his knees. Her eyes burned when he tilted his head back and licked his lips then raised a brow. Holding her tongue for no more than the second it took to curse herself, she whispered, "Please, Master."

* * * * *

As soon as Madison opened the door to her apartment and saw Aunt Louisa decked out in black leather pants and matching vest, she flung herself into her aunt's arms. Only her aunt would turn away a client for her. Only her aunt would ask no questions when she called and asked her to come over immediately. The familiar strength in her aunt's warm embrace seemed to fortify her, something she needed desperately after her time with Drake.

"I must be in the wrong apartment. My niece would never wear a dress like..." Aunt Louisa stilled then leaned back and frowned down at Madison's chest. "What's this all about?"

Backing out of her arms, Madison turned and walked into her kitchen. "I made your favorite."

"Maddy." Aunt Louisa met her as she entered the living room.

Holding a plate laden with melon and cheese wedges in each hand, Madison could only stand and inwardly groan as her aunt ran her fingers down the front of her dress until they touched the chains.

"Chains? My Maddy wearing chains?" Aunt Louisa plucked open a button and slipped one long finger in then hooked a chain and dragged it into view. "And I had such hopes you'd make a fine Domme one day."

Feeling the tug on her nipple, Madison heard the phrase Drake had repeated all morning as he tugged on her chains. Property of Drake Williams. She wondered if her aunt heard the bell chiming that she belonged to him, that no one could make her scream or cry like he did. She shimmied away and set the plates on the bistro table in front of the window. "Do you want iced tea or soda?"

"Maddy, you know I hate your sugar-laden version of iced-tea." Sitting down at the table, her aunt adjusted her bra, plopped a chunk of melon into her mouth then coughed as if she were choking. "Did I just hear a bell? Please tell me this is just part of your training."

Madison poured iced tea into two tall, ice-filled glasses and brought them to the table. "Of course, it is."

When she sat down, she realized too late that she had forgotten about her plug and grunted when it surged up on impact. Glancing up, she found her aunt once again frowning. "What?"

"I know that sound, Missy." Aunt Louisa arched her brow as she tapped long, red acrylic nails on the glass tabletop.

"I don't know what you're talking about," Madison muttered.

"No? You think I don't hear that little grunt every time one of my subs sits down? You think I don't know why they grunt?" She reached across the table and grasped Madison's wrist. "Shit, Maddy. A butt plug? Why the hell do you need that to train for this story? They don't allow anal sex in the club, dammit!"

Madison pulled her hand away. "Really? That bastard." Picking up her glass, she brought it up to her mouth, but the clinking of the ice rattling as the glass shook had her slamming the glass down. "I...I..." She met her aunt's searching look head on. "I think I'm in trouble here."

Raising the glass of iced tea Madison had poured for her, Aunt Louisa snorted. "You think? I can't remember the last time you asked me if I wanted this crap and today, you asked then gave it to me after I reminded you that I hate it. Okay, break out the wine."

An hour later, pleasantly buzzed by the wine and snuggled on the couch beside her aunt, Madison continued her long tirade on Drake's so-called training methods. "Then this morning, he said we were going out to breakfast then made me sit facing the restaurant. Oh God, Aunt Louisa, he made me sit with my legs open the entire time."

Aunt Louisa popped a cheese wedge in her mouth and chewed, a pensive look on her face. Finally she swallowed and shook her head. "If I know Drake, he sat in front of you. The man never could get humiliation training right. Am I right?"

Shocked, Madison nodded. "Well, yeah, but it was still damn humiliating."

"Really? I'm sure no one saw a thing."

Lifting her head, Madison scowled. "He kept banging my legs so the bell would tinkle. Every five seconds! Ring. Ring. Then him telling me that I belonged to him and making me repeat it. I belong to you. My body belongs to you. I'm your sweet slave."

"Sweet. Never heard him say that before. Go on."

"Isn't that enough?" Shifting away from her aunt, Madison stood up and paced over to the window. Glancing out, she realized that she had expected to see Drake waiting down on the sidewalk. What she didn't expect was the sense of longing and disappointment when she failed to find him there. Before he had dropped her off, he brought her to the brink of orgasm again, then left her there, unfulfilled, needy and horny as hell. Bastard.

"Look, judging by everything you've told me so far, Drake is acting exactly the way I'd expect him to. Well, a little too giving and kind, but acceptable."

Madison spun around then moaned and grabbed her breasts. "This is normal?" Her throbbing nipples felt like they were the size of grapes. "Is this safe?"

"Of course. He knows what he's doing, Madison. I don't understand why he's taking your training for this job so fa..." With a delighted laugh, Aunt Louisa pushed herself up from the couch and wagged a finger at Madison. "Get over here."

Madison hesitated. She loved her aunt more than any other woman in her family, but the woman had a way of dominating that made them butt heads at times. "Why?"

"I'm not sure what's up, but I think he's digging in."

"Digging in?"

"Tell me something. Did you have to ask permission to have lunch with me?"

Heat flared over Madison cheeks. "I told him I had to feed my cat and bring it to a neighbor's for the week."

"The week?"

The heat intensified. "Well, I'm kind of staying with him while I train."

"Maddy, get your butt over here."

Unable to stop herself, Madison took one more look out the window. "I'm dying here, Aunt Louisa," she whined as she crossed the room. "This is so not me."

Aunt Louisa took Madison's chin in a firm grip. "Listen, Maddy, you remember one thing. You have total control."

Madison snorted. "Yeah, right."

The grip on her chin grew painfully tight. "I mean it. You think those big lugs that kneel at my feet have no control? You think I can do anything I want to them, without them having any say?"

"I thought that's why you did it. To get off on the control."

Her aunt released her cheek then tousled Madison's hair as if she were a silly child. "I do. But I'm well aware that my control is only there because they allow it. I have no foolish notions that my subs have no say. Contracts, Maddy. They sign contracts and change them when *they* feel the need. Plus, there are the safe words."

When Madison just stared back, her aunt continued. "I don't know what Drake Williams has up his sleeve, nor will I interfere with your training in case his plans are for your safety, but you must always remember that you have the final say in everything he does. Got it?"

"Hell, he doesn't act like I have say."

"Neither do I, dear. When I tell my sub to shove his ass up so I can whip it, he'd better get it as high as he can! The sub's power is subtle, hidden, understood. The Domme's power, or Dom's in your situation, is in your face for you and all to see. He is in control from the minute you sign away your rights, but you have the right to take them back if you are not happy with how he uses that control. Understand?"

Nodding, Madison stole a glance at the clock. Her heart rate sped up at an alarming rate when she noticed that her time away from Drake would end in just ten minutes. Again, as she had done so many times in the past, her aunt seemed to read her mind.

"You can't wait to get back to him, can you?"

Aunt Louisa's knuckles brushing down Madison's cheeks slowed her racing heart. "Crazy, huh?"

"No, not crazy. The man is a natural dominant and gorgeous." Planting a kiss on Madison's forehead, her aunt drew up her shoulders. "Well, I have my favorite client kneeling in my dungeon waiting for my return. All this talk has me itching to get back to him and those pink cheeks."

Madison watched her walk to the window and peek outside then jerk away.

"Better get your butt in gear. He just stepped out of a cab."

Her heart leapt to her throat. Every erogenous zone tingled in anticipation. "Don't let him see you. I'll never hear the end of it if he knew I panicked and...if you..."

Opening the door, her aunt waved over her shoulder. "I'll just wait in the foyer until you two leave. And Madison? Lighten up. You might enjoy this."

* * * * *

The heat wave still held the city in its grip. While most in Central Park sought shelter from the sweltering sun on one of the benches lining the shaded paths, Madison ran down to the pond. She caught Drake's longing glance at the cool interior of the surrounding trees before joining her.

"If you're hot, we could sit there. Thanks to you, I'm quite comfortable."

"Thanks to me?" He wrapped his arm around her shoulders and steered her to a bench close to the water.

She spun around. "This dress is so thin the slightest breeze goes right through it. And as per your orders, oh mighty Master," she bowed, revealing her breasts, "I have nothing else on."

"I think you just proved that to the couple behind you."

Shooting a glance over her shoulder and discovering that they were alone, she punched him in the arm. "Ow! Your muscles are hard."

Drake snagged her waist and drew her down onto his lap. "Slaves do not punch their Masters."

Although his voice sounded gruff and he glared at her, Madison could see that his lips quirked up. After another decadent night under his rule, another night without him introducing her pussy to his cock, she couldn't help herself. She wrapped her arms around his neck and gave him what she hoped was a phenomenal kiss. Lifting her lips just enough to speak, she murmured, "I just took without asking. Will I be punished tonight, Master?"

"Do you think you deserve to be punished?" He nibbled her lower lip.

"Oh, definitely. At least twice." She felt his erection grow beneath her. Taking Aunt Louisa's advice, Madison had returned yesterday determined to lighten up and enjoy her slavery. As usual, following her aunt's advice proved a wise choice. Her introduction to Drake's flogger early this morning convinced her that punishment had definite merits.

Groaning, he lifted her up and set her down beside him.

"I love the way you do that. Lift me up like that."

"Like what?"

"You know. I'm so tall, but you make me feel, oh, I don't know, like I'm petite, like I don't weigh that much."

"Madison, you're tall but slender. Here, put some meat on those bones."

Feeling happier than she had in years, she took the muffin and container of coffee. As she picked a blueberry from her muffin, she felt Drake stiffen.

"Hey, Master D. Where've you been?" A sultry voice slithered down Madison's spine.

Chapter Seven

As Madison glanced up, Drake gripped her knee. The woman standing before them was stunning. Legs that seemed to go on forever peeked out from shorts that, judging by the front, revealed a substantial amount of her butt. The bikini top barely covered her breasts. Long blonde hair, pale blue eyes, collagen-enhanced lips and a face too perfect to be real made Madison's stomach sink. Painfully aware that she had gone out without makeup and with her hair in a messy ponytail, she wondered if Drake found this woman attractive then mentally smacked herself in the head. Of course, he did. Only a gay man wouldn't.

Drake set his coffee on the bench beside him and slung his arm over Madison's shoulder, drawing her closer. "I've been around, Giselle. And you?"

Giselle glanced down at Madison and smirked. "Girlfriend, you'd better run home before Drake, here, gets out his whips and chains."

"Maybe I like whips and chains." Madison jutted her chin out.

"Yeah? Wait 'til he grows tired of those and takes out the big guns." She scowled at Drake. "Then you realize you're just another toy."

Drake's grip tightened on her shoulders. "Madison will never be any man's toy, Giselle. That's where she and you differ."

"We'll see." She turned walked up to stand in front of Drake, angling herself so her back faced Madison. "You hear about the subs getting hurt at Train Me?"

"Thought you weren't into that anymore," Drake answered as he shifted his hand then drew circles on Madison's neck with his thumb.

Giselle stuck her hand out revealing an engagement ring with a massive diamond that couldn't possibly be real. "I'm not. But I stayed friends with some of your pals' subs, Drake. Carol got hurt real bad in there last night."

Madison tried not to wince when Drake's fingers dug into her skin.

"Is she all right?" His voice was so cold, so menacing an icy chill slid down Madison's spine.

"She'll live. Word's out some reporter's going to go in." She glanced over her shoulder at Madison then back to Drake. "Carol said the creep kept asking her if she's a reporter, said she had the right color hair and eyes." She frowned at Madison, then blinked and turned fully toward Drake. "You work at a magazine. You hear of this reporter? Same coloring as your new pain slut, here."

"Listen, you anorexic bitch," Madison struggled to rise, but Drake held her down and cut off her next words.

"Don't know anything about a reporter, Giselle, but I'd stay out of it, if I were you."

"Oh, you don't have to tell me. Carol said he beat the shit out of her, telling her that she should have taken his warning seriously. Carol thinks he meant what happened to Mistress Louisa because word's out that she trained the reporter."

"Mistress Louisa?" Madison choked out. Her coffee and muffin tumbled to the ground.

Giselle jumped back just in time to avoid being splattered with coffee. She adjusted her bikini top until it covered the bottoms of her breasts and exposed more cleavage. "She's in the hospital. Hit and run. Poor old bitch."

If Drake hadn't shot her a warning glance, Madison would have flattened Miss Perfect. Gritting her teeth, she watched out of the corner of her eye as Drake leaned closer to

Giselle. Madison missed what they discussed. The pounding of her heart drowned out all other sounds. The smell of coffee mingled with the overpowering sugary scent of whatever perfume Giselle doused herself in and made Madison's stomach roil. Visions of her aunt looking like the women in the photos she'd seen in Rob's office made it lurch. She stared down at Giselle's petite, sandal-clad feet, wondered what the woman would do if Madison upchucked all over them.

Finally after fluttering her ring under their noses, Giselle bid them farewell. Drake firmly held Madison down until Giselle disappeared down a path. As soon as he relaxed his hold, Madison shot off the bench and took off running across the park.

She felt Drake's hands grab her around the waist and lift her into his arms. His warmth and strength surrounded her, but all she could think of was getting to Aunt Louisa. "Let me go!"

"Madison, wait. She exaggerated just to get to you. I never get rough with my subs."

His subs? Was she just one of many? It didn't matter.

Nothing mattered except Aunt Louisa. Blindly she punched and kicked at him as she struggled for freedom. "Oh God, Drake, oh God! Put me down."

"Dammit, Madison, calm down!"

She had to get to her aunt, had to get away from Drake, from becoming just another pain slut, just another sub. How many subs looked like her? How many would end up in the hospital? Or die?

Would Aunt Louisa? Was she already dead? Her heart felt as if some had shoved a knife in her chest and twisted it. "Let me go!"

No matter how hard she fought, Drake wouldn't release her. She kneed him in the balls and brought him down, but his grip only tightened. Finally exhausted, defeated, she crumpled against his chest and let the tears fall.

"Please, don't cry. You're breaking my heart." He kissed the top of her head. "What's wrong? Where were you running?"

"My aunt. I have to see my aunt." She tilted her head back and gazed into midnight blue eyes. "Let me go, Drake. Please, let me go to her."

Drake's eyes narrowed. "Your aunt? You're losing me here, Madison. Why do you suddenly have to go see your aunt?" He wiped the tears from her face with the back of his fingers.

"Mistress Louisa." A fresh deluge of tears flowed from her eyes, casting Drake in a swirling blur. When he frowned, she squeezed her eyes closed. "She's my aunt. Oh God. Rob! He'll think it's his fault."

"Mistress Louisa is your aunt?" His grip loosened then crushed her with its intensity.

The pain of his embrace cushioned her from the agony tearing into her heart. Welcoming his strength, accepting that without it, she would have crumpled to the ground in a useless heap, she felt it seep into her body, heard his heart rate kick up a notch yet remain steady enough to ground her own racing heart.

She nodded, wiping her tears onto his shirt. "And Rob's mother. He never acknowledges her. Even changed his last name." She dropped her forehead onto his chest. "I don't even know what hospital she's in."

"I'll make a few calls and then we'll go see how she is."

Breaking free of his embrace, she swiped away at her tears. The man amazed her. They hardly knew each other, yet he just assumed that she would want him, maybe even need him to get through this.

What had happened to the woman she had been before Drake? The woman who would never need a man's strength just so she could stand? The woman who, instead of falling apart and weeping in a man's arms, would have set to work investigating and uncovering who had discovered the link between her and her aunt and how. She had told no one. No one.

Madison choked on a sob, refusing to accept what she could not deny. "How did he know?"

Drake frowned but didn't answer.

"Aunt Louisa would never have told anyone about my job. She told me that first night that somehow word got out about me training, but not that it was for this story, not that I was a reporter. How did he find out? Only me, Rob and..."

She backed away. For all she knew, Drake had been the one.

Her heart sank. For all she knew, he was the man responsible for harming those girls.

It all made a sick sort of sense now. The way he had demanded Rob drop the assignment, and his refusal to admit she could pass for a sub. He had wanted a week. A week to keep an eye on her? A week to break her will and force her to give up the assignment?

She held her breath, took another step back. Her heart roared in her ears. "Don't touch me."

"Madison?" He stood up, still wincing from her attack. The side of his eye had already started swelling where she had head-butted him.

She almost moved to touch him, almost looked into those eyes that could make her forget everything. Make her forget the woman she had fought all these years to become.

Unmindful of anyone who might see, she reached under her dress and unlatched his chains. Tossing them on the ground, she swallowed the lump lodged in her throat. "Don't follow me, Drake. This game is over."

He clenched his fists at his side. "I don't know what the hell is going on, but you gave me a week. I own you, Madison Garrett. Now pick up the damn chains, and let's go find your aunt."

His voice rumbled, his muscles visibly tensed, but his eyes held a plea that nearly sent her back into his arms and control.

Shaking her head, she turned and fled.

* * * * *

"What the hell are you wearing?"

Madison swung away from NY Presbyterian Hospital's information desk. "Marco?"

Peering through her tears at the blurred shapes of her brothers barreling toward her, she braced herself for the usual friendly punches and bear hugs. When their massive arms wrapped around her without so much as a stinging jab, she melted into their embrace. As she had as a little girl, she sobbed against their muscled chests and allowed them to hold her up and kiss her tears away until she had the strength to speak. "Is she okay? Please, tell me she's all right."

When no one answered, her legs gave out. One of them, probably Lex judging from the beard scratching her temple, shoved the others away and held her against his chest.

"She looks bad, Maddy. Real bad." Lex looked down at her with shimmering eyes. "But the doc says she'll be fine."

The musky scent of Lex's cologne swirled around her head, but the rank odors that brought back too many memories of her own visits to various emergency rooms when she had been stabbed or beaten made their way in.

Pushing away from Lex, she palmed away her tears. "Take me to her."

"Not with you dressed like that. You look like a whore," Lex muttered

"What the fuck?" Christopher glared at her chest and the telltale bumps. Before she could back away, he ran his hands down her back. "She's not wearing a bra!"

"Shit, Chris." She glanced at the people in the chairs around them and cringed. "Why don't you tell the rest of the hospital?"

"Like they need him to tell them. Your teats are poking a hole in this tissue paper." Marco grabbed her chin. "What the hell's going on Maddy?"

Staring into the handsome face she had seen marred with rage too many times, she answered in a soothing voice. "It's just a job, Marco. I'm in disguise."

"Disguise? What kind of disguise shows more of you than we saw changing your diapers? Huh?" His eyes darkened, his right eyebrow shot up into a sharp, inverted V. "You're not playing a hooker again, are you?"

"No!" Madison tried to pry his fingers loose. When he refused to let go of her chin, she snarled, "Get your hands off me, Marco, or your wife will have to look elsewhere for a baby."

"Let her go, Marco." Lex's voice broke through the haze of anger enveloping Madison and Marco.

As soon as she felt the fingers holding her chin relax, she spun around and ran to the elevators. Of course, the three bears followed. She jumped when she felt Marco's hand sweep up the side of her thigh and hip.

"No underwear. My baby sister's wearing no fucking underwear!" Marco growled.

"Who did this? That weasel, Rob?" Chris sputtered, punching the elevator doors a second before they opened.

Wiping his spittle off her arm, Madison drew back her shoulders and strode into the elevator. She swatted Lex's hand away from her hip. "I like going commando."

"Like hell, you do." Lex stabbed the button marked with a three.

"You're not letting her go in like this, are you, Lex?" Chris elbowed past Madison.

"Yeah," Lex sighed then turned on Chris, "You gonna try to stop me?"

"Yeah, think you can take me and shortie, here?" Marco draped his arm over Chris's shoulder.

"I'm warning you, Marco. Call me that again and you'll pay. You've only got a quarter inch on me." Chris ducked out from under Marco's arm then drew himself up to his full six feet and glared into Lex's face. "We're getting her out of here before anyone sees her like this."

"Like hell you are." Madison smacked the back of Chris' head.

"I'm letting her see Aunt Louisa before we take her home and get her dressed. And that's that." Lex took a step toward Madison.

She watched Marco and Chris sweep in front of her and block Lex. Who would think these men had wives, children and profitable businesses?

"Nobody 'lets' me do anything." She frowned. "I mean..."

Ignoring her, the men continued to stare each other down until the doors swung open. Darting out before they could stop her, she ran down the hall. Glass instead of walls separated the patients from the nurses. Madison's heart sank when she realized her aunt's condition warranted a room in ICU. She peeked in each room as she shuffled between walking and running. Skidding to a halt a few feet past the last room she checked, she felt her eyes burn and her mouth grow dry. She would never think the woman lying in that bed was her aunt, but few women had hair the color of bourbon streaked with gold. And few would have a cop sitting outside their door.

As she approached the door, the cop stood and moved to block it.

"Let her in." Marco's voice left no room for argument. The cop dropped back down onto the chair. "And keep your dirty eyes off my sister's ass."

Madison held out her hand. She couldn't go in without them. As much as she hated the way they always bossed her around, she needed them at a time like this. She knew it and they knew it.

They were gruff, overbearing and downright bearish, but they were always there for her with a shoulder, a hug and a smile.

Marco wrapped his hand around hers and led her in. When she reached her aunt's side and her knees buckled, Lex caught her. While she cried on his shoulder, Marco and Chris rubbed her back and kissed her temples, cheeks, shoulder. All three vowed the person responsible for hurting their aunt would pay.

Madison prayed Drake hadn't leaked out word of her plans for Train Me, Chain Me. The three bears would pulverize him before he threw a punch. Guilt over her accusation swamped her. The Drake she had come to know over the past few days wouldn't do this. God, he had nearly taken Rob's head off for suggesting she risk getting beaten.

Madison stepped out of Marco's arms. "Oh my God, Rob! He must be freaking out."

"The weasel, as you can see," Chris swept his hand out toward the empty room, "didn't even show."

She couldn't imagine Rob not being at his mother's side. "Are you sure he knows?"

"He called *us*. Thought he should stay away," Marco muttered, pulling a chair up to the bed for her.

"Stay away?" Madison sat down and took hold of her aunt's hand. It felt lifeless, cold. The lump in her throat grew. "Why the hell would he say that?" she whispered.

Scowling, Lex leaned against the wall and crossed his arms. "Why do you think? You know Rob."

Chris paced. "The fucking weasel. He's worried."

Marco walked over to the window and peered out. Mimicking Rob's voice, he whined, "There'll probably be reporters there. I can't chance having my picture in the paper with her. Could you imagine what that would do to the magazine?"

"No." Madison shook her head then glanced at Aunt Louisa. "Does he realize she's in ICU? He probably—"

"He knows." Lex pushed away from the wall. "Why do you always stick up for him? The man is slime. Even if he wasn't worried about bad publicity, he'd leave her here alone. You know Rob and germs."

Marco punched the wall a little too close to the window as far as Madison was concerned. "The fucking bastard's probably glad she got hit."

"Marco! How can you say that?" Madison shot a worried glance down at her aunt. Thankfully her eyes remained closed.

"How? Oh, Robbie Rabbit would have done this himself if he wasn't such a wimp. She's so popular with her boy toys because she's got beauty and balls, Maddy! If Aunt Louisa is scarred, she can kiss Mistress Louisa goodbye. And you know damn well how Rob's been praying for that all these years." Marco looked at Lex and Chris for support. They both grimly nodded.

Madison watched her brothers stare at her aunt. Like her, they loved the aunt and the infamous Mistress Louisa. Unlike her, they couldn't understand why Rob found it so hard to accept his mother. "You're wrong. Rob loves Aunt Louisa. Sure, he's embarrassed. But he still loves her."

Lex strode to the door and flung it open. "Believe what you want, Maddy. He's not here, and in my book, that brands him a bastard. We'll go get some coffee and give you some time alone."

Chris and Marco followed him into the hall.

Madison knelt beside Aunt Louisa's bed and started to pray.

For her aunt.

For Rob.

For herself.

*****

Drake had checked nearly every hospital in the city. Realizing he didn't know Louisa's last name, he tried calling the police and asking for the name of the woman recently involved in a hit and run, but they refused to give out any information. He called all the Mistresses, Masters and subs he knew and with each call became more and more determined to find Madison and lock her up indefinitely.

Giselle had not exaggerated. According to word on the street, his little slave's days were numbered. Some of the Masters, those having no clue of the abuse taking place at Train Me, had heard a reporter planned to expose the identities of all Masters and subs, to unmask them in a national magazine and ruin their private and public images. Too many people wanted to stop her, too many wanted to teach her a lesson. And thanks to a chatty Master-in-training, word of her training session with him had even leaked out.

By the time he found Madison kneeling at the bed of her battered aunt, he wanted to haul her over his shoulder, carry her home and lock her in his room. Then he would go out and kill every Dom he had spoken to, every man who dared imagine his hands on her body. Afterward, he would go back and spank Madison's sweet butt until she promised never to go undercover again.

But when she turned to him, her tears still glistening in her red-rimmed eyes, her lashes spiked from those already shed, he took the chains he had carried since she fled and shoved them in his pocket.

When she rose and revealed her red knees, when she entered the hall and bit her trembling lower lip, he held out his hand. "Let me help you, Madison."

She glanced at his hand then up to his eyes. "I didn't even recognize her."

He brought the hand she ignored to the back of her head when her body slammed into his, kept it there for the eternity it took her to stop crying. His heart broke even as it swelled with relief.

"Who the hell are you?" a masculine voice from down the hall boomed.

"Get your hands off my sister," another roared.

"I know him! I saw him once at Aunt Louisa's club. He's one of the...is that your collar around my sister's neck?"

Drake turned his head then almost laughed. Three men who looked more like linebackers than bears charged down the hall, shoving each other out of the way in a race to be first. His laughter died a sudden death when he realized all three carried tightly balled fists.

Before he could do or say anything, one grabbed Madison and pulled her free, a second landed a numbing punch to his jaw and a third sank his fist into what Drake had foolishly thought was an impenetrable wall of abs. His breath whooshed out of him. He knew he was going down. The ceiling lights flashing before his eyes gave it away. As the back of his head hit the floor, he heard a scream—Madison's?—and blacked out.

When he came to, he opened his eyes to a sight more beautiful than any angel sent from heaven. Madison, her eyes somehow greener, her hair afire from the lights overhead and her lower lip snagged between her teeth, stared down at him. No angel could hope to compare.

"Drake? Can you hear me?" she yelled, breaking the spell and hurting his ears. "Drake!"

"I hear you." Raising a hand, he probed his aching jaw. "That's gonna leave a bruise."

Madison laughed and helped him sit up. "It already has, tough guy. Um, correct me if I'm wrong, but you never even landed a punch, did you?"

He glanced around the hall as he stood. "I take it those were the three bears?"

Madison brushed off the back of his pants. "Yup. Now you know why Rob has an order of protection against them. When I interned at *Exposed* during college, Rob sent me out undercover…as a hooker. I was just eighteen."

"Eighteen?"

She thumbed toward her aunt's room. "They took Rob to the corner I was trying to work. Beat him up in front of the ladies and left." She continued to fuss over him. "With our clothes."

"I hate to admit it, but I think I like your brothers." Drake brushed his knuckles over her damp cheek. "How's Louisa?"

Madison slumped. "She's real bad. The cop said whoever did this got out of the car and kicked her a few times before leaving." She stared into the room. "They have a description, but it's vague."

Her lower lip trembled. Drake rubbed the pad of his thumb over it and felt his heart shift.

"Madison," one of her brothers walked out of the room and stared at Drake's thumb until he lifted it from her lip. "ICU visiting is over."

"Come on, we'll take you home," another said as he followed.

"She's coming home with me," Drake stated with enough force to leave no question about his intentions if these brutes interfered. Which was pretty damned brave and a little stupid, considering he could still feel the force of their punches. Still, he held his hand out, palm up. "Let's go, Madison."

Madison took a step up to the glass and stared in at her aunt. He kept his hand out, not quite sure what he would do if she refused.

"She's coming with us," one of her brothers declared in a soft voice that reeked of power and dominance.

Drake turned and, keeping his hand out, stared down the men who had just flattened him as if he were nothing but an annoying fly. When he felt her hand slip into his, he closed his eyes for a second to relish the feel of her choosing him over them, him over freedom.

Her brothers took a step forward.

Drake tensed, prepared to fight every one of them if that's what it would take to keep hold of Madison.

Madison clenched his hand. "Back off, bears."

Drake watched the three men draw up their massive shoulders. Before he could say or do something he had no doubt would land him on his back again, Madison stomped her foot.

"I mean it. Back off."

Amazingly they did, casting each other furtive glances.

Madison allowed him to lead her out of the hospital.

Once inside a cab, she crawled onto his lap. Drake cradled her, acutely aware that he had succeeded in getting her into the habit of sitting on his lap for comfort, at least.

No matter what he said or how many times he kissed her damp cheeks, she cried the entire trip home. She didn't ask where they were going, and when they arrived, silently followed him inside. Seeing her like this—so broken, so defeated—destroyed him.

She watched silently as he made her coffee.

Later when she was holding her mug in trembling hands, her words shattered him. "I want to trust you, Drake. I just can't help but wonder if you're somehow involved."

Drake felt as if his entire world shifted into another dimension. Somehow, after only a few days, the woman in his arms had become an essential part of his life, the air he breathed. A few days. No. A few hours. Those few hours he had scoured the city searching for her. Those few hours he had faced losing her.

He intended to enslave Madison Garrett, permanently. Without her trust, Drake doubted he would succeed. Trust, so important in any relationship, so crucial in a Dominant/submissive relationship. How could he ask her to relinquish her freedom and follow every command if she didn't trust him? He placed his mug on the table then squatted down before her. When she avoided looking into his eyes, he gently grasped her face in his hands and forced her to. "I've known Louisa for years. You trust her, don't you?"

She nodded, swallowed a sob.

"When you walked into that first session, you felt safe, right?"

Again she silently nodded.

"You felt that way because you knew she'd never send you naked into the arms of someone who would hurt you." He rested his forehead against hers. "She trusted me to be gentle, to take care of you."

He let out a long, silent breath when she nodded. She wrapped her arms around his neck then slid off her chair and onto his lap, almost unsettling him.

"It's my fault she's in that hospital, Drake," she mumbled into his neck.

"No, Madison. Don't you dare think that. Whoever did this is responsible." Lifting her, he cradled her in his arms.

"I'm so tired."

He carried her upstairs to his room. Setting her on the edge of his bed, he took out her ponytail and ran his fingers through her hair. He undressed her and fought the urge to replace his chains. When he lifted the down comforter, she kissed his cheek before climbing onto the bed. He drew the comforter up to her chin. She snuggled into her pillow, hugging his to her chest.

When he turned to leave, her soft voice called out his name. "Drake. Hold me, please?"

He didn't realize how much he needed to hear those words until she voiced them. Easing under the comforter, he gathered her into his arms, hooked his legs over hers. She clutched his shirt as if he would leave if she let go.

As if he could. For the first time in his life, Drake knew what it felt like to be possessed, bound to someone as if unbreakable chains wrapped around his body and soul. When he felt her lips press against the hollow at the base of his neck, he closed his eyes against the emotions engulfing him.

No one but Madison could do this to him. "Promise me you won't run off and do anything foolish, Madison," he whispered. "You're so much like my sister, Cassidy."

Madison raised red-rimmed eyes and sniffed. "I thought you only had one sister...Ginny?"

"I do. Cassidy died when she was eight." He closed his eyes, welcomed the familiar pain that had dulled over the years to a subtle, gnawing ache in his chest.

"How did she...I'm sorry, I..."

Looking into her red-rimmed eyes, he sighed. He never discussed that day. His greatest sin. His skeleton in the closet, one he had no intention of taking out. She would leave if she knew.

"Drake?" Madison's warm palm pressed down over his heart.

One glance down into her eyes, one touch of her lips and he had to tell her. To trust her. If keeping him from feeling responsible for yet another death kept her out of Train Me, Chain Me, then he'd risk losing her respect, risk the whole world discovering his greatest sin. "When I was twelve, I took her to a park near our house. Like you, she was too brave for her own safety. She swore she could climb to the top of a maple tree. Swore she had done it before. Like a fool, I believed her. At her funeral and for weeks afterward, everyone insisted it was God's will, an accident. I knew what they were thinking. It was my fault she died."

"Oh, Drake, no." Tears pooled in Madison's eyes. Her warm hand cupped his cheek.

Flinching away, he glared at her. "They were right, Madison. I was the oldest. My parents had depended on me to protect her. If I'd put my foot down and let her know who was boss, she never would have died. I broke my mother and sister Ginny's hearts. I failed them…in the worst way."

When Madison opened her mouth to reply, he crushed it with his and drowned himself in her sweet taste. He had meant to soothe her, to explain why he couldn't, wouldn't allow her to set foot in Train Me, Chain Me. Her legs embraced his. Her fingers raked through his hair then caressed his cheeks. She took control of their kiss, softened it until he moaned beneath the butterfly wings fluttering over his lips. The pain piercing his heart ebbed. Tears kept prisoner since that fateful day broke free.

Later, when Madison's breathing steadied and the weight of her body bearing down upon his increased, he silently vowed he wouldn't fail her.

When he awoke, once again her absence rocked him. The red haze of the waning sun set the room aglow. Swinging his legs over the bed, he heard the faint tinkle of her bell and turned toward the sound. Madison, wearing nothing but her collar and chains, gazed out the window, her cheek pressed against the glass.

"I put them back on. If I'm going in, we'd better get back to work."

His heart slammed against his ribs. "Don't be a fool. I uncovered three more subs he's beaten, three with the same color hair and eyes as you! He'll make you the second you walk in." He crossed the room. Standing behind her, he added, "I'll find a way to make him pay, Madison. You have my word."

"*I'll* make him pay." Her back stiffened.

"The hell you will." He reached out to grab her arms, but she jumped back.

"No! You touch me and I forget who I am, what I am." She shook her head. "You only own me until Saturday, Drake Williams. After that, I'll go wherever and do whatever I please."

"Fine." He stalked her into a corner. When she shot out her chin, he grabbed her shoulders and spun her around. "Get in the bathroom, slave. It's time for your bath."

* * * * *

Sitting in the lukewarm water, Madison inwardly trembled as she waited for Drake's return. He had stripped her, lifted her unceremoniously into the hot water then left almost forty minutes ago without a word. The anger shimmering in his eyes frightened her more than anything he had done to her so far. His silence and impersonal touch hurt more than any punishment she had encountered at his hands.

Although the thought of entering Train Me, Chain Me terrified her, she was more determined than ever to go in and bring down anyone involved in the abuse and her aunt's attack. Drake seemed to have forgotten her skills when it came to disguise. Hair and eyes were the easiest to change.

The rest she would leave up to him.

She couldn't just promise not to go. He would never believe her. But he might feel he succeeded if, after one, maybe two more days of resistance she succumbed and promised to let him handle everything. She would become his sub, his slave and his possession. She would bury her rage, her guilt, her soul and trick every Dom, even Drake, into believing the old Madison Garrett no longer existed.

Then she would make the bastard who had hurt her aunt pay.

By the time Drake returned, she shivered in cold water. He silently washed her. His anger rolled off him in waves she could almost feel pummeling her. How she wished she could soothe him and promise to be the meek, compliant slave he sought. To remain home while he scoured the city, while he uncovered the bastard who had hurt her aunt and the others.

But Madison knew that she would lose herself if she gave in. How many times had he called her his she-cat with desire setting his eyes afire? Would that fire die if she gave in to his dominance completely?

Grabbing her arms, Drake lifted her out of the chilled water, laid her on the cold tile floor and clamped a long bar to each knee, splaying her legs wide. Her eyes focused on his hard features as he shaved her, but no matter how hard she silently willed him to meet her gaze, his eyes remained on his work.

Back in the bedroom, a muscle along Drake's jaw twitched as he undressed. Madison, manacled to the bedpost, shuddered when she beheld the muscles straining across his back when he turned down the comforter. She had never seen him so tense, and his refusal to meet her eyes or break the suffocating silence with even a command revealed just how close he was to losing his temper.

The idea of him flaying, spanking, or torturing her while his rage hovered so close to the edge of his control sent tremor after tremor through her body and ice-cold dread flowing through her veins.

When he turned, his eyes focused on her lips. "You're bleeding."

Madison's lungs seized. Until he spoke, she hadn't realized just how hard she had been biting her lip. "I...I'm a little scared."

"Of me?" His brow turned crimson as it furrowed over the bridge of his nose.

She wouldn't have thought it possible, but his lips thinned even more than before. "You're angry."

"You're damn right, I'm angry." He breached the distance between them.

She instinctively flinched away, but he only reached up to unbuckle her manacles.

As soon as she was free, she straightened and glared at him. "I'm going in no matter what you do or say. This silent treatment and any punishments you've got planned for tonight won't change a thing. This BDSM shit is training for my job, nothing more. The only thing that scares, or r-rather concerns me is whether your anger will affect our training in a harmful way."

Drake pointed to the bed and, with a menacing voice, ordered, "Get into bed. Now!"

Sauntering past him, she threw him a contemptuous glare. Heat from his body swept down the length of her side as she squeezed between him and the bed. It amazed her that his mere presence could arouse her even now.

Moving to the far side of the bed, she lay on her side with her back facing Drake. The cool satin sheets banked her desires. When the mattress sank behind her, she inched closer to the edge to keep from touching him, from giving in to the urge to turn and snuggle into his embrace. Hooking her waist, he brusquely dragged her from the edge until her back slammed into his chest. Her body welcomed his. Her mind revolted.

After a few failed attempts at prying his arm away from her stomach and his hand from her breast, she slumped. "Let me—"

"Go to sleep, slave."

Tears burned her eyes, tears she neither welcomed nor understood. Why his anger and disappointment should bother

her was beyond her comprehension. That morning they had shared an emotional intimacy that had enveloped her in warmth. Now, although he spooned her—holding her against his body—a cavernous void dwelt between them. Her body still strummed with need. She had never felt so bereft of warmth.

Sleep eluded her. She couldn't get Aunt Louisa's swollen face out of her mind. Her tears continued, her nose ran. Her refusal to sniffle and sob openly strangled her.

A long while later, Drake's hushed voice sliced through the silence. "The day you face my anger secure in the knowledge that I would never hurt you with either my hands or words is the day you will truly be my slave."

Blinking into the darkness, she pondered his words. She didn't know why, but deep down inside, she knew Drake would never strike her in anger. But truly be his slave? Had that been his intention all along? Not to train her for a job but for him? From the way he talked, she would never be free of his chains. She would have to trick him into letting her—

"Go to sleep, Madison. We have a long day tomorrow. One you'll need all your energy and wits for. One, I'm afraid you won't like."

Chapter Eight

༄

The next morning, Madison awoke as Drake lifted her into his arms and carried her to a bath. She sighed, needing a warm bath. Needing Drake. Her sigh turned into a shrill scream when he lowered her into cold water.

A robot, void of emotion or tenderness, he washed and, although she couldn't imagine much hair had grown overnight, shaved her again. When he finished brushing her hair, she thought they were through and rose to leave the bedroom.

A gruff, cold order sent her into to the bathroom. He rubbed lavender-scented lotion over every inch of her skin, rouged her nipples and replaced her collar with a blue one. A large, blue metal teardrop hung off the front D-ring. Emblazoned in white were the words, "Property of Drake Williams".

Her loins turned molten at the site of her reflection. He latched similar tags to the loops hanging from her nipples and clit. Leaning her over a tilted bench, he spanked her until her entire lower region strummed with heat. Something cool and thin moved over her right butt-cheek. Turning her around, he knelt before her and with a permanent marker scrawled over her mound the same words engraved on her tags.

"Getting a little obsessive, aren't we?" she muttered then yelped when he tipped her over the bench and spanked her until she writhed and begged for release to come.

He spoke not a word as he worked, only teased and tormented her, spanking and soothing, nipping and licking. Repeatedly he drove her to the brink of an orgasm then snatched her away with a firm reminder that she not come without his approval.

Before they left the bedroom, he inserted an egg-shaped object into her, pushing it deeper and deeper.

Now, sitting across from him as he stared into his mug, she could only wonder at the reason behind the morning's preparations. She felt ridiculous covered with his signs of possession. And the thin wire hanging from her pussy frightened her to no end. She had heard of people using electricity for pain play and prayed this wire had nothing to do with that.

Finally Drake raised his head. He took a small remote out of his shirt pocket. Cold, determined eyes met hers. The remote dropped onto the table with a deafening bang. Fear and the strong scent of lavender overwhelmed her. He pressed a button. The egg sprang to life, vibrating just enough to unsettle her.

"Remember, slave, you must never come until I command it," he coldly reminded her over the rim of his mug. "Now, eat your breakfast."

After she managed to force a slice of toast down her throat, he turned a dial on the remote and the vibrations increased. She whimpered, almost knocked her mug off the table. Gripping the edge of the table until her knuckles turned white, she held her orgasm at bay. Out of the corner of her eye, she saw his finger move. The vibrations grew so powerful she felt them all the way from her clit to her anus but still, she denied herself release. His eyes shone with pride when her teeth sank into her lower lip and sweat dripped down her temples.

"Come for me, my sweet slave."

She had intended to hold out for a moment more, to prove to him that she and not he controlled her body. At his tender command, she shattered.

"Wash the dishes, slave."

Rising on jelly legs, she silently cursed him and did as she was told. Halfway through the first dish, the vibrations returned. He reached between her legs and activated the butt plug. She held on as he brought her to the brink repeatedly. When she sank to her knees, he stood up, stared down at her tense body, then spun the dial. Madison reached out and grabbed onto his legs. She felt the buzzing go down her thighs and up to her breasts. "Please, Master, let me come," she sobbed, digging her fingers into his thighs.

"You live to come." The vibrations started rising and ebbing, like waves crashing onto the shore. "One is never enough. Two are never enough." Lifting her, he carried her to the chair and sat her down. The plug surged up and almost sent her over the edge. Pulling over a chair, he spread her legs and pointed down. She looked. The wire quivered.

"Come!"

Her body fractured into a million pieces. Convulsing in her chair, she lost track of where one orgasm ended and another began. Through the haze, she watched his finger sliding back and forth over the remote, heard him repeat over and over that she lived to come, that one was never enough.

"Please, Drake, make it stop. I can't take it anymore."

"Master!" he barked.

"Master. Please, please, Master," she choked out.

He rose, came around the table, tilted her head up and kissed her lips, swallowing her cries. "You will only come for me, Madison. Others might pleasure your body, others might make you wet with desire, but you will only come for me." He reached down and slowly pulled the egg out. "Only me, my sweet slave."

Before she could answer, he returned to his seat and let out a weary breath. Sweat dripped from the hair hanging over his furrowed brow. "Just how much research into BDSM have you done, Madison?"

She blinked and tried to catch her breath. "Not much. That night at my aunt's was the beginning."

"I thought you never went in blind." Disappointment laced his words.

"I thought my aunt would tell me all I needed to know," her voice cracked, "eventually."

"She's fine. They're letting her out tomorrow."

Madison gasped. "How do you know?"

"I called before you woke up. Now—"

"Thank you, Drake, but I'd really like to go visit her."

"And I'm not letting you go anywhere near that hospital."

"Letting? You're not *letting* me visit my aunt?" her voice rose.

"As per her orders. She's afraid the nut that put her there did it to find you. I agree. You should never have charged over there yesterday. For all we know, you were followed here. You can call her later, but you will not go near her or leave my side until this creep is caught. Understood?"

Madison nodded. "If what you say is true, then she's safer away from me."

Rising, he refilled his mug. "I've already explained why and how a sub receives her pleasure by pleasing her Master. What you don't seem to understand is that much of the pleasure they both derive is not from hurting or humiliating, but from trusting. The sub, or slave, is putting her entire being—body and soul—in the hands of her Dom or Master. She trusts him to care for her, to be responsible for her pleasure and well being."

He sat down. "Have you any idea how it feels to trust someone so completely that you allow them to strip you of your freedom, your ability to walk away permanently? You allow them to wield a weapon and torture your senses until they burst free from your control. Trust, Madison. Trust that under no circumstances would your Master harm you. Trust that your Master would do anything to ensure your safety."

"Well, isn't that what I've already done? With you?"

"I thought so." He stared meaningfully at her clenched hands then continued, "As a Dom, I've spent years mastering my control, learning ways to ensure my sub's safety while in my care. Last night, I didn't speak to you for a reason."

"You were punishing me?"

He smiled, though his eyes remained somber. "A Master never touches his sub while he is angry. I must maintain control of my hands or a whip or any weapon so that I give just enough pain to stir pleasure. I have to listen to every sound you make, gauge every move your body makes so I can see your line between pleasure-pain and real pain. Some welcome severe pain, but even they have lines. Crossing that line, even for a moment, means I failed. It means I no longer deserve your total trust. And it is your total trust, Madison, which gives me pleasure in my domination. Even when you scream from the pain. Your refusal to use your safe word, your trust that *I* know better than you when to stop arouses me to unbearable heights."

"I—" When he scowled, she closed her mouth.

"Anger has a way of slipping into a person's actions and words. To take responsibility for the gift my sub has offered me, I must not touch or speak to you until I calm the beast, so to speak. So, last night, I remained silent as I prepared you for bed."

Madison frowned. "But you did touch me."

"You are my slave. I have a responsibility to care for you as I would myself, better than myself. I will always give you all you desire, all you need to survive, to be happy."

Her brothers would kill for each other. Knowing that, it had always shocked and terrified her that they could easily and brutally fight each other when enraged. "Have you never lost control?"

"Oh, I'm not perfect. But you have my word that where you're concerned, I will leave if I do."

Madison felt lighter as it struck her that she believed him.

"Everything in me wants to lock you in a cell until someone else exposes the Master responsible for the abuse at Train Me. Unfortunately you are strong-willed and determined enough to find a way out. You may find this hard to believe, but I find your strength your most attractive quality."

Beaming, she leaned her elbows on the table. "When do we start?"

"I wouldn't be so quick to smile. You haven't done your homework. Just trust me, Madison. Everything I do from now on will be to prepare you. I'll hate subjecting you to some of it, but I have no choice. I'm responsible for your safety." He lifted the egg. "Come here, slave."

Madison stood before him and wondered why he still seemed so grim.

"Go upstairs, brush your teeth and use the toilet. Then meet me in the bedroom." He slid the egg up into her pussy.

Halfway up the stairs, the egg started vibrating with a vengeance. Groaning, she steeled herself against another oncoming orgasm.

"Madison."

She turned and ruefully smiled down at him. He looked so handsome standing at the foot of the steps looking up at her. "I know, Master. Not until you tell me."

* * * * *

When Madison stepped out of the bathroom, Drake forced himself to still the need to shove her back in and nail the door shut. Kneeling before her, he laved her clit until her moans filled the room, her juices dripped down his chin and her legs trembled.

"I-I'm dying here, Master. Please, let me come." Her breasts rose and fell. Her eyes shimmered with the intensity of her arousal.

Instead of giving her the command he knew she expected, he pulled out the egg. Her legs nearly buckled, but he didn't dare touch her. If he was right, he had stimulated her to the point where one misplaced touch could send her over the edge. He stood and tied a blindfold over her eyes.

"This is a test of trust." Hooking a leash onto her collar, he tugged until she took a tentative step forward. "Now, follow my lead and instructions."

By the time they reached the living room, she seemed to have grown more secure and barely hesitated with each step. Leading her to the dining table he had brought into the room earlier, he lifted her up onto it.

"Lie down on your back, slave."

Her tongue darted out to lick her lips when he bound her wrists and ankles to the legs of the table. Gazing down at her a moment longer than he should have, a moment that nearly shred him of the control he needed to carry out this session, he whispered in her ear, "In Train Me, Chain Me, you will not be allowed into a private dungeon until you have spent time in the main playroom. That is where you and your Dom will interact in public. Where he'll share you to lure the abuser."

At her gasp, he ran his knuckles over her rosy cheeks. "They know how you look, Madison. No wigs this time. You'll dye your hair black, get waxed before so no nubs give you away and wear dark brown contacts."

Stepping back, he nodded to his friend, Andre. Drake's nails dug into his palms when Andre ran his tongue over Madison's nipples until her breathing increased then licked his way down to her clit. Watching his friend suck on her until she squirmed was the hardest thing he had ever done.

He knew Madison thought he suckled her clit. Bending over, he kissed her sweet mouth.

Madison froze, filled her lungs with his breath. Her lips quivered beneath his.

Andre laved her breast.

"No!" She wrenched free of his kiss then pulled at the manacles that bound her. "Drake, please, no. Oh, God, Drake."

Her tears seeping out from under the drenched blindfold nearly undid him. He brushed his lips over her ear. "They all know me, Madison. Word got out that I trained the reporter. No sub is safe with me until someone catches this nut. You've left me no choice."

She twisted her hands as she tugged against the manacles as Andre sucked her nipple deep into his mouth. "Please, Drake. Make him stop!"

"You were fine with the trainee at Sweet Submissions. This is no different," he whispered.

"It is." Madison turned her face away. "I am…"

Andre moved to the foot of the table and glanced up at Drake.

"I can't go in with you, Madison, and I won't place you at the mercy of a stranger. Before I remove your blindfold, I want you to know that I would trust Andre with my own sister. He has been my friend since we were kids and is a respected Dom."

He untied then slid the blindfold from her eyes.

Madison raised her head and glanced at Andre. Drake knew she didn't see a trusted friend, understood that all she saw was a tall, muscular man she'd never met standing at the foot of the table and staring at her exposed pussy.

"Continue, Andre."

At his command, Madison gasped. She jerked her hips back when Andre lowered his head.

"Madison, look at me."

Her head swung to the side, instinctively following his command, but her eyes rebelled, pleaded.

His nails pierced his palms, gave him the strength to go on. "They are *all* trusted friends."

"A-all?"

Drake stepped aside to reveal the five men sitting in the living room. Andre grabbed her hips and buried his face between her thighs.

"No!"

Her wail tore at him. He had done this. Telling her over and over that she belonged to him. Only him. Years of protecting his subs from public rooms and the touch of others left him unprepared for the jealousy that gripped him at the sight of another man's hands and mouth on Madison.

Invisible chains he had yet to understand bound him to her and demanded he end this session, end her suffering and his.

Logic and his responsibility as her Master demanded he force her to explore every scene she might encounter in the public room at Train Me, Chain Me. At a private club, they had more freedom than at most public clubs.

"Your reaction is exactly the reason why I've done this. If you'd gone in there tonight, you would have blown your cover immediately."

He leaned over and kissed the corner of her mouth, then added, his voice stern, "You will not pursue this assignment if you do not continue your training. I'll lock you in a cage until they catch him. Do you understand?"

He watched her expression change, her eyes harden as his words sank in. She opened her mouth to speak then closed her eyes and nodded.

As he brushed a damp tendril of her hair from her forehead, he added, "It's all right to feel aroused by Andre. Your body is still sensitive from this morning. That was part of your preparation for this. You will give in to the arousal, my sweet slave. They'll know if your pussy doesn't weep that it's a sham. And open your eyes. You have to show that you are used to men watching you."

She shook her head emphatically.

"Open your eyes, slave!" he demanded.

She peeked at the men. Her gaze darted down to the bulges in their pants before she shut her eyes tighter than before.

"Punish her, Andre."

Andre nodded at two of the men. They approached the table. Each grasped one of her knees and spread her legs wider. Andre took out a horsehair whip and swatted her pussy until her crimson lips were swollen, until her juices pooled on the table and she begged for release to come.

Drake gritted his teeth. Andre ignored her pleas and went to stand at side of the table then proceeded to whip her breasts until they were covered with pink stripes, until she opened her eyes and stared at the men who now stroked their freed cocks. Her eyes widened when the two who had been lucky enough to join in plunged their fingers into her weeping pussy.

Drake felt her shame as if it were his own. Her pink stained cheeks filled him with guilt. Tremors racked her body, yet her eyes looked to him, not Andre, for permission to let go. The remaining three men stood up, surrounded her and watched closely.

"Do you want permission to come, slave?" Andre asked, his voice void of all emotion.

Drake forced himself to smile down at her and nod.

"Yes, Master." Her ragged voice shook him, but her eyes, remaining focused only on him, almost shattered his resolve.

"Then come, slave," Andre ordered in a voice that left no room for doubt over who ruled this session.

When she didn't, Andre tugged on her chains, shoved his finger into her wet channel alongside the others' fingers and pumped in opposition to their motions. "You have my permission. Come for me."

A low growl rumbled from Madison. Her body glistened with sweat, muscles rippled beneath her glowing skin. She shook her head.

"Suck her tits and clit," Andre said to the three men watching. "Come, slave."

When she still held on, when the pain of her restraint twisted her face, Drake's gut clenched. "Come for me!" he ordered, desperate to end her suffering.

Madison screamed. Her hips shot up and still she held his gaze. Her body convulsed so violently, he released her bonds and cradled her to protect her from the hard table. He carried her to the couch and sat with her on his lap. Kissing her face, smoothing his hands over her breasts, between her legs, reclaiming what belonged to him alone, he silently thanked God that she hadn't come for Andre.

Taking their cue, Andre and the men moved to leave.

"Same time tomorrow," Drake called to them, before giving Madison his full attention. "Are you all right, Madison? You're not hurt, are you?"

She shook her head, keeping her face buried in the crook of his neck. The heat of her cheeks seared him.

"But one of them needs a manicure," she mumbled. "It felt like a knife slicing into me."

He gently probed her pussy. When his finger came out smeared with blood, he ground his teeth against the tide of anger that overwhelmed him. "I'd understand if you wanted to hit me."

Again, she shook her head.

Dropping his head onto the back of the couch, he gazed at the table. He would never forget the image of her splayed on it while Andre's head moved between her legs and other men touched her.

Damn, she was *his* slave.

If he thought he had any chance in hell of convincing her, he would insist she hold off training until the end of their week. During that time, he would make sure she gave herself up to him and no one else. "Did you enjoy it?"

"It was humiliating."

"You didn't answer my question. Did you enjoy other men pleasuring you?"

"Only you touched me tonight, Drake."

He felt her smile against his neck as she snuggled deeper into his embrace.

"I'll let you in on a secret, my sweet slave. I hated every moment until you came." He kissed the top of her head. "For me."

"I'm cold, Drake."

"A warm bath with some Epsom salts will help." Rising, he carried her as he might a fragile infant upstairs.

Tomorrow, he would find out who dared draw blood from his slave.

* * * * *

As Drake prepared her bath, Madison sat huddled under the comforter he had draped around her. She went over what had happened downstairs. Only Drake's presence and her ability to convince herself that every mouth was his, every touch his had kept her from losing her grip on her sanity. It had shocked her that she couldn't, wouldn't, come without his command. Recalling his constant reminders that she belonged to him and only him, she wondered if he had somehow brainwashed her.

"Are you all right?"

She looked up. He stood in the doorway of the bathroom, his face etched with concern.

"I'm fine."

With a nod, he returned to the bathroom.

She wondered if he knew that his eyes had shimmered with unshed tears when the others incited her body. Afterward, when he had held her in his arms as if she were a babe, she had felt like one, content that someone other than herself would tend to her every need, soothe her wounds.

Sitting alone in the bedroom, so tired it took an effort to remain erect, she longed for his return. When he finally did, he stood in the doorway to the bathroom and stared at her until she shrugged the comforter off her shoulders and held out her arms.

He crossed the room, slid his hands under her knees and shoulders then lifted her into his arms. Not waiting for permission, she brought her lips to his and slipped her tongue into the moist heat of his mouth. He allowed her to control the kiss while he carried her to the bathroom and lowered her into the warm water. When he finally pulled away, she opened her eyes and gasped.

Dozens of white candles cast a golden glow in the room. Something brushed against her tender breasts. She glanced down. Rose petals floated on the water, surrounded her, clung to her skin. Their sweet scent filled her lungs. When she turned to thank him, her words died in her throat.

Drake stood naked beside the tub, his skin amber in the candlelight. The multitude of flickering flames cast shadows that marked the definition of his muscles. His cock jutted out in her direction from a bed of black hair. Obviously her body was not completely worn out, she mused, clenching her inner muscles against the aching void that opened.

"May I make a request, Master?" she asked, blushing as if she were a virgin, as if three men had not just fingered her while three others sucked her nipples and clit.

"As a reward, you may request anything, my sweet, beautiful slave." He stepped into the tub and, nudging her forward, sat behind her, then drew the softest cloth over her breasts.

"I want..." she hesitated, frowning down at his hand as it soaped the cloth. "I have an ache and..."

The foamy cloth slid down her arms, over her shoulders. His lips and tongue teased their way around her neck as the cloth moved over her stomach. "Go on."

"I want you."

Drake's growl rumbled through her back and found a home between her legs just as the cloth grazed over the tender flesh there. A mixture of pain and pleasure shocked her. She whimpered and closed her thighs on his hand.

He stilled. "Did I hurt you?"

She turned her head and kissed his jaw. "Just a little."

"You're still tender. Maybe we should wait." Drake withdrew his hand and draped the cloth over the side of the tub then, grabbing the hand spray, wet her hair.

Madison moaned contentedly while he lathered the shampoo and massaged her scalp, sighed when he rinsed her and sent warm water coursing over her back and heavy breasts. She ached all over with need.

"Master?" she asked, tilting her head back on his shoulder and licking the water that dripped from his jaw.

"What do you say we forget about the training for the rest of this evening? Tonight, we're just Drake and Madison."

Shifting until the hairs on his chest tickled her breasts, he stole her reply along with her breath in a kiss that let her know he would be her Master no matter what names they used.

Snuggling into his embrace, she wondered if even this—the candles, the tenderness—were all part of his plan. A plan that would keep her out of Train Me, Chain Me. Suspicion nibbled away at her. She wanted to trust Drake, needed to believe he too, felt his heart crack with every kiss.

But someone had leaked word of her identity and assignment. Only two, other than herself and Aunt Louisa, knew enough to talk. Rob wouldn't sabotage his own magazine. He had put the assignment on the table. And while he might not like his mother's lifestyle, he was her son. Madison could not imagine him doing or saying anything that might harm her.

That left the man holding her in his arms. The man so intent on keeping her out of Train Me. The only man she could ever imagine shedding her armor for.

Tonight, as the Doms had meandered out of the living room, she had heard one mention that two more subs matching her description were beaten. Her throat closed. She had to escape and finish her assignment before anyone else got hurt.

As if he read her thoughts, Drake tightened his embrace.

Chapter Nine

෨

"She still asleep?"

Drake nodded and handed Andre a mug of coffee. "She rarely wakes before five."

"So she's the sane one."

"Someone hurt Madison last night. Someone with nails."

Andre held out his hands, revealing two long ragged nails. "Yeah, sorry pal. But you didn't give us much time to prepare."

"It won't happen again, Andre." Drake held his gaze as he slid nail-clippers across the table. "Cut them. Now."

Andre flipped open the clippers. "Sure, Drake. You know I'd never harm one of your subs. God, what was with all the tags and markings?"

"Just making sure everyone understood she was taken."

"Oh, I don't think you'll have to worry about that." Rubbing his hand over his jaw, Andre raised his brows. "Wanna tell me why you dragged me out of bed?"

Drake stared at his friend. He thought of his sister Ginny's description of Andre. "Blond curls framing a face too angelic for those lifeless gray eyes". A chill skittered down his spine.

He and Andre had known each other since they were kids, and while he trusted Andre with his life, his friend had taken the previous night further than they had discussed. He had seen something in Andre's face when Madison had refused to come for him, something he couldn't put his finger on.

Drake knew he had broken a rule when he had ordered Madison to come. The session belonged to Andre. Drake had no right overstepping his authority. But instinct and the way Andre's face had hardened, demanded he end the session.

Now, looking into Andre's bleary eyes, he wondered if he had only imagined that odd expression. Seeing Madison responding to those men had bothered him much more than it should have. He had to admit, he had been searching for some excuse to bring the session to an end.

"Last night didn't work, Andre. She's still set on going in."

"So let her." Andre peered at him over the rim of his mug. He took a sip and set the mug down. "That woman has more balls than most men I know. Whatever made you get involved with her?"

"You wouldn't understand." Remembering the first time he had seen Madison, Drake couldn't help but smile. He would never forget the way her eyes had shone with anger when he told her she could never seduce the Masters at Train Me, Chain Me. And when she grabbed his balls, he would have kissed her right there if he hadn't been in so much pain. He rose to refill his mug. "There's something about Madison."

"She's no Kitten, that's for sure." Andre downed his mug and held it out to Drake. "Fill me up, will ya?"

"She's a lioness, Andre. But when she's at my mercy, she's so damn sexy and purrs like a cat." Thinking about her naked and manacled to his bedpost made him harden to the point of pain. "Look at this!" He pointed to the huge pup tent in his sweats. "I can't even talk about her without getting a hard-on."

"Well, just don't let her get to your head. She's not the type to stick with a domineering jerk like you."

Sliding Andre's mug across the table, Drake slumped into his chair. "I know."

"She enjoyed last night."

Drake peered at his friend.

Andre's face hardened. "Dammit, Drake, you saw her come. I never saw a pussy spill so much juice."

For the first time since they were young boys, Drake wanted to slam his fist into Andre's face. "She came for me."

"True." Andre took a pack of cigarettes from his pocket. After lighting one, he let out a long stream of smoke then asked, "So, are you going to tell me what this pre-dawn meeting is about, or not?"

"I need another session out of you." Drake felt his stomach churn just picturing what he had planned.

He thought his friend might refuse. Andre hadn't handled another sub since his marriage. His wife, though, seemed to have grown more daring since robbing her Master of his freedom. On more than one occasion, Drake had watched his friend stand by and grimly watch while a group of Doms tortured his horny wife. He would never forget the look on Andre's face the first time she had asked if Drake could join them. Drake had refused before Andre could respond. Spoiled by her Master, Andre's wife kept badgering him for one night with Drake. Although Drake continued to refuse, a rift formed between him and his friend and nothing he did seemed to close it.

Maybe that was what he saw last night. Maybe Andre's odd malicious glance had nothing to do with Madison and everything to do with his wife's desire for Drake.

"Fine. When do you need me?" Andre stomped out his cigarette.

"Give me two more days with her." Drake had planned on having Andre head another scene today. But this next session might just be the one to drive Madison away from him permanently, and he just couldn't let her go. Yet.

They spent the next hour going over what Drake had planned. He made Andre repeat everything—amount and positions of the contact points, voltage limits and number of jolts. When he felt his friend had no doubt about where he wanted this session to go, where he wanted it to end, he rose from the table. "Thanks, buddy."

Andre draped his arm over Drake's shoulder as they walked to the door. "You know I'd do anything for you. Brothers 'til the end, right?"

Andre raised his hand. The jagged scar across his palm never failed to stir the same emotions in Drake it had when he and Andre had first made their pact. He raised his own hand and pressed his scar to Andre's. "'Til the end."

Trudging up the stairs a few minutes later, he hoped the session they laid out never came to fruition. Sharing Madison with other men made him sick to his stomach.

His guilt over last night still weighed heavy on his shoulders when he crept into his room and glanced at his bed. Madison lay spread-eagle on her back, her cheek resting on his pillow, her flaming hair concealing her face.

This morning he would take her. This morning he would please her and make up for last night. Recalling how she had waited for him to release her orgasm and how she so openly admitted that she had felt no one's touch but his, he wished this relationship could someday be more than just part of her job. But knowing Madison, she would never embrace a life of enslavement. Even only a sexual one.

He slipped out of his sweats. Taking hold of the silk sashes he had tied to the bedposts before going down to call Andre, he wrapped them around Madison's wrists and ankles. She stirred but didn't wake. Leaning over, he peeked between her legs. Still slightly swollen from last night, her outer lips pouted and revealed the coral folds of her pussy in such a way that his mouth watered.

Dawn set the room aglow. He slid open the night table drawer and removed the feather he'd bought the day he decided to train the willful journalist who bragged that she could bring any man to his knees. At the time, he thought she meant with the jewel-crushing blow she had given him in the elevator.

Now, overpowered by emotions he had never felt for another woman, he wasn't so sure.

He leaned over and blew a stream of cool air over her nipples. They pebbled in response.

Madison sighed and shifted slightly.

"Now, my sweet slave," he whispered, letting his breath flow over her breasts, "now, you'll learn about a different kind of torture. A sweet, gnawing pain that comes from within."

Sweeping the feather over her breasts, up her legs and along those coral lips, he watched her breathing grow faster, watched her body start to writhe. Her tongue darted out and moistened her lips a second before her eyes opened. She smiled up at him then, realizing her arms and legs were restrained, frowned.

"Is this another lesson?" Her voice cracked, her eyes darted about the room as if she expected to find Andre and the others lurking in the shadows.

"Yes and no." He teased her clit with the feather.

Madison drew in a hissing breath. "Yes and no? What the hell does that—?"

He slid the feather over her nipples.

"Oh, God that feels good." Grinning, she closed her eyes. "Whatever it is, just keep doing it."

"This lesson is a freebie. One you don't need for the assignment, but I thought you deserved after last night."

"Sure. Whatever you want, Master." Madison peeked out from one eye. "Just you and me, though. Right, Master?"

His chest swelled. It felt damned good hearing her say that. Too damned good. Did she even realize how easily "Master" slipped over her tongue? How often she called him "Master" last night although he had told her she could call him Drake?

"Just you and me, my sweet slave," he whispered.

He bent over and took her nipple between his teeth. He gently grazed his teeth over the pert tip and trailed the feather over her wet pussy until her groans filled the room and her arms and legs fought for freedom.

"Open your eyes, my sweet slave." When Madison's lids rose and revealed crystalline green eyes that burned with desire, he straightened. "See what you do to me. What pain I go through every minute in your presence."

He felt her gaze sear him as it left his face and meandered down his body. Her eyes flared at the sight of his erect cock. It jerked as if she had touched it. Grew more engorged when she licked her lips. The feather floated to the floor.

"Look up, slave."

She hesitated, as if she couldn't tear her eyes away from his cock. When she finally glanced up at the mirrored ceiling, she gasped.

"I look..." she whispered then closed her eyes.

"Beautiful. Look, Madison." She opened her eyes. He rested his finger on her ankle. "I'm going to untie you, but you mustn't move. In your mind, my will is more powerful than any chains. Do you understand?"

Madison met his glance in the mirror and nodded.

He freed her ankles and wrists, taking his time, needing every minute to shore up his control. "I want you to remain exactly like this. Spread open for your Master's pleasure." He swept his palm down her body, his skin a hairsbreadth away from hers. "Your body belongs to me, slave. You know that, now. Don't you?"

Again she nodded, her eyes focused on their reflection. "Yes, Master."

Bending over he skimmed his tongue up her inner thigh then drew in a deep breath. "I should share you. It's selfish to keep such a sensuous dish to myself. Would you like that?"

Her eyes widened, her breathing increased. A soft whimper accompanied her reply. "Yes, Master."

"So, you enjoyed last night."

Madison stilled. "No, Master."

He lifted his eyes, wondering how in one breath she could say she would welcome his sharing her then in the other say that she didn't enjoy the exact same thing. She met his gaze, her own confusion etched across her face.

"Why, Madison?"

"I...I think because I could see that you...you were not enjoying it." She smiled, her eyes caressing him. "You hated it. I guess I understand now about my pleasure coming from giving you pleasure."

Drake lowered his head so she wouldn't see just how much her comment affected him. He held back a primitive roar of victory. "Do you see that chair, Madison?" He nodded to the plush, satin armchair in the corner.

He brushed his nubby cheek against her nipples. "I should set you on my lap."

Grasping her inner thighs lightly, he spread them farther apart. "And hold your legs open, so wide it hurts. And then, while I fuck your sweet, virgin ass, I should gift a hundred men with one taste of your cum. Each man's tongue will experience one lick, one kiss. One per man, Madison. One hundred men. One hundred hot, wet tongues. One hundred mouths kissing the sweetest pussy. Would you like that?"

"Yes, Master." Her pussy dripped with the ambrosia he had become addicted to.

"Today, you may come at will."

Madison groaned in response then whispered, "Thank you, Master."

He lapped the sweet elixir, delving his tongue between her swollen folds as he made his way at an excruciatingly slow pace up to her swollen clit. He kissed it, drew it into his mouth, let it slide free. "One…"

He only lost count once but doubted Madison noticed. Twice her hips shot off the bed and her pussy slammed into his mouth while her muscles convulsed around his tongue and her juices flowed down his throat.

When he finally raised his head, she lifted hers from the pillow and glanced down at him.

Madison scowled. "That's only ninety-six, Master. I've got four more coming to me." Her head dropped back down and her hips wriggled. "Come on. Your slave's waiting, here."

Chuckling, Drake lowered his head and supped on her until she screamed. Rising up on his hands and knees, he planted butterfly kisses all the way up to her mouth. "They can taste you, Madison. But only your Master can possess you."

When her inner lips kissed the tip of his cock, he stilled. "Say it. Only I will ever possess you. Only me."

Her nipples tickled his chest with each breath she took, tangled in and tugged the hairs. Seconds felt like hours as he nudged her moist folds. Her gaze caressed his forehead, his cheeks and his mouth then captured his eyes.

"Only you will ever possess me, Drake. Only you."

He savored the spell she had woven around him for a moment longer then plunged his cock deep into her burning pussy. Drake thought nothing had ever felt so good. So, fucking perfect. It took all his control to keep from exploding immediately. Her hips rose and her muscles drew him in deeper.

"Don't move," she whispered into his mouth, holding her hips firmly up to his. "Please."

"God, you feel so good," he growled against her lips. "So damn good."

"I want to touch you, Drake. Please let me touch you." Her voice slid like honey through his mind and enveloped his senses. "Please, release me, Master."

One glance brought home with glaring proof just how much he dominated this she-cat. How many times had she come? Screamed from the force of her orgasms? Her arms and legs remained exactly where he had placed them. Invisible chains. He burrowed deeper, let her gaze into his eyes and see the power she held over him. "You're free to do as you please, Madison. It seems I'm no longer the Master here."

He felt her lips quirk up as he slid his tongue over them.

"You are so wrong, Drake." Her hands cupped his face, and she peered into his eyes. "So very wrong."

Her thumbs touched where their lips met. Feeling them did him in.

"Tell me what you want, Madison."

Her eyes darkened. "Make love to me, Drake. Make me cry when I come."

He burrowed deeper then started to slowly pump into her, trying to make each thrust a caress. Her nails scratched his scalp as she raked her fingers through his hair and held his mouth to hers. Plunging deeper and faster with each thrust, he rode the waves of pleasure that made her shudder beneath him.

When she screamed out his name and came apart in his arms, he released the fierce hold he maintained on himself and filled her with his seed.

His orgasm shook him with its force. White flashes of light he had only seen the few times he had taken a punch to the jaw burst before his eyes. Every inch where her body touched his branded him. Dragging her hips with him, keeping his cock deep inside her so that he could feel every spasm squeeze him dry, he sat back on his haunches.

She wrapped her legs around his hips, her arms around his shoulders. Peered down at him with tear-filled eyes and a soft smile.

"That lesson wasn't too bad, was it?"

He smirked when she answered by covering his face with kisses.

Her warm lips grazed his temple then brushed his ear. "I didn't quite get this lesson, Master. Maybe you should show me again," she whispered. When his cock surprised him by hardening in response, she added, "See, the little fireman agrees."

He leaned back and glared into her face. "The little fireman? *Little* fireman?"

"Oh, fine." She rolled her eyes and ground her pussy onto him. "The big, fat, amazingly long python agrees."

"That's better." He took her again, this time surging up into her while he nibbled on her hard nipples and sucked in the soft flesh of her breasts until they bore the signs of his possession.

He felt his cum and her juices coating his balls. Their sweat mingled, their breaths swept into each other's lungs. Everything he was became a part of her as he accepted all she offered.

This time he had no control. This time she led the dance, constantly bringing him to the point of exploding then holding him at bay. By the time they both climaxed, he thought he would rip her in two with every thrust.

She slumped against him, panting. Cradling her in his arms, Drake took them both down to the mattress. Hating to do it, he slid out of her pussy and pulled the covers over them.

Madison snuggled against his chest. He felt her heart beat in time with his. His back stung, and he realized she had scratched him. He concentrated on the slight sting rather than face the agonizing truth that he could never truly possess Madison and would soon have to set her free.

"Drake?" She shimmied up until her face rested in the crook of his neck and her body molded to his.

"Hmm?" He kissed the top of her head.

"Was it ever like that for you?"

He could feel her breath still. Grinning, he shook his head. "Never. How about you?"

Her warm lips pressed against his Adam's apple. "Not even close."

Content, he started to doze.

"Drake?"

"Your Master needs sleep."

"The only part of being your slave I'm not sure I can accept is this sharing thing. Do all Masters share their slaves?" She ran her fingers through his chest hair.

The only part? His heart slammed into his chest. "No. And slaves never have to do what they don't want to."

"If...if I were truly your slave, would—"

"No one would ever touch you again."

"So you never shared?" She shifted and looked up at their reflection in the mirror above the bed.

He met her gaze. Held it. "I'd never share you."

She smiled and closed her eyes. Just as he started to doze off, her soft voice again broke the silence.

"Okay."

Drake drew her tighter into his embrace and prayed she meant what he thought she did. "Okay?"

"Okay...if it pleases you, Master."

After a long while, he closed his eyes. "Okay."

A phone rang somewhere. A distant phone. He wondered why no one answered it.

Chapter Ten

ಸಂ

"Drake. Drake, wake up!" Madison giggled when Drake's eyes opened then squeezed shut to block out the glaring light of the midday sun.

"How'd you get out?" he mumbled, then rolled onto his stomach and proceeded to snore.

"What? Oh, damn!" Blood encrusted scratches striped his back. She ran her finger alongside one.

Drake rose up on his elbows and squinted at her. "Damn, it was only a dream."

When he rolled over and hooked her finger, she lay down beside him. "A dream? That great sex? No way. That was definitely real."

"Actually I dreamt I had you locked up in a cage."

"Me? In a cage? That must have been some dream." She bit his chin then kissed it.

Drake tucked her hair behind her ear. "You turned into a lioness and bit me every time I tried to pet you."

"Yeah, that sounds about right."

He glanced over his shoulder then licked her lips. "Seems I bedded a she-cat this morning, one with claws."

"Bedded but not caged."

His laughter rumbled through her, warming her. "No, never caged."

She had never seen a man so beautiful. She loved his hair loose and flowing over his shoulders. Loved the way it fell over his eyes no matter how many times he raked it back off his forehead. His tiny nipples peeked out from the hair dusting his chest. Leaning over, she licked one.

Drake jerked but let her have her way. "You know why you'll be punished, don't you?"

Swirling her tongue around the small nubbin, she nodded then raised her head and reached down to glide a finger along his hard cock. "I touched without asking. Think I can make you forget punishing me?"

"Not likely. I have a good memory."

"Oh, I forgot. Your sister, Ginny, just called." When he rolled his eyes and groaned, she nodded, "That's right. You were supposed to be there a half hour ago."

"I totally forgot." Smirking, he sat up and rubbed his hands over his face. "It's the Annual Williams Barbeque slash Ginny's Birthday Bash."

Scooting off the bed, Madison looked down at him and wondered if he planned on taking her or locking her in the house. He had not let her out of his sight since her aunt's attack. "So…"

"So, I have to go. You do *not* want to get Ginny angry." He flopped down on his back and groaned. "The woman makes you look tame."

While he looked delicious, lying there naked with his morning woody rising up from that soft thatch of black hair, she knew there was no time for another romp. Turning away, she strode to the bathroom. "I'll start the shower."

"Whoa! I take care of you, remember," he called from the bed. "Start the tub. If you're going to meet my crazy family, then you're going to smell like the sweet rose you are."

She spun around in the doorway to the bathroom. "Are you saying I smell?"

"You're damn right you smell." He rose from the bed and stalked her. "You smell of sex, slave. You reek of it."

She backed into the bathroom until the cold sink hit her bare butt. "Well, if I do, so do you...Master."

He placed his hands on the sink, trapping her. "Then I suggest we shower together."

Madison purred and rubbed her body against his. "But what if I bite?"

"Bite away."

His hand burrowed into her hair and held her head firmly in place while he entranced her with a possessive kiss. Raising his head, he gazed into her eyes. "I think it's time for your punishment."

Tossing her over his shoulder as if she weighed no more than a small child did, he carried her down the hall to another, larger bathroom. Black and white marble covered the walls and floor in a dizzying checkerboard pattern. A white pedestal sink, sunken Jacuzzi and massive eight-spigot shower stall took up most of the bathroom. She caught a peek of a toilet inside an alcove.

"Drake, there's no time."

"There's always time." Leaning over, he turned on the shower. Water sprayed toward the center of the stall from three walls. Steam billowed up from the floor. "Like hot showers, slave? The feel of hot water pounding your clit and nipples turn you on?"

"You're a sick man, Drake Williams, a sick man with wonderfully sick ideas."

Grabbing the chains hanging from her breasts, he leered. "Oh, my sweet slave, you haven't seen anything yet." He tugged the chains, then left. When he returned a few minutes later, steam filled the bathroom, but she could still see the handcuffs and vibrators in his hands.

Her skin tingled as thousands of goose bumps rose up in anticipation.

Placing each item on the counter, Drake led Madison into the shower. Hot water struck her from every angle, thousands of needles. The sheet of sweltering water cascading down her body enveloped her. She sighed as muscles tender and tense from her night of training relaxed.

"Look up, slave." An order. A husky, bone-melting order.

Tilting her head back, she groaned. Chains hung from the ceiling.

Jealousy, ridiculous yet burning, struck. "How many women have hung from those?"

"Master!"

"Master." Eying the chains, she frowned. "How many?"

Grasping her wrists, he raised her arms and handcuffed each to a chain. Hooking her chin with his finger, he tilted her face up to his. "You, my sweet slave, will be the first to try these out."

Her lips twitched, but she kept the smug smile from showing.

He squatted before her then looked up and smirked. "You sound jealous."

Madison sputtered as she tried to come up with something to put him in his place. A sharp yank on her ankle that unbalanced her and had her hanging from the chains, left her speechless. The cold kiss of metal around her ankle followed by a clink and the inability to pull her leg away from the wall, brought a growl of anger to her lips even while her body strummed with excitement.

"Drake Williams, what are you doing?"

"I really do have a bratty slave." After securing her other ankle, he knelt before her and stared at her gaping pussy until she moaned. "Very well. Do you know why you are being punished?"

"What? No!" Madison searched her mind. What had she done? Said? What would her punishment entail?

His open hand shot up between her legs. Madison squeezed her eyes shut. The force of his palm striking her pussy shocked her. Screaming, she yanked on the chains.

"Do you know why you are being punished?"

Again, his palm struck.

Another scream. Her mind ceased to function. Drake slapped her with more force than he ever had. She struggled to remember her safe word or at least uncover what she had done to deserve this, but each time one or the other was almost in her grasp, she lost sight of it from another stinging smack. The heat of the water combined with the burning aftereffect of each slap. No pain compared to the pain of holding her orgasm at bay until he gave her permission to release it. She knew that his ability to control her orgasms had nothing to do with her training for the assignment, knew she could come if she chose to, but she wanted to give this to him. To see that look of pride in his eyes.

Tears streamed down her cheeks. Tears shed because she enjoyed every strike of his hand, embraced the way the burn spread deep into her channel and reverberated through her clit.

His voice boomed in the shower. "Why are you being punished, slave?" Standing beneath the assault of the hot water shooting out of the showerheads, Drake appeared completely unaffected. His control and power humbled her and made her crave his touch even more.

Hiccupping, realizing she struggled to spread her legs wider, she sobbed, "I touched without asking? I didn't say Master?"

Another swift, stunning, exquisite slap. "You are forgetting your manners. What does a slave say when her Master is kind enough to punish her so that she will grow and learn to be a good slave?"

"Thank you, Master."

"See that you don't forget."

Madison sighed, relieved, despondent that her punishment would end.

The jarring sound and pain of more slaps—stronger with less time in between, striking her pussy, ass, inner thighs—kept her breathlessly crying out "Thank you, Master."

An orgasm built. An undeniable orgasm she struggled to contain. Tremors shook her body. Her mind seemed to detach from all but each successive smack ringing in her ears, each surge of fire, her voice, Drake's.

"Can you do it, my sweet slave?" The hard, demanding voice now slipped into her dazed mind like warm honey. Seductive. Devilish. "Is my beautiful, sweet, red and swollen slave strong enough to wait for my permission to come? Shall I test her?"

Growling, Madison wrapped her hands around the chains and fought to prove that, yes, she was stronger than anything he meted out.

"Answer, your Master!"

"Yes, Master. Test away." Her orgasm almost took flight from the wicked fantasies swirling through her mind.

The raspy, hot, wet touch of his tongue on her clit almost did her in.

The sudden, swift removal of her butt plug nearly sent her over the edge.

A long vibrating, clit buzzing vibrator shoved into her pussy while his finger surged up into her anus and his teeth closed around one nipple shattered her resolve and shredded her control as if it never existed.

Screaming, she convulsed, yanked on her restraints and sobbed uncontrollably. Drake continued gnawing on her nipples and pumping his finger into her ass. The vibrations deep within her pussy and over her clit buzzed even stronger. One orgasm rolled into another. Their chant from their training session at Sweet Submissions rang in her ear, although she heard not Drake's voice but her own. One was never enough. She could never have enough. She needed her Master's cock. She would never get enough. The touch of his cock nudging her raw inner thighs threw her into an orgasm so powerful, she closed her eyes against the burst of white light blinding her.

A tongue slid up the side of her neck. Teeth skimmed over her earlobe. A soft, gentle voice murmured in her ear.

"Madison…do you know what you just did?"

Realizing her eyes remained closed, she opened them and met his smug smirk. "I came without permission?"

She felt something slither down her stomach and glanced down. Suds covered her body, slid down when he moved to the side and the water struck her skin. Frowning, she wondered how he managed to wash her while he had both hands between her legs.

A sharp nip to her nipple sent electric jolts of pleasure running through her stomach to her clit. Her inner muscles clenched.

"You did come without permission, slave, but you did something else." His hands smeared more soap over the tender skin between her legs.

She realized a strap held the vibrators inside her. "When…" Gasping, she looked down at his head while he suckled on her nipple. "Drake?"

"Master," he mumbled, never fully releasing her nipple.

Sighing, Madison shifted until her nipple popped from his mouth and he glanced up. His eyes burned with desire. "Did I faint?"

Drake just continued to stare, his lips thinning.

"Oh, fine, Master…did I faint?"

His smile, one that met his eyes and creased his cheeks, warmed her in the oddest way.

"Well? Did I?"

Rising up, licking a scalding trail up to her mouth, he spoke with his lips brushing over hers. "Madison, my sweet, you screamed. You cried. And you fainted. I told you. I never break my promises."

His lips hovered over hers. She could see in his eyes that while he reveled in his ability to bring her to such heights, he worried over her reaction. Drake had taken her as close as possible to her pain threshold, her limit, that invisible line he so often spoke about without once crossing it. She remembered how she had listened to him talk about pleasure and pain in Rob's office that day that seemed so long ago, how she had longed to know what it felt like scream, cry and even faint from such a powerful climax. How she had doubted she would ever experience such an orgasm. How he had promised just that if she gave him a week.

Staring into his eyes, she whispered against his lips, "Thank you, Master."

Instead of kissing her, Drake dropped to his knees. Madison watched as he freed her ankles then stood and did the same to her wrists. She wrapped her arms and legs around him just as the tile wall slammed into her back and his hot cock rammed into her pussy. He pounded into her like an animal, like an out of control beast, striving with each thrust to go deeper and deeper. Her muscles clenched around his heat, welcoming each painful lunge. Tension coiled in her womb. Water dripped from his hair onto her face, slid between their lips as she fought to deepen their kiss, taste and sup on as much of Drake as she could.

His hands held her so firmly to him, she thought she would soon melt into his hard body and lose herself in his possession. Groaning as she fought to hold off her orgasm, sounding more like an animal than a woman, she tangled her fingers in his hair and held on for the most amazing ride she ever imagined.

Drake tore his mouth from her. Staring into her eyes, his own shock over the frenzy that had overtaken them etched into his face, he asked a silent question she somehow understood.

"Not without your permission, Master." She blinked away the tears blinding her and smiled. "Not ever without my Master's permission."

Were those tears in his eyes? Water?

Drake looked up at the ceiling a moment then let out a loud, rumbling roar that nearly made her break her vow. Thankfully he met her gaze once again and this time spoke through the laughter that echoed in the shower stall, "Then come for me, my sweet slave. Come all you want."

An hour later, feeling naked in her jeans and tee shirt without the familiar pressure of her chains, Madison stood in her own bedroom and fingered her neck. She couldn't believe it, but she had grown used to Drake's collar. Her neck felt bare without it.

"How long does it take to throw on some clothes?" Drake yelled from her foyer. "You know, you had plenty of clothes at my place."

"Nothing I could meet your family in." Taking one last look in her full-length mirror, she went to join him. The denim scratched her skin and felt too confining to walk comfortably in. As she reached the top of the stairs, she yelled, "You've ruined me! I used to love these jeans and…"

Drake stood at the foot of the stairs looking up at her. His eyes shone with the hunger that always dwelled in their depths when he looked at her. Wearing a white, button-down shirt and jeans, standing there with one foot on the first step and an arm draped over the banister, he looked more handsome than any man she had ever laid eyes on.

"Damn." He murmured, starting to climb the stairs two at a time.

"What? Is something wrong?" She twisted and turned, checking out her outfit. Running her fingers through her hair, she searched for a wayward strand. Her heart swelled when he suddenly swept her into his arms and crushed her lips.

"We'll never get to my sister's if you keep looking at me like that," he growled into her mouth. "And I like the jeans."

"You do?" She hated the way such a simple compliment made her giddy. "You know, I thought, maybe, since I never met them, I should wear something nicer." She pushed out of his arms, convinced that her tan trousers were more appropriate.

"Forget it." He snagged her hand and led her down the stairs. "Massapequa's at least forty minutes into the island. At this rate, we'll get there just in time for the cake."

When they finally exited off the Long Island Expressway, Madison's stomach started to churn. Meeting Drake's family shouldn't matter. Their relationship was only temporary. Still, she couldn't stop worrying about her outfit or checking her make-up in the visor mirror.

"You look beautiful, Madison."

"Do they know about you? About Master D?" She picked at the zipper on her purse.

"Does your family know your sexual preferences?" He raised a brow.

"No..." She glanced out the window and drew in a shuddering breath. "So they have no idea that you're, well, a dominant?"

"No, Madison. And they'll have no idea that you're anything other than the gorgeous woman I brought as a date."

Biting her lip, Madison touched her neck.

"Feel good without it?"

Before she could think about the telling motion, she shook her head. She waited for him to laugh or come out with a smug remark. He merely stared at her until the honk of a horn returned his attention to the road.

Five minutes later, he turned down a street lined with quaint old storefronts. When he parked, Madison fumbled in her bag and reapplied her lipstick. "Is this too dark? Damn, I should have taken the lighter shade."

"Keep pouting like that and we'll both be wearing lipstick. Anyway, they'll be too busy looking at your eyes to notice whether your lipstick is too dark or not." Getting out, he walked over to her door and opened it.

"My eyes?" She flipped up the visor mirror, stared at her eyes, then gnawed on her lower lip. "Too much eyeliner?"

"I meant your eyes are...well...captivating."

Stunned by his compliment and the flush of color splashing across his cheeks, she mutely stared up into the midnight blue eyes that had captivated her the first time they met. Feeling her insides turn into warm honey, she reached up and smoothed her palm over his cheek. "My eyes are nothing special, but thanks."

Drake held her hand to his cheek then brought it to his mouth and kissed her palm. Tingles ran up her arm while an ache lodged deep in her chest.

She glanced out at the stores. "Why'd we stop here?"

"I have to get a gift."

"You didn't get a gift for her? Drake!"

"Yeah. What can I say? I forgot." He held her hand as she stepped out of the car, continued to hold it as they walked up to a jewelry store. "Ginny would never let me live it down if I didn't bring a gift."

Inside the store, Drake released her hand. "Why don't you browse while I take care of this?"

Before she could say anything, like maybe she would rather help him with his sister's gift, he strode toward the back of the shop and leaned on the counter before a svelte, top-heavy woman wearing more gold and diamonds than Madison thought the store displayed. Watching them between her lashes as she pretended to check out some earrings, she nearly choked when the woman glanced her way then motioned Drake toward a narrow door behind the counter.

Tapping her nail along the glass top, Madison leaned over and tried to see where they had gone. She caught an occasional glimpse of the bimbo walking to a cabinet and switching one flat, black velvet box for another, but nothing else. Finally they emerged.

"What do you think?" Drake held out a wide box and popped open the lid with a flick of a tiny gold button.

She glanced down and gasped. A thick linked choker made up of three strands of green stones the likes of which she had never seen lay on a bed of red satin. "Oh! It's beautiful. What are those green stones?"

The woman took the box and tilted it toward the fluorescent lights. "Green cat's eye tourmaline. See. When the light hits it a certain way, a golden band emerges, like a cat's eye. There are thirty-six tourmalines. And," she flipped over a tiny satin flap Madison hadn't noticed and revealed a teardrop diamond dangling off the middle of the bottom strand, "a full carat, teardrop white diamond."

"What do you think?" Drake asked, rubbing his knuckles down her cheek.

Madison ran her fingers along the strands then looked up at him and prayed her envy did not show on her face. "It's stunning. She'll love it."

He hooked her chin and turned her to face a large oval mirror. "She'd better. I expect her to wear it every day. Unless, of course, I find something else that matches her she-cat eyes."

Madison's throat closed. "Oh, Drake, I couldn't..."

"The diamond has been waiting here for years. The choker arrived this morning, as planned."

"This morning? As planned?"

Nodding, he lifted the choker from the box. "Hold up your hair."

"But it must have cost a fortune." Her fingers trembled as she lifted her hair.

"I'm sure it's worth every penny." His warm breath flowed over the back of her neck. His lips touched the whorl of her ear. "Street collars are priceless, secret treasures."

The choker cooled her heated skin as he clasped it around her neck. She watched him in the mirror, entranced. Kissing her at the base of her neck and sending chills down her spine, Drake held her gaze in the mirror and whispered in her ear again, "Wear this in public, Madison. Feel it and remember that you are mine. My..." He kissed her earlobe never taking his gaze from the reflection of her eyes. "Sweet..." He kissed her sensitive skin below her ear. "Slave."

Forgetting the jeweler, she leaned back into his arms and closed her eyes. His erection pressed into her butt. How decadent, she thought. How utterly decadent. Madison Garrett, girl most likely to knock a guy out, a sex slave possessed by a magnificent man who could enslave her with just a look. It struck her that she would miss Drake and his possession when their time together ended. Turning in his arms, she smoothed her cheek over his lips. "Thank you, Drake. I love it. But it seems so expensive...for the few days we have left."

"I've been thinking about that." He wrapped his arms around her waist. "I think we need to seriously renegotiate the length of our agreement."

She couldn't breath, wouldn't allow herself to jump to the wrong conclusion. "Why? Don't you think I'll be ready by the end of the week?"

He spoke against her mouth. "This has nothing to do with Train Me, Chain Me." He bit her lip then licked away the pain, "This is about you belonging to me."

If she had found the words to answer, she would have probably said something stupid like, "You had me at hello."

Thankfully he stunned her with a kiss that left no doubt in her mind that he had seen her answer in her eyes.

After he paid, they left the store and headed to his sister's house. Madison spent the rest of the trip thinking about this new turn in their relationship. Drake seemed equally self-absorbed.

"Penny for your thoughts," she murmured, admiring his profile.

He pulled up in front of a small ranch. "I'm wondering if my family is going to see more to this than there is."

Madison opened the door. "What do you mean?"

Taking her hand, he started up the path to the door. "You'll see."

The door opened. Madison swallowed the lump in her throat. As she forced herself to smile at the young woman holding open the storm door, she felt her eyes burn. His words pierced the euphoric bubble that had surrounded her since their time in the shower. See more than there is? Had she totally misread his feelings? His intentions?

"Hi, Ginny." Drake leaned over and kissed his sister then wrapped his arm around Madison's shoulder and stated, "This is my friend, Madison."

His friend? Madison held out her hand and willed it to stop shaking. "Hi, I'm —"

"Hey, Mom! Dad! Drake brought a *girlfriend* home." The woman, who looked nothing like Drake, yelled so loud Madison doubted the jeweler back in town missed the announcement.

As squeals and clapping came from behind the house, Drake groaned. He shot her a meek smile. "I warned you."

In the next few minutes, Madison received bone-crushing hugs from Drake's parents and so many aunts, uncles and cousins she lost track.

When Drake's grandmother admired her choker, Madison cast Drake a furtive glance. All hell broke out. Men patted him on the back and women surrounded her for a look as if the necklace was an engagement ring.

She lost track of Drake as they all made their way through the house. So many tall men with black hair filtered out the back door that she couldn't be sure which was Drake. She gave up trying to follow the rich timbre of his voice. Obviously most of the Williams males inherited that gene.

The smell of fresh baked pies brought her to the kitchen table. Leaning over, she drew in the heavenly aroma and sighed.

Something hard pressed into her butt, something she couldn't mistake for anything but an erection that felt too small to be Drake's. When she moved to step away, an arm snaked around her waist and pulled her back.

"Something told me Drake would bring his latest toy."

Recognizing Andre's voice, Madison jerked free. Without turning, she ran to the back door. A blush burned her cheeks, tears filled her eyes. Was this just another stunt to humiliate her into giving up the assignment? Did Drake even know Andre would be here? Did he think it wouldn't matter one way or the other to her?

By the time she found Drake, she had already decided to leave. When he turned with a welcoming smile then rushed up to her and clasped her face in his hands, she almost kneed him in the groin.

His smile vanished. "What the hell happened? You're red as a beet."

"I want to go," she said, low enough so only he would hear. "I want to go, now."

"Did one of my cousins come on to you?" His voice turned to steel as he glanced around the yard. "Tell me which one. I'll beat the shit—"

"Andre's here. How could you?" She glared up at him. "You take me home, or I'll embarrass you in front of your whole family."

"Andre?" He smiled down at her. "You must have mistaken someone for him, Madison. Andre never comes to Ginny's birthday. She's hated him since high school."

"I *talked* to him. He said he came..." She looked down to hide her tears.

"What?" Again his voice hardened.

"He said he came because he knew you would bring your latest toy," she mumbled.

"Now, I know that wasn't Andre. He wouldn't—"

"What? Call me a toy? Shove his dick in my ass in your sister's kitchen?" She ground out her words moving closer and closer, keeping her face hidden from his family. "Why not?"

Drake tilted her head back and glared into her eyes. "Because he knows I'd beat the fucking shit out of him if he did."

"You made me his toy. You let him and his friends shove their fingers up my pussy. Why on earth would he think you'd—"

"The collar," he ground out, as if she would understand, should. "My God, Madison, didn't you research *any* of this? You said you didn't go into your assignments blind. I thought you knew..." His eyes strayed to her new choker.

When he wrapped his fingers around her upper arm, she could feel his anger and the tension reverberating through them, yet his grip remained gentle. Still, she did not appreciate his manhandling her in public. And when he led her toward an empty corner of the yard like she was a wayward child, it brought back memories of the way her brothers had so easily dragged her around in her youth.

She dug in her heels. "Let go."

With a withering look, he released her arm.

"The collar," he said, his voice so low she had to lean closer to hear, "is the most valued and meaningful piece of equipment in our world. It says so much more than mere words."

She reached up and touched the warm stones encircling her neck.

"All collars set boundaries. Limits. When you agreed that first night to wear the one Louisa gave you, I thought you understood. That was a Protection Collar, Madison. It told the trainee and anyone else who might see it that as long as you wore it, you were under her protection. No one could touch you unless she allowed it that night. And for that night, she gave you to me. Only me." His eyes darkened.

"But the trainee…"

"That trainee touched you because *I* permitted it."

"Oh." She peeked over his shoulder at the yard and wondered what the hell this had to do with Andre. The man grabbed her ass not her collar.

"Oh?" He shook his head and rolled his eyes. "When you agreed to let me train you, I switched collars. Do you remember? I removed Louisa's and put on mine."

Heat pooled between her legs. How could she forget? The touch of his fingers on her neck. The sound of the buckle. The look of triumphant power in his eyes. "I have a vague recollection of it. But about Andre—"

"The night he came over, I explained our arrangement. I fucking covered you with my signs of ownership." Drake rubbed his knuckles down her cheek and smiled. "Don't blush. I told him you had agreed to wear my Collar of Consideration and be my slave for a week. The collar told him that you were now off limits even out of my presence." His eyes grew more intense. "It told everyone that for the time we agreed on and possibly longer, I owned you."

"I understand, Drake. Now can we deal with Andre? I don't like him."

She gasped when he slid his finger under her choker and twisted it until she felt the edges of the settings dig into her skin.

"I thought you understood what this meant when you accepted it."

"I did!"

"I don't think so." He grabbed her arms and drew her closer. "I thought you'd researched BDSM and realized that when a Dom gives his sub a special collar, one unlike any other, that it is considered to some a Training Collar. Others consider it a different form of the Consideration Collar. But everyone realizes that when a Dom gives his sub or slave a one-of-a-kind collar with a symbol or initial, it's a sign that the couple has entered into a commitment. An emotional as well as BDSM commitment. Each of the collars you've worn has had a silver tear-shaped tag inscribed with my initial."

Madison smirked. "Like a dog tag."

Drake didn't laugh. "Exactly like a dog tag. There is one hanging from the clasp. A teardrop. Inscribed. Still, I had the jeweler put that diamond on your choker and made her promise not to make any others exactly like it. My sign of ownership, Madison." He dropped his hands from her arms and glanced over her shoulder at his relatives. "After this morning..."

She balked at the word "ownership", but the morning's passion and the intimacy she shared with him still warmed her with his every glance. She could still hear the solid "okay" that had meant so much. It had lingered between them, bound them like nothing else.

The chains were back in Drake's brownstone, but what they had shared had created invisible, stronger ones. She thought of her past lovers, of the way they had scurried around to please her and avoid raising her temper. Madison could not imagine ever needing to please such a man but now, seeing the disappointment in Drake's face, she searched for something that would make him smile.

"You thought I knew your gift meant we're moving in a new direction. That we've renegotiating the length and depth of our relationship."

"My ownership, you mean." His eyes sparkled with pride and power.

She pressed her chest into his and felt his heartbeat race. "Oh, Drake. I didn't have to do research to know that."

"And?" He gazed down into her eyes.

A bee buzzed nearby. The hum of conversation grew distant.

"I'm wearing it, aren't I?"

He grinned as he lowered his head. "So, you realize that every Dom you meet in public will see my choker and know that you are mine? That when they see that diamond, they'll know that you have forfeited your freedom to me?"

His lips fluttered over hers as he spoke, the gentlest caress while his voice grew more and more possessive. By the time he finished, she would have forfeited her entire bank account for that mouth. Not bothering to answer, she rose up on her toes to close the scant gap between their lips. Drake held her in place.

"Answer me." His voice rumbled with authority.

"I'm forfeiting my freedom…to a certain degree." She nipped his lip before he could stop her.

His eyes twinkled. "That's my she-cat." He ran his hand down her back, pressed her hips into his and took possession of her mouth.

Too quickly he ended the kiss and frowned as he looked into the yard. "Now, do you understand why I find it hard to believe Andre would touch you or speak to you so disrespectfully?" Drake flicked the diamond. "A teardrop, Madison. Sweet pain. I've talked about it with him, about my putting a diamond one on a collar when I made it this far with a sub. When I found one I wanted to keep. I've never done it before, Madison. Never." His eyes swirled with anger. Pressing the diamond into the hollow of her neck, he spoke through clenched teeth. "He knew what this meant."

Without another word, Drake kissed her forehead and stalked away. Madison watched him charge up the steps and swing the screen on the back door off its hinges. The diamond weighed heavily on her skin. Rooted to the spot by his admission that he wanted to keep her, she did not move until front door slammed and someone screamed.

Chapter Eleven

Madison rushed to the front yard. Someone screamed again. Pushing people aside, she made her way to the front of the crowd. Drake stood on the lawn, blood dripping from his nose. Andre sat on the ground, his jaw swelling.

"Madison, come here," Drake called, swiping blood from his nose with the back of his hand. "Would somebody give me a goddamn napkin?"

Feeling everyone's eyes on her as she went to him, she silently cursed him for making a spectacle of her. When she stood before him, he caught the napkin one of his cousins tossed.

She took it from his hand and gently wiped the blood away. "You big jerk," she muttered. "Now, what are you going to do?"

Drake grinned down at her. She watched him lower his head and expecting him to say something, turned hers to the side. When his palm caught her cheek and turned her face back to his, she murmured, "Drake, your whole family's watching."

"I know."

"But I thought you didn't want them to think—"

"I changed my mind." He kissed her, his lips firm, demanding then soft and tender.

Drowning in the desire his kisses always wrought, she slid her hands over his shoulders and held on. She felt the hard ridge of his cock press into her stomach, felt his arms pin her to his hard body. Accepting that she'd become addicted to his kisses, she let him have his way with her mouth. When he lifted his mouth from hers, he ran his thumb over her bottom lip. Their eyes met.

"Andre has something to tell you. Don't you, Andre?" Drake still looked only at her.

Madison no longer cared about Andre. Drake had made a stunning statement by kissing her like this in front of his family. Her heart felt as if it would burst from her chest.

"I'm sorry," Andre muttered.

Madison glanced over her shoulder.

Andre rubbed his jaw and smirked. "No one told me. I tried to tell Tyson here, that I came up from behind and didn't see the damn choker."

Drake glared at him.

"He did, Drake." Too many relatives stood nearby. Did they realize what Andre was talking about? She prayed they didn't.

* * * * *

Later, Madison sat on the front porch and watched the men gathering for a game of football. They argued comfortably with each other over teams as the late afternoon sun peeked through gray clouds. She itched to join them but doubted Drake or his family would understand that she had spent most of her life playing street football with her brothers and father.

Ginny stepped out of the front door. "My mother just told me something you might like to know."

"Really?" Madison smiled and patted the concrete beside her.

"She heard how the fight started." Ginny lit a cigarette and let the smoke stream out as she grinned.

Since she and Ginny seemed to hit it off, she doubted the woman would be so happy if she were going to mention Madison's involvement with Andre and the other Doms. "She did?"

"Drake came charging out of the house like a bull. He told Andre he had heard what he did to you and that after he beat the shit out of him, he would make sure everyone heard Andre apologize to his girl. His girl. Do you believe it? I don't think I've ever heard Drake say that. Well, not since high school." Shaking her head she laughed. "Anyway, Andre laughed and said you were just a fling, and Drake—now this is the good part." She took a long drag and shook her head, still grinning.

Madison wanted to wring her neck and shake the rest out of her. Instead, she calmly asked, "Well? What did he say?"

She sidled closer to Madison. "Drake yelled that you were much more than a fling...so much more, that if Andre didn't apologize, their friendship was over. That's big, Madison. They've been inseparable since they were kids."

A little bit of fear and something that felt a lot like love hit her so suddenly, she couldn't catch her breath. She told herself to be reasonable, that Drake had fallen for Madison the slave, not the real Madison.

She brushed some of Ginny's stray ashes from her jeans and wistfully watched the men play. Drake caught her eye a few times. Before long, she got so involved, that when one of Drake's uncles bowed out, she jumped up and, without thinking, yelled, "I'll take his place."

Drake's father chuckled. "Football is too tough for women."

Already halfway across the lawn, Madison came to such an abrupt stop, she almost fell. She opened her mouth to argue but Drake's booming laughter cut her off.

"I wouldn't get on Madison's bad side, Dad. She's got a sharp tongue," he threw her a wink, "and an odd habit of going for the family jewels."

Mr. Williams eyed Madison. "You saying you know how to play football?"

Madison walked up to the men. "I've played with my brothers since I was eight. Even played on Pop Warner."

Mr. Williams stared at her then shook his head. "I don't know. We play rough."

Drake strode over to her, his face grim. "I hate to do this, but he's right."

Her eyes met his. "Please, Drake. Don't."

His warm hands cupped her face. "I wouldn't dare risk something so delicate."

"I am *not*—"

"So fragile." His fingers slid through her hair to the back of her neck.

"Fragile?" Tears burned her eyes.

"So special." He held up her choker. "Ginny can hold on to this while your playing."

A half hour later, sweating and happier than she had been in a long time, Madison leaned into the huddle with Drake.

His father panted as he went over the play. He glanced out of the huddle. The others were lining up. "They put Andre opposite Madison's position. You want me to move her, son?"

Drake looked into Madison's eyes. "Madison?"

"I know how to take him down." She ran her arm over her sweaty brow. "I'll just hit him below the belt."

"Way below the belt, Madison." Drake hooked her neck and kissed her. "Hit him *way* below the belt. Get that she-cat I love out and curl her into a ball. Then hit him in the shins and lift. You got it?"

Grinning like a fool, she saluted Drake. "Way below the belt, sir."

"You win this for me, Madison." Drake's father winked. "That man has taken down our quarterback too many times."

"Hmmm...I feel a bribe coming." She nudged Drake.

"Oh," Drake's father laughed, "I think we can arrange a thank-you kiss, can't we, son?"

Later in the bathroom, she and Drake washed away some of the sweat and grime from their faces and arms. Patting her face with a towel, Madison giggled. "I really took Andre down, didn't I?"

Drake grabbed her by the waist and hoisted her onto the edge of the sink. He shut the door and twisted the lock.

"I thought you broke his neck. Scared the shit out of me."

"Me too." She felt her pussy heat when he took hold of her knees and spread her legs. "Good thing I held back a little when I lifted."

"It made me horny as hell, watching my little slave throw a man twice her size over her shoulders." He ground his hips into her crotch.

Her clit pulsed. Needing more, she pulled him closer. "I think you're exaggerating. I am not little and he is not nearly twice my size."

Drake's eyes darkened with desire as he ran his fingers over the choker once again encircling her neck. "Take off your shirt, slave. Time for your reward."

She yanked her shirt up, baring her stomach.

"Slowly," he ordered in a voice so husky it sounded more like a growl.

Keeping her eyes on his as they feasted on her body, she ever so slowly lifted her shirt over her head. When she moved to unclasp her bra, Drake grabbed her hands.

"No. I take over from here." He removed her bra then twisted it around her arms until it bound them behind her back.

Taking a brush from the small basket on the counter, he ran the bristles over her breasts and swallowed her cries with his mouth. Each time she thought she might be approaching the line between pleasure-pain and real pain, he seemed to read her mind and stop. Then his mouth would soothe her until she wriggled with need. Over and over, Drake tortured her.

When she thought she could not possibly take any more, he unzipped her pants and yanked them off.

"Did I give you permission to forgo underwear?" His hand reached for the brush.

Her pussy lips pulsed in fear and excitement. "I like going commando." When he arched a brow, she quickly added, "Master."

Staring intently between her legs, Drake scraped the sharp bristles over her inner thigh. By the time the first bristle touched her dripping pussy, her whole body trembled.

"Spread you legs wider for your punishment, slave."

Biting her lip to stem the moans strangling her, she spread her legs until he nodded his approval. Drake continued to stare for a few moments then took hold of her ankles and raised her legs until her heels rested on the edge of the counter.

"Remain in this position, slave. In fact, I want to see you spread your legs wider after each blow. And do not let those legs fall." Menace and desire glazed his eyes. "Not a sound, slave. No words. No pleas. A test of total control. If you fail, I'll punish this pussy until your screams bring in everyone, until they all see how you offer yourself to your Master."

A whimper slipped free. She swallowed and stared at the brush as it moved up to her pussy. Afraid it might hurt more than she could handle or enjoy, she sighed when the blow was not as brutal as she had expected. After the first few strikes, Drake instilled more and more power into each one. Her tender flesh thrummed from the impact of hundreds of stiff, sharp bristles. She writhed, spread her legs wider and made not a sound. Driven to the point of thrashing her head from side to side, she felt her heels slipped from the edge of the counter. Immediately Drake stopped.

Her stomach clenched. He wouldn't. She heard no sound coming from the hallway, but a picnic table full of his relatives was just outside the window. Too afraid to ask, trusting that she knew him, that he would never follow through, she waited and watched him drop the brush onto the counter.

"Does you pussy hurt, slave?"

Again, that whimper, that odd sound she had never made before Drake, had never found impossible to silence before Master D. "Yes, Master."

"Does it burn, slave?" When she nodded, his fingers caressed her. "It's so red. So pretty like this. Do you think you can take more?"

Eying the brush, she shook her head. "No, Master, please."

He lifted the brush. "Spread your legs wider."

Without a thought or moment's hesitation, Madison spread her legs.

A wicked grin tilted Drake's lips. "That's a good slave."

He dropped his head and planted a wet, open-mouthed kiss on her pussy. His tongue delved inside her then licked away the sting from her lips. When her whimpers turned to sighs, he stood up and stepped back.

Madison watched him free his cock and almost grabbed hold of it, almost shoved her hips forward so it could fill that void only he created, only he could fill.

But she remembered her place. The knowledge that she was at his mercy made her body burn even hotter.

He decided when to please her.

He decided when to punish.

He ran his finger down the cleft of her pussy. "You're always so wet for me, Madison. So fucking wet."

She watched him lick his finger and thought she would come from the sight. "Please, Drake."

"Tell your Master what's wrong, slave," he whispered, "Tell me."

"I need you, Master." When he flicked her clit, she bit her lip to keep from crying out.

"Shh, slave. There are people right outside this door. Now tell me what you want. I want to hear those dirty words coming from my she-cat's mouth." He flicked her clit again.

Sharp trills of pleasure-pain tore through her. Gasping, she snagged his gaze, held it and whispered against his lips, "I want your cock in my pussy. I want you to slam into me so hard I scream."

Drake crushed her mouth. His tongue surged between her lips and caressed every inch of the inside of her mouth. It was like their kiss in the shower, a lover's kiss that made her head swim. When he thrust his cock into her harder than he ever had before, she gasped, drawing in a large draft of his breath. His air filled her lungs, his tongue probed her mouth and his cock burrowed deeper into her greedy pussy. He possessed her so forcefully, so totally that she thought she would faint from losing herself.

"I want you to fuck me, slave. Like you wanted to that second night we trained." He bit her lower lip. "Remember?"

Madison nodded. Her mind tumbled back to that night. How he had affected her like no other, even before she had known Drake and Master D were the same man. "Oh, God, yes. Please."

Lifting her off the counter as he continued to surge in and out of her, he carried her to the toilet. "Please, what?"

"Please, Master." She pulled the seat cover down with her foot.

"Aren't you ashamed doing this, Madison? Fucking in my sister's bathroom so close to my family?" He sat with a groan.

Straddling him, Madison nodded. "It is bothering me, a little."

"Then why are you letting me do this?" He rubbed his nubby cheeks over her already tender nipples.

"I can't...I can't say no to you."

Drake grabbed her hips and drove her down hard onto his lap then immediately tortured her breasts with his nubs until they were red and throbbing. "That's right, baby. You have no say. I fuck you when and where I want. It's not up to you is it?"

She gasped for air, fought the orgasm she felt coming on. "No, no, Master."

"So don't let anything bother you, Madison. This is out of your hands. All you have to do is enjoy it. Take the pain." He bit down hard on her nipple.

She stifled a yelp, felt his teeth sink into her again and gritted her teeth to stop from screaming out, to stop from coming before he gave permission. She wanted to offer that gift, that control, that obedience from now on.

"Take the pleasure, my sweet slave." He suckled away the sting.

Madison felt him swell inside her. "Please, let me come with you, Master."

"Then come for me now, Madison." He surged up into her.

Madison ground her teeth and swallowed the scream that lodged in her throat as she came apart in his arms. His hot sperm filled her and still he pumped her with more. She smiled as she calmed and wrapped her body around his.

Drake kissed her neck. "I don't think I'll ever get enough of you, Madison Garrett. Not ever."

* * * * *

Later, washing out the cake plates in the kitchen with Ginny, Madison watched through the window as Drake said goodbye to Andre. It amazed her how quickly they had gotten over their fight.

Curious, she asked, "They've known each other a long time, haven't they?"

"Just since they were in pre-school," Ginny slid the dish she had just dried between the wooden slats of the dish rack. "Blood brothers 'til the end."

"Excuse me?" Madison rinsed another plate and held it above the sink until the excess water dripped off.

"You know that scar on Drake's palm?" Ginny asked in a conspiratorial voice. She ignored the dish Madison held out and sat at the table.

Madison had seen the nasty scar but hadn't really paid it much mind. She had a couple scars herself that she would rather not explain. Now, intrigued, she turned off the faucet, set the dish in the drain and joined Ginny at the table. "I've seen it."

Lighting a cigarette, Ginny blew out a stream of smoke then explained, her voice low, her eyes darting between the back door and the archway into the dining room. "They did that to each other when they were ten. It was Andre's idea." She held up the pack of cigarettes to Madison. When Madison shook her head, Ginny continued, "Well, you know how kids like to merge blood and become blood brothers?"

Madison nodded. "But that's a nasty scar."

"Yeah, they both are. Seems Drake only pricked Andre's skin. Andre grabbed Drake's hand and explained that if they were going to be real blood brothers they had to cut down to the veins. This way their blood really merged. Sick, right?" She glanced over her shoulder toward the back door and lowered her voice. "Before Drake knew it, Andre had cut open his whole palm then did the same to his own."

"No!" Madison leaned forward on her elbows.

"We nearly lost them. They both needed surgery. Sick."

Drake poked his head in the door. "Ready to go?"

"Gimme a minute, okay?" She smiled as sweetly as she could, then as soon as he closed the door, turned back to Ginny. "Why are you telling me this?"

Ginny frowned. "No reason. Just shooting the breeze."

"Ginny. I can tell there's more." Madison reached across the table and covered Ginny's hand with hers.

Pulling her hand away, Ginny stood up. "I'm just warning you. Andre's sick. If you marry Drake, he'll cut you too."

Madison did not know what to respond to first. The ridiculous notion that she and Drake were even contemplating marriage, or the idea that a grown man would consider re-enacting a childhood ritual with his friend's wife. Which she had no intention of becoming. Well, not right now, at least. "That was when they were kids, Ginny. Just kids doing something adults would never do."

"Yeah? Then in high school, he got me." She shoved down her jeans. Slashed across her hipbone, raised and pink, was the letter "A".

"Andre did that?" Madison's stomach roiled. "Has Drake seen it?"

"Are you kidding? He'd kill him. And knowing my family, I'd be disowned if Drake ended up in jail."

Madison shuddered, recalling how Andre had used her the night before, how someone had scratched her. "Still, that was so long ago. What makes you think—"

Ginny leaned down and whispered. "I saw his wife one day at the gym. In the locker room. She wasn't too pleased to discover that she wasn't the only one wearing her husband's initial."

"Hey, Madison. You coming or not?" Drake called from the hallway.

She and Ginny jumped up. "One second, Drake."

As Ginny hugged her and continued whispering in her ear, Madison struggled to keep from throwing up everything she had eaten that day.

"She showed them off like they were some kind of trophy. He'd marked both her breasts with an "A", Madison, with the horizontal line going right through her nipples. I got off easy, don't you think?"

Chapter Twelve

The next night Drake wondered what could have caused the rift that now yawned between him and Madison. She had seemed to enjoy his family, laughing at their antics, playing with his niece and nephews. Even bonding with Ginny. Not an easy thing, considering his sister tended to keep to herself.

But then, as they drove home, he couldn't seem to get the conversation flowing. She stared out the window and met his questions with the briefest answers. When he asked if anything was wrong, she said "nothing" in the way every man knows means something big.

Even during their time in the tub that night, she seemed distant. So distant, he just washed and shaved her without a word. Her silence ate away at him. Her distance simply left him lonely and oddly bereft of her companionship.

The next day, he brought in an escape expert who taught her how to slip free of manacles, handcuffs and a man's arms. Madison's determination amazed him. She practiced until her skin bled. At one point, the expert made her manacles too tight. Madison sobbed as she tried repeatedly to pull her hands out, but when Drake moved to comfort her, she turned away and faced the expert with cold determination. Her calm request that the expert show her how to get out, even if it mean breaking her hands, shocked and sickened him.

Uncomfortable about approaching her while she was acting so strange, Drake decided to forgo any submission training that night.

Sliding under the covers next to her, he moved to turn off the light. Her soft voice stilled his hand.

"Ginny mentioned how you got that scar on your palm."

Cursing his sister, he mumbled, "Is that what's been bothering you all day? It was nothing."

"Not according to her. According to Ginny, you and Andre nearly died." She reached out and took his hand. Everything in him told him to pull away. The scar had been the one and only time he had doubted Andre. Over the years, he avoided that memory because recalling it meant seeing again how his friend's eyes had looked when Drake had screamed in pain. "Kids do stupid things, Madison. Then they get over it."

"You really trust him?" Her voice shook.

Rolling over, he took her into his arms. "I'd trust him with my own sister, Madison. Doesn't that tell you all you need to know?"

He watched her open her mouth to reply then close it. Instead of snuggling against his chest, she rolled to her other side, offering him her back.

"What's wrong, Madison?" He lifted a lock of her hair and rubbed it between his fingers. "This can't just be about a boyhood pledge. Andre didn't say or do anything else, did he?"

"No. He was...very respectful."

"My family?"

"No, they were wonderful. If anything, I felt so phony. Letting them go on believing there was something...something special between us."

He touched her shoulder and felt her stiffen.

"Please, Drake. I'm so sore from that guy's exercises and my hands are cramping. I just want to go to sleep."

Lying on his back, Drake stared up at the mirror and saw that her eyes remained open. "You don't have to go through with this, you know. Promise not to go to that club, and you're free to leave."

"I'm going in." Madison turned over and stared up at him. "And I don't want to leave you, Drake."

"Just remember, when you're cursing me tomorrow, that I gave you the opportunity to end this." Angry with her for forcing him to carry out the day he and Andre had planned, he got up and strode from the room.

* * * * *

Madison awoke to the sound of metal clinking and something cold embracing her ankles. Blinking into the sunlight glaring through the window, she grinned at the shadowed form bending over the foot of the bed. "This couldn't wait until I woke up, Drake?"

"Drake had to go out on business," the shadow said in a familiar voice.

Cold, sweaty dread swept over her body. "Andre."

Sitting up, Madison clutched the blanket to her chest. How could Drake just leave her like this? Her heart kicked into overdrive.

"You're not here for another lesson, are you? Where's Drake?" She tried to pull her foot away. "Drake!"

"God, relax." Andre slid his hand under the covers and retrieved her other ankle.

Watching him lock a manacle to her ankle then retrieve her leash from the dresser, Madison recalled how he had shoved his hard dick into her at the barbeque.

She held the blanket tighter to her chest. "Where's Drake?"

"That, I can't tell you." He tugged until she released the blanket, then he unhooked her choker, buckled a leather collar around her neck and hooked the leash to it. "Stop covering yourself. You have to get used to walking around naked if you're planning on entering the club's playroom. Come on."

"I have to walk around naked?"

The sharp tug on her leash shocked her. Every part of her training at Drake's hands had seemed more of an erotic fantasy. The memory of her conversation with Drake's sister had her scooting further back on the mattress.

"I said, 'Come'!" Andre raised his free hand. She watched the whip strike her leg, expected a slight sting then yelped when it hurt much more than when Drake punished her.

"All right!" Madison leapt out of the bed and followed him toward the bathroom. "When's Drake coming back?"

When Andre didn't answer, she pulled back on the leash. "He is coming back, isn't he?"

"Drake called. I came. Other than writing down your morning rituals and a few other instructions, we didn't talk."

Madison froze. Morning rituals? Yanking the leash out of his hand, she spun around and ran. Something pulled her feet out from under her but just before her face hit the floor, Andre's arm snaked around her waist and hoisted her up.

"We're chained together. One of Drake's instructions. I guess he figured you'd run."

She glanced down then scowled up at his amused expression. Somehow, she hadn't noticed the two slender chains hooked to her manacles. Andre lifted the legs of his trousers. Her chains were hooked to similar manacles around his ankles.

"I'm not peeing in front of you." She wished her voice would stop shaking. "And...and I'll be damned if you're going to...to...well, take care of my morning rituals."

"I'll turn my back while you pee." Andre chuckled as he turned and pulled her into the bathroom. "But I will wash you, and I will shave you." Andre pushed on her shoulders until she sat on the toilet. "You have two minutes."

Burning with shame, she relieved herself then stepped into the tub. She couldn't help but notice the difference between Andre's touch and Drake's as he washed her body. Drake's touch incited every nerve, inflamed her very soul.

Andre's treatment reminded her of the way she had washed her childhood dog. Even when he shaved her, his brows furrowed with concentration and his fingers moved methodically. His fingers never caressed her as Drake's had, never strayed to test for proof of her arousal. When the razor nicked her, she yelped and held her breath, expecting him to try to carve his initial in her skin.

In a strange way, she was glad there were no tender kisses to her inner thighs to lessen the impact of her humiliating position as he shaved her anus. Her mind kept insisting that it didn't matter who trained her, as long as she learned how to act when it was show time. Then Andre shifted her plug to remove the hairs under the flat base and Madison's face felt as if she sat in a sauna with too many lava rocks piled in the well.

How many times had Drake done the same thing, telling her that only he could touch her virgin hole? Why had he bought her the choker and told her it meant she belonged to him if he had planned to hand her over to another?

"Why is he doing this to me?"

Andre paused.

Madison closed her mouth. She hadn't meant to actually voice her question.

"He didn't do this. You did. I've never seen Drake look like he did when he left this morning." He returned to his task of baring her of any hair. "I could ask you the same thing. Why do you insist on spreading your legs for strangers? Why are you doing this to him?"

"Him? What have I done to him? I don't see him holding his legs up in the air." She turned her head to the side and stared at the drops of moisture gathering on the mirrored wall. Drake had left? "Damn him."

"If Drake had his way, no one else would ever touch you." Andre rinsed and toweled her off, then grasped her hand and yanked her up to her feet.

Oddly no longer embarrassed by her nudity, Madison moved closer. "He told you that?"

"He didn't have to. This morning, even as he told me what to do, he looked at me as if he wanted to kill me. I've never seen him quite so possessed." Andre seemed annoyed and glared down at her. "You changed him."

Madison couldn't stop grinning.

Until she strode into the kitchen and saw two men eating breakfast at the table. Again her face burned. She recognized them. They were two of the men from the other night.

Andre made her kneel beside his chair and beg for every bite of food until her plate was clean. When they then led her into the living room, she expected them to tie her to the table and tugged feebly back on her leash, but Andre delivered another stinging lash and led her to the couch.

Minutes dragged by. Occasionally one of the men—it didn't matter which—would stroke her inner thighs or breasts. When an hour had passed and she could no longer deny that their brief, fluttering caresses were arousing her, the man to her left bent over and started to suckle at her breast.

Andre stood up and turned on the TV. He flicked through the channels then stopped at an Oprah rerun. "Watch the show, slave. There will be a test at the end. If you fail, you'll be punished."

She watched as the other man, the one with a crew cut, slid into the space Andre had vacated then proceeded to suckle her other breast. Keeping her eyes on the show, she tried to block them out, tried and failed to still the trills of pleasure spiraling through her stomach.

Something was terribly wrong. She didn't *want* to react. She suddenly recalled Andre rubbing some kind of cream over her nipples and clit, sinking it deep into her pussy while they were in the bathroom. Each place where he had spread the cream now strummed with need.

"Cradle them to your breasts, slave."

His command thrilled and terrified her. When she touched the men's heads and felt them moving in her hands, liquid heat pooled between her legs. Andre knelt before her. As if obeying a silent command, the men pulled her legs apart. She expected him to cover her with his mouth or sink his fingers deep into her. Instead, he motioned for two men she hadn't noticed. They came out from behind the couch and knelt on either side of Andre.

"Look," Andre said, his voice hard and insulting "see how Drake's slave weeps from the touch of strangers. Her juices are soaking the cushion."

Hearing him, she suddenly realized that Drake would see the wet spot. If he didn't, something told her Andre would point it out. Her frenzied mind screamed. He would know that someone other than him could arouse her. The other night, she had told him that the only reason she had responded to their touch was because she had maintained eye contact with him and imagined only he touched her.

She had seen his reaction when she told him that no one but he had touched her that night. How would he react to her dripping for these men in his absence? How could she explain?

"Please...stop."

They ignored her. If anything, they sucked harder and harder until it hurt then bit her tender nipples. Something cold touched her inner thigh, slid down between her outer lips. She strained her head to see what it was, but the two heads at her breasts blocked her view.

"Keep your eyes on the TV, slave, or your punishment will be severe," Andre warned, his eyes holding none of the sympathy she had seen briefly in the bathroom.

Her thoughts scattered. The cold pressed against her clit then started to heat up. Vibrate. Just as she started to tumble into an orgasm, she heard Andre's stern warning.

"Do *not* come without permission."

Madison ground her teeth until she thought they would crack. Her legs started to tremble. The men at her breasts raised their heads and placed odd discs over each nipple. Feeling something slither into her, she started to lean over and peek down. Two firm hands grasped her shoulders and held her in place, but not before she saw the black wire disappearing into her body. Her eyes widened and fear sucked all the air out of her lungs when she realized the same type of wires were attached to the white discs adhered to her nipples and clit.

"Oh, Christ," she croaked out through her suddenly dry throat. "This looks dangerous. Listen, I don't think Drake would approve."

The men ignored her. Andre slid a black metal box in front of his knees.

"Andre, please don't." Madison struggled against the hands holding her shoulders to the couch and the ones forcing her legs apart. The discs heated. After a few seconds, whatever they had slid into her pussy heated. Her eyes focused on Andre's fingers wrapping around a dial. She watched as the dial slowly turned. "Andre, please, this is...oh!"

A minute electrical charge zinged her.

"Tell me, Madison. Have you ever fantasized about having more than one man pleasuring you?" Andre's voice drew her attention away from the wires. His eyes bored into hers. "Before you started training?"

"Hasn't every woman?" she replied.

A larger charge zapped her. Her clit twitched.

"Answer with 'yes, Master' or 'no, Master'," the man with the crew cut warned. "And remember the test."

"Yes, Master." Her eyes strayed to the TV. She had no idea who sat beside Oprah. Oh she was going to be punished for sure.

"Do you like being Drake's slave?" Andre asked, his gaze flicking to the box then back to her.

Squirming against the hands holding her down, she hesitated.

Were there right and wrong answers?

Did Andre want her to bare her feelings here or answer the way a good slave did? "Truth?"

Another charge, this one stronger, longer left her gasping and hungry for more.

"Only the truth, slave." Andre's voice held an edge of anger, although she had no idea why. "Do you like being Drake's slave, spreading your legs for him, doing everything he demands?"

A heated blush swept down the length of her body. "Yes, Master, I do."

"When your week is over, will you welcome your freedom?"

"No, Master," she whispered, somehow knowing that Andre would have seen the truth even if she had lied.

"You like this?" Andre swept his hand over her. "Giving yourself to strangers, feeling them touch you?" He shoved his finger into her pussy, then held it up. "Entering you whenever they want with whatever they want? Strangers?"

He spat the word out. His eyes condemned her. She was just about to ask him what the hell his problem was, when he startled her with the next question.

"You're a virgin, aren't you?"

The muscle ticking in his cheek sent a chill of apprehension down her spine.

"Who the hell told you that?"

Three consecutive charges streaked through her, connecting to each other as they sent her closer to orgasm then she thought she could control. "No, Master!"

Someone nudged her plug. She cringed. Oh yes, there she definitely was a virgin. She had promised that treat to Drake, feared following through, but couldn't imagine anyone else touching her there, entering her there.

"Are you a virgin?"

"Y-yes, Master."

"I think taking your tight ass will please me. Would you like that?"

The fingers on her shoulders dug into her flesh.

She watched Andre's hand move. Shoving her hips back into the couch, she shook her head. "No, Master."

The plug began to vibrate.

"No!"

Her desire plummeted. The two holding her legs pulled her butt to the edge of the cushion. Andre sent another series of electrical charges through the wires and although her body quivered in response, her mind searched for some way to escape.

"It won't hurt, slave. Your Master has prepared you well, and now your body craves my possession." Andre spun the dial then shoved the box aside.

The charges, just shy of painful as he moved between her legs, surged through her body. She thought she climaxed, but nothing mattered except preserving herself for Drake.

"No," she wailed, thrashing against the hands that held her. "Let me go. Tomato! That's my safe word. Tomato!"

"Why?" Andre asked, his voice too cold, too detached. "Do you want someone else? Him?"

He pointed to the man with the crew cut.

When she continued to fight and shake her head, he pointed to the man holding her other leg. "Then him? You prefer him to me? Answer me, slave!"

Madison blinked away the tears that blinded her. "No, none of you!"

"Not even me?"

The sound of Drake's voice softly asking from behind her sounded so surreal she thought she had imagined it. She flung her head back and saw him gazing down at her with the ever-present hunger filling his eyes. "Drake. Oh thank God."

His hair dripped with sweat. Lines of tension creased his brow and the corners of his mouth. She vaguely felt someone peel the discs away and pull the wire out of her pussy. The hands holding her shoulder—how did she not see that they were his?—trembled.

"Don't let him do it, Drake. Please. I can't. I won't."

Andre wrapped her hair around his fist and yanked her head until she looked into those lifeless eyes. "You didn't answer his question, slave."

Madison threw him a scalding glance. "Yes, with him. Okay? Only him."

Without a word, Andre released her hair and started packing away his wires.

Still, Drake remained silent. She thought of her body responding while her mind had not. Turning on the couch, she rose up onto her knees and brushed the damp hair from his eyes. "Drake? He hurt me. He whipped me."

"Who did Oprah have on her show?" He ground out the question, his voice so cold she thought his breath would drip ice.

"I don't know. Drake, what's wrong? Talk to me."

"Show the men out, slave. Then come upstairs." Without another word, Drake strode from the room.

She heard him stomp up the stairs. Turning, she cast a questioning look to Andre.

Chuckling, he stood up. "Got me. It took all my nerve to go as far as I did with him shooting daggers at me. Then again, maybe I do know what's wrong."

As the men gathered, she huddled on the couch, somehow more aware of her lack of clothing than when they had her splayed open. Andre sat down on the couch. "Admit it. You've got it bad for Master D."

Got it bad? A shudder ripped through her body. After tonight, after experiencing just how far this could go, her feelings for Drake terrified her. How many times could she go through this without losing herself completely, without losing her mind?

Grabbing a throw pillow, she hugged it to her chest. "This is a job for us. Nothing more."

"Yeah, right. He heard your answers, Madison. He's not stupid." Andre leaned back and crossed his legs. The other men quietly left. "He knows you were trying to save yourself for him."

"I never said that."

"You didn't have to." A loud thump from the second floor drew Andre's gaze up to the ceiling. "Sounds like he's pissed all right."

"Why's he so angry?" She dropped her chin onto the pillow. "Why did he leave? He knows this isn't easy for me. This submission thing. You'd think he'd be happy that I admitted I liked being his slave."

"Maybe he realizes he's brought you too far."

"Too far? How so?"

The Andre who had frightened her, who had treated her so roughly seemed like a completely different man from the one who sat beside her. "Our life is now in your blood, Madison. You came for a bunch of men. Not an easy thing for some Doms to see, but we're bound to our slaves just as much as they're bound to us. When they want strangers…and they *all* do…they *all* have to spread their legs for strangers," he kicked the black box and stood up, "we have no choice. We reward them if they are good slaves. We bring them to the clubs and let other men pleasure them. Maybe Drake just realized why some of us find that part of our life unbearable."

"But I said I only wanted him. God, I lost it when I thought…you know." Madison glanced down at her hands.

"I doubt he believed you."

Madison looked up. Anger simmered in Andre's eyes.

He crossed his arms and then spoke quietly, as if he were imparting a great secret. "You fucked up royally, tonight, Madison."

"What? I did not."

He grabbed her chin and forced her to look up into his eyes. "If you freak out like that in the club, they'll know you're a fake." He gave her chin a painful squeeze before releasing it. "It's obvious you can't handle this job."

"What?" She jumped up. "I fucked up? I came, dammit."

Needing to see Drake and uncover the real reason for his anger, she threw the pillow at Andre's face and stalked out of the room.

When she entered the bedroom, the shimmering glow of candlelight shone from under the bathroom door. Relieved that he was not angry, that he was obviously setting up for another romantic bath, she walked up to the door. The handle turned halfway then stopped. She could hear the water filling the tub.

Jiggling the doorknob, she called through the door. "Drake, something's wrong with the door. It won't open."

He didn't answer.

"Drake. I can't open the door." She knocked, wondering if the sound of running water muffled her voice. When he still didn't answer, she pressed her face to where the door met the jamb and yelled, "Drake! Open the door."

Nothing. Grumbling to herself, she wondered how men held so many powerful positions in the world when they were nothing but overgrown babies. She walked to the bed and slid beneath the covers. Glaring at the door, she waited for him to get over his anger and come out.

The door downstairs slammed shut. A minute later, the sound of a car pulling away told her that Andre had left. Drake remained locked in the bathroom.

"Damn men with their overgrown egos," she yelled at the door then punched her pillow and settled in for the night.

Sleep eluded her. Her anger simmered as she watched the minutes flick past on the alarm clock. She sat up and stared at the door. Too much time had passed, too much time listening to that damn tub filling. It had to be full by now.

Her heart skipped a beat. What was he doing in there?

Tossing aside the covers, she tiptoed to the door and pressed her ear to the wood. Only the sound of running water met her ears.

"Drake, if you don't open this door, I'll break it down. I will!" She rested her head against the wood. "Please, Drake, you're scaring me."

She slid down the door to her knees and tried to peek under it. Her eyes skimmed across the tile floor, past the toilet, past the wall of the tub. Something lay wedged against the rest of the door, blocking her from seeing anymore of the bathroom. Telling herself to calm down, she rationalized that Drake had probably tossed his shirt onto the floor before stepping in the bath.

Flattening her hand, she slipped her fingers into the tight space beneath the door. The wood scraped her skin away and still she pushed her hand further in. When the tips of her fingers touched cloth, she snagged it with her nails and dragged it toward her. The cloth only gave a little.

Sweat trickled down between her breasts. "Damn you, Drake. If this is some lesson or trick, I'll…"

A sliver of water seeped out from under the door. Another wider one appeared.

"Oh shit! Drake!"

Madison jumped to her feet and started slamming her shoulder into the door. When that failed to budge it, she raced down to the kitchen and searched the drawers until she found a knife. Just as she turned to leave, something landed on her head. She raised her hand. Water.

She glanced up and a whimper skipped up her throat. A stain spreading across the ceiling sent her charging out of the kitchen and back up the stairs.

"Please, let him be okay," she cried to the empty house as she skidded into the bedroom and rushed over to the bathroom door. The puddle had already spread five feet into the room. Thin crimson lines swirled through the water. She flung open the closet and snatched her cell phone from her bag. After calling 911, she dropped the phone and returned to the bathroom door. The knife slid in her sweaty palms, but she managed to wedge it behind the molding and wiggle it until the door popped free. "Hold on, Drake."

She shoved against the door. It gave.

Opened a couple of inches.

Stopped.

"Shit!" She could see part of one of Drake's legs, but nothing more of him, nothing to calm her racing heart.

"Drake. Wake up, dammit," she screamed through the crack. Squatting, she shoved the door again. Her stomach sank when his leg moved with the door a scant inch like a dead weight. Reaching her arm as far through the opening as it would go, she gave his thigh a sharp pinch.

He didn't even flinch. Her heart slammed into her ribs. Sobs tore at her throat, but she refused to release them. Like the signature on a death certificate, they would validate a loss she could not, would not accept.

Madison Garrett did not cry or sob or scream. Madison Garrett did not give up.

Still squatting, she curled into a ball and shoved until her shoulder throbbed and the door moved enough for her to squeeze through. When she did, her feet slid out from under her. Her butt slammed onto the tile floor. Pain shot up her back, but her scream had nothing to do with her injury. Blood surrounded her, clung to her bare butt, her legs and the corner of the sink. She tore her eyes away from that crimson smear and stole a peek at Drake.

Sprawled on his back, his head under the pedestal sink, he looked as if he were sleeping peacefully. Blood seeped from beneath his head. His chest barely rose.

Madison dropped to her knees and let her sobs rend the night.

Chapter Thirteen

※

"I am not letting some faux-hawked, just-out-of-school kid touch him, Nurse Pat-ter-son." Madison jabbed her finger into the plastic nameplate of the hefty, six-foot nurse trying to intimidate her by puffing out her triple-E boobs. "You get someone with gray hair and wrinkles, or these babies will deflate before you can say breast reduction!"

"Oh God, Madison, who are you bullying now?"

Hearing Drake's weak voice behind her, she spun away from the nurse and rushed to the gurney they had brought him in on. She cupped his pale, cold cheek in her hand. Tears burned her eyes when he smiled up at her.

"Drake."

"I slipped. My head hit something."

Swiping at a tear that landed on his cheek, she grinned. "Yeah, I figured that out."

His smile faltered. "I'm sorry. Andre took that further than he should have. I let my curiosity get in the way of keeping tabs on the voltage. And then I saw the mark on your leg and realized that he had whipped you. If I didn't leave, I would have killed him."

"It only hurt at the end. I...I..." She didn't know what to say. Her face burned as she recalled how her body jerked from her orgasm. "I didn't want to...come...but that machine. A- and I think the cream he used. I'm sorry."

His lips thinned. "Any fool could tell that you didn't enjoy it. Damn, Madison, if that happened in the club and the abuser was there, *you'd* be in the hospital."

"I know. If I knew you were there, I would have—"

"Enjoyed it? Not fought?" He grasped her wrist and held her hand to his chest. "Let me take your virgin ass for the first time with an audience?"

She leaned over. Through the thin dress she had thrown on in front of the startled paramedics, she felt the heat of his chest against her breasts. Her bell chimed. "I belong to you, Drake. Take me wherever and whenever you want."

Pressing her lips to his, she felt her heart stutter. When had she fallen for him? When had her enslavement become one of the heart instead of just the body?

His tongue slid between her lips, caressed the sensitive flesh behind them. She tasted him, drew his tongue deeper and sent a telling moan into his mouth. She could feel his heartbeat racing under her palm.

"I thought I'd lost you," she whispered against his lips.

Breaking the kiss, she rubbed her cheek against his and let him feel her tears, let him hear her weep.

Drake's arm wrapped around her and held her close. "You don't have to go into the club, Madison."

Staring into his eyes, she wanted nothing more than to squeeze onto the gurney and offer him her warmth and total obedience. Instead, she straightened. "I have to go in, Drake. You know that."

Drake pushed up on his elbows. "Madison, you don't understand. I noticed something tonight—"

"Last night, Drake. We have been in this damn emergency room for hours. I watched them bring in his latest victim this morning."

Someone cleared his throat.

Palming away her tears, she turned away from Drake. An elderly man in a white doctor's coat stood at the foot of the gurney.

Madison kissed Drake's cheek. "I'd better let him have his way with you. I'll come back later."

"Madison, wait."

She backed away as he struggled to rise. Blowing him a kiss, she turned and ran down the hall.

* * * * *

That night, while Drake lay in a hospital bed downtown, Madison dyed her hair black in Rob's guest bathroom. When she stepped into Rob's den, she could tell by his expression that, once again, she had worked magic with her disguise. Her slender nose now had a wide bridge. Collagen puffed her lips, and blue contacts hid her green eyes.

"Well?"

"You didn't get any of that stuff on the towels, did you?" Rob wrinkled his nose. "And what's that god-awful smell?"

Flopping down onto his ivory leather couch, she shoved her shoulder against his and giggled. "You're such a Denton."

The Dentons, one side of mother's family, never ceased to amaze her. Like her mother, they were puritanical neurotics who wasted their lives worrying about cleanliness and germs. The other side of her mother's family, like her aunt, bucked like a wild horse against the constraints of society. Madison used to believe she hovered somewhere in the middle but after nearly a week with Drake, she seemed to have passed her aunt by a mile.

"I don't like this." Rob stood up and started pacing in front of the windows. Behind him, Manhattan's skyscrapers twinkled against the moonlit sky. "I don't like going behind Drake's back."

"God, Rob. The man is in the hospital holding on to life by a thread! We can't bother him with this."

"By a thread? You said he was fine." He shoved a lock of hair off his furrowed brow.

Madison bit her lip. "Well, sure, he's fine. But his condition could turn with the slightest rise in blood pressure."

"No one will believe this. I look ridiculous." He turned and glanced at his reflection in the window.

She had to agree with him on that score. The black leather pants that had clung so alluringly to Drake's muscular legs and outlined the long ridge of his erection hung loose on Rob's scrawny legs. Drake's broad, sinewy chest and washboard abs had made her mouth water. Rob's only had a few hairs to take one's mind off the sunken sternum and slight pooch of a belly. "You look fine."

"You don't look so bad yourself. I might go straight for a body like that."

"Yeah, right. I saw your latest boyfriend, Rob. That pretty boy face blows me out of the water." Only slightly embarrassed by her nudity after exposing herself to so many men—ten if she counted the paramedics—she stood up and rouged her nipples before snagging them in the loops of her chains. She tugged on the chains to check the tension. After a few adjustments, she tugged again.

"Would you cut that out? You're making me ill." Rob strode to the coat rack and yanked off a black raincoat. "Well, if we're going to do this, we may as well get going."

"You know the drill, right?"

"We go to that festering den of STDs, I try not to touch any of the sluts spreading AIDs to those poor men, and you catch a beating. Is that right?" Rob wiped spittle from his lips with the back of his hand.

"Well, not in those words, but..." Madison frowned. "Shit, I always knew Train Me, Chain Me wasn't your cup of tea and that it bothered you that your mom owned it, but," she slid her arms in the coat he held out, "I never knew you hated it so much."

"Hate it?" He opened the door and held it open for her. As she passed, he leaned over and whispered, "If I thought I could get away with it, I'd burn that Tower of Babylon down with everyone in it."

The hairs on the back of Madison's neck rose. Watching Rob lock the menagerie of deadbolts then wipe them clean with antiseptic cloths, she wondered how he viewed her. "Uh, Rob, maybe I should go in alone. I wouldn't want you to...uh...bump into any of those...uh..."

"Sluts? They like getting slapped around, don't they?" He grabbed her upper arm and led her to the elevator.

"No, not really." Her mouth went dry when she glanced up at his face. She had never seen Rob so determined looking.

His eyes had narrowed to slits, his lips were compressed and white and his fingers dug into her arms. "Don't be stupid. They like it."

The elevator door opened.

Rob's grip tightened as he practically shoved her in. "At least they're not like my mother."

The doors slammed shut. Madison almost sighed with relief when Rob pressed the button for the lobby. She didn't like this side of him. Oh she had seen him angry. She had seen him sputtering with rage every time her brothers wrestled him to the floor just to prove they could. But she'd never seen him sizzle with loathing, never seen his eyes burn with fury or heard his voice drip with contempt. It was downright frightening.

As they waited for a cab, he continued. "At least these sluts don't make a grown man lick their feet." He turned eyes on her that seemed glazed as if he were drugged or seeing something other than her face. "I walked in on her once. When I was twelve. You didn't know that, did you?"

Madison could only shake her head. Deep down inside, she loved Rob. Always had. Tonight, she feared him. Tonight, she felt her chains under her coat and regretted wearing them in his presence.

"Train Me, Chain Me was under major renovations. Mother's favorite client, some bodybuilding fireman, couldn't wait until it reopened. Three thousand, Maddy. Do you believe it?"

"Huh?"

A cab pulled up. Sliding in, she hoped Rob would drop the story rather than air it in front of the driver. Once they gave the address, the cab pulled away and the driver started whistling.

"He paid her three thousand to humiliate him in her apartment. My home!"

"Rob, my arm." She could swear his nails had pierced the coat and now sliced through her skin.

Rob glanced down at his hand, and although he kept hold of her arm, he loosened his grip. As he continued to speak, his grip once again tightened. "I came home from school. With friends, mind you. And there's this man—his body epitomizing what each one of us prepubescent fools dreamt of having—this muscle-clad Adonis is on his knees, licking my mother's feet while she whips the hell out of his welt-covered ass."

"Rob, you're hurting me." Madison started to pry his fingers loose. She glanced at the back of the cabdriver's head. The man kept whistling some strange, lilting tune.

"What is wrong with these people?" He grabbed her other arm and forced her to turn toward him. "You like it too. I could tell when you put Drake's chains on. You like being beaten. Being his slut. You!"

"It's just a job, Rob. I'm back to being plain, old Maddy after tonight." She blinked, sneaking a quick glance down, gauging the distance between his balls and her hands.

"I'm not so sure." He held her gaze. "I always hated how you were just like my mother."

"What?" She almost laughed. Almost. "I've never been a Mistress. God, I'd crack up if some guy asked me to spank him."

"No. You're much worse. My mother's domination is a game for her and her clients. 'We're just playing a game, sweetie. Bruno's been a bad boy and now I'm punishing him.' God, I almost threw up."

He glanced down at her hand and smirked. Before she could anticipate his move, he released her arms and grabbed her wrists. Pushing her back until she lay half sprawled on the seat, he held her hands over her head. "It was never a game to you, Maddy. You've made me and every man you met crawl on our bellies and lick your feet."

"Rob, let me up. Okay? This is me. Maddy. I love you, you dopey oaf." She forced her lips to turn up into a smile.

Rob blinked. "I'm so sick of this, Maddy."

"I know, Robby Rabbit." She hoped her childhood pet name for him would sink in, release the boy she had once shared campouts and sleepovers with.

Switching both her wrists to one hand, he grazed his fingers down her cheek. "I knew, the minute he entered my office, that Drake would be the one to bring you down. I just knew it. But he went too far, Maddy. Now you're the one crawling. You're the slut licking someone's feet just so he'll stick his cock in you."

"See," Madison smirked, "that's where you are so wrong. I told you, Rob. This is just a job. A role." She felt the bone-breaking grip around her wrists loosen and hurried to make her point. "My relationship with Drake is purely a teacher-student one. And I strongly, very strongly oppose screwing one's teacher or boss."

Rob stared at her, through her.

"And remember, Rob, I don't screw for the sake of a story. Never have and never will. You know that!" She chuckled, although most of her wanted to scream at the whistling cabbie to pull the fucking cab over and help her out.

"Really, Maddy? This is just for the story?"

When she nodded, he closed his eyes. After a very long minute, he released her wrists and sat back. Madison sat up and backed into the corner of the seat. Praying the door wouldn't swing open, she pressed her back against it and watched Rob go through some strange breathing routines.

As they pulled up in front of Train Me, Chain Me, he turned to her and smiled. "Ready?"

She wanted to jump out of the cab and grab the nearest cop. Rob needed help before he killed someone. A little voice insisted she was first on his list. She peered at the deserted downtown street. No bouncer stood outside the unmarked door of the club. No cop walked this beat.

Rob opened the door and held out his hand. "It's show time, Maddy. You're going to owe me big time for this. God, I hate this place."

Knocking in the sequence of taps and pounds her aunt had drilled into her head, Madison prayed the night would go as planned. The door opened. Rob reached into the pocket of his raincoat.

Maddy tensed, expecting him to whip out a machine gun and wipe out all the sluts in the club, including or at least beginning with her. Of course, there was always the chance, the more probable chance that he would whip out a can of Lysol and wipe out all the germs in the club. She relaxed when he gingerly drew out a black, hooded mask and dragged it over his head.

Peering at her through the holes, he ordered in a voice that bespoke an authority Rob just didn't possess, "Move, slave. Tonight I share."

"Yes, Master." She followed him into the club. Masters, Mistresses, subs and slaves milled around the bar. Madison wasn't surprised that no alcohol lined the shelves below the bar mirror. Drake had explained the dangers of mixing alcohol and punishment. A sub might be too intoxicated to tell the difference between pleasure and real injury. A dominant might lose touch with his control of whatever weapon he wielded.

Wails and moans echoed over the din of conversation and music. Nudging Rob until he glanced away from a scantily clad group of men, she nodded to the coat check.

Few of the patrons paid much attention to her, although she did note that a number of Doms did glance her way and nod at Rob in approval. Until he gave them the go ahead, she was untouchable, unapproachable.

As planned, Rob hooked a leash to the collar he had bought that afternoon then led her into the playroom. Surrounded by alcoves featuring one means of restraint or another, they searched for a vacant one then made their way to it.

"I don't like this," Rob murmured in her ear as he manacled her to a St. Andrews Cross. "I'm getting bad vibes, left and right."

"Of course, you are. You're entering a world you've despised your whole life, Rob. Get over it." She didn't admit that she felt the same vibes. Now splayed out, she felt too vulnerable to help Rob or herself if things went wrong.

She told herself that here, in the main playroom, no harm would come to her. She told herself that Drake would understand why she had defied him. As the Doms approached and Rob spread the word that he would share her and that the Dom able to make her cry would get the pleasure of private dungeon time, she told herself that she had trusted the wrong man and stepped in some bad shit.

But she didn't panic. She didn't even break a sweat.

Until one of the Doms slapped Rob on the back. "Well, if it isn't Master Steed. I heard you've been making the rounds here."

Master Steed? Rob, her wimpy, sick little cousin a Dom? Recalling the scene in the cab, Madison started to yank at the manacles.

Rob brought his face up to hers. "What's your problem, Maddy?"

"Master Steed? What the fuck is going on?"

"You got me. He must have me confused with someone else." Grinning wickedly, he added, "I like the name. Don't you?"

He didn't wait for her reply. She realized that rather than chance letting the real abuser slip through her fingers, she had to trust Rob. She watched him converse with a group of Doms. When they lined up, horsewhips, paddles and objects she had yet to experience clenched in their hands, she regretted coming in without Drake.

* * * * *

Watching the nurse through his lashes, Drake wondered how long it would take for the sedative they gave him to wear off. When Madison had glanced back at him one last time before leaving the emergency ward, he had seen the look of a hunter in her eyes. The look he imagined she had no control over. It had taken three security guards and the jab of a needle to get him back on the gurney. Just before darkness had engulfed him, he prayed he was wrong, prayed Madison wasn't going in alone.

Hours passed while they fussed over him.

"A concussion," the doctor stated in a bored voice then left after telling him to take it easy.

By the time the sky darkened, Drake could think clearly.

As soon as the nurse left the room, he dragged himself out of bed and rummaged through the plastic bag with his name scrawled across it. He grabbed his cell phone and prayed his friend could be trusted. Prayed the bizarre idea that had formed in his head last night had been just that. Bizarre. Conjured up out of the jealousy of seeing his slave, his Madison come at his friend's hands.

"What's up?" Andre's voice crackled through a bad connection.

"She went in, Andre. Madison went in without backup." A wave of dizziness hit him. Sinking to the floor beside the door, he held the phone to his ear. When Andre didn't reply he repeated himself and added, "You've got to go in for me, buddy. I'm stuck in the hospital."

"What happened? Are you all right?"

"I'm fine, just bumped my head. I need you, Andre. They drugged me and until I can shake it, I need you to go in and help her." He waited, checked his screen for signs of a cutoff and then growled into the phone, "Andre, dammit. I need you."

"Sure, buddy. Anything. It may take awhile for me to get there. I'm home."

Before the line went dead, Drake heard the familiar sounds of Train Me, Chain Me's main playroom.

* * * * *

Still reeling from the latest Dom's caning, Madison peered down at the pink stripes marring the front of her legs, stomach and breasts. The next Dom held a cell phone to his ear. She recognized him as the one who had called Rob Master Steed. So far, none of the Doms had been overtly rough. Her skin burned but not too much.

Other than learning that public flogging was definitely not her cup of tea and that, without Drake, none of this turned her on, she had uncovered nothing.

Rob performed perfectly. Among other things she felt he just did not have to do, he ordered her around, making her jut her hips out so the hairs of the whip could strike her pussy. She figured she had herself to blame. Rob was only getting back at her for years of what he considered domineering abuse.

While the next Dom talked on his cell phone, Rob wiped the sweat dripping down her body with a cloth that smelled like ammonia.

"Having fun?" she asked, through clenched teeth.

"Actually I am. You?"

"Keep it up, Rob, and you'll pay when I'm free."

"Now, Maddy, whoever said I'd free you?" He twisted her nipple until she yelped.

Her mind shut down for a moment as pain shot through her breasts. Way over the line pain.

"Cut it out, Rob, or I swear I'll break your nose when we get out of here."

"You don't get it, Maddy." Rob's eyes glittered. "Once this place sinks its teeth in you, you never get out."

Her heart stilled. Oh no, not Rob. Yet, it made sense, seemed so obvious that she wondered how she hadn't thought of it before allowing him to restrain her.

Rob's hatred for the club, the lifestyle and his mother's role in it. A sob strangled her.

The Dom who had been talking on his cell flipped it shut and strode over to Rob. Madison tried to focus on him, but sweat dripped into her eyes. She watched the two men standing close and talking in hushed terms. When Rob turned and strode out of the playroom, Madison blinked away the sweat and tried to figure out what the hell had just happened. The Dom unlocked her manacles and silently led her away.

"You cost me a pretty penny."

Recognizing the voice, Madison drew in a hissing breath. "Andre? What are you doing here?" She followed him through a door. "I think Rob's the abuser! He's acting so weird. How did you know it was me?"

Andre ignored her. She had to run to keep up with him as he pulled her by the leash downstairs then along a dimly lit hall.

"Andre, answer me."

"Your scars gave you away. I'm here to help." He neither turned nor slowed down.

When he opened a door, she slipped past him then, planting her hands on her hips glared into his masked face. "Did Drake send you here? I'm telling you, it's Rob. He just hurt me. And you should have seen him in the cab. And he's talking crazy."

He gently nudged her until she faced a marble St. Andrews Cross. "He's coming down here. Just do as I say."

Pushing her against it with his body, he ignored her cry of shock when her raw flesh touched the cold marble. With a speed that amazed her, he manacled her wrists and ankles.

"Andre!"

"I told you, I'm here to help."

"It's Rob, isn't it?" Tears burned her eyes at the thought of Rob being responsible for the injuries she'd seen in the pictures. Madison watched him stare at the manacles binding her wrists. "Would you answer me?"

"Not yet." He reached up.

She couldn't see what he did behind the marble, but she felt the manacles pull her arms up and out until she thought they'd pop out of the sockets. "Too tight, Andre."

He didn't reply, didn't relieve some of the pull on her arms. Instead, he squatted by her right leg and did the same thing until the edge of the marble cut into her foot and she cried out in pain.

"Andre, what the hell are you doing?" She cursed when he silently went to work tightening the restraint on her other leg until she yelped. "Would you loosen these things before he gets here?"

Something ripped behind her. She tried to turn her head, but strapped this tightly she could barely lift her chin enough to ease the pain of it pressing into the hard marble. When he yanked her head back and sealed her mouth with duct tape, Madison realized she'd made a terrible mistake, one that just might cost her life. Rob wasn't the abuser.

The man Drake trusted, the man he considered his brother had fooled them all. Scalding tears filled her eyes.

And she'd allowed him to bind her.

Cold sweat sheeted her body. She heard drawers open, heard metal clanking. Dragging one long breath through her nose into her lungs after another, she considered slamming her head into the marble until she passed out. No one had to tell her she stood on the precipice and would soon tumble into hell. She had seen the pictures of Andre's victims.

"You do realize, Madison, that unlike the others, you know who I am."

The sound of someone striking a match sent a strangled scream up her throat.

Chapter Fourteen

ಐ

The cab driver sat at a red light. Drake tossed another fifty over the seat. "Pass it. And drive faster."

"Any faster and I'll be flying."

"Then you'd better fucking fly."

Watching the blur of pedestrians and cars out the window, Drake downed the last of his coffee. The damn sedatives made his arms and legs feel like lead. Hopefully the NYPD would beat him to the club and save him the humiliation of standing by helplessly while Andre tortured Madison.

"I won't lose my license for any amount. You got that, pal?" The cabbie leaned over and turned on the radio.

Billy Idol belting out *White Wedding* made the staples in Drake's head vibrate. Reaching out, he grabbed hold of the headrest behind the cabbie and hauled himself up.

"Listen, pal, put the fucking pedal to the metal before I throw you out of the cab and drive myself." He slumped back and added, "And shut that damned radio off."

When they finally arrived, Drake scanned the street but found no sign of police. He knew his speech slurred slightly from the sedatives, but he expected them to send at least one car to check out his story. Heaving his legs out of the cab, he used the door to pull himself up. As soon as the door slammed shut, the cab screeched away.

A wave of dizziness threatened to send Drake crashing into the gutter. Weaving, he made his way to the door. He squeezed his eyes shut and forced his brain to center on the complicated series of knocks and taps that would gain him entrance. When the bright lights inside met his eyes, he blinked and found himself on the floor surrounded by Doms, Dommes and subs.

"You okay, boss?" Sam the youngest bartender held out his hand.

"I told you not to call me that, Sam." Drake took his hand. The bodybuilder practically lifted him off the floor.

"Sure, boss. You need a drink?" Sam wrapped his arm around Drake's waist.

Drake took a step, swayed then, leaning all his weight on Sam's arm, shook his head.

"No, boss, maybe you're right. Looks like you've had enough, already."

"Get me to a chair, Sam."

"Sure, boss."

"And stop calling me boss."

"Sure, bo...ah...sir."

When he felt the hard chair strike his ass and Sam's hands release his armpits, Drake realized he must have blacked out again. He couldn't hold himself up. How could he hope to fight Andre?

"Sam." He hung his head between his legs to ward off another wave of dizziness. Before Sam could once again announce to those nearby that Drake was the anonymous owner, he ground out, "Get the men. We have a shredder."

"Sure, boss."

By the time the bouncers stood waiting for his instructions, Drake felt well enough to attempt standing on his own.

"Get downstairs!" he yelled at the men. "Check every room and find the sub with the red hair and gre—"

"Are you looking for Maddy?" Rob's face appeared as he looked over one of the bouncer's shoulders. "Because if you are, her hair's black now."

"Rob? Dammit, did *you* bring her in here?" Drake clenched his fists, ready to break Rob's nose. "Where is she?"

"Relax." He squeezed between the men and grinned. "I sent her down with your friend."

"Andre?" Ice-cold fingers slid down Drake's spine. Even after realizing that Andre had lied about being here during their phone conversation, he still wanted to believe his suspicions were unfounded. "Did he tell you his name?"

"Well, not exactly."

Drake shoved him aside. "Get down there," he yelled at the men still standing around.

"But he showed me the cell phone screen to prove that you'd just called him." Rob held up a wad of twenties. "And he gave me money to make it look real."

"What?" Drake stared at the money. "We don't pay for subs like they're some prostitutes!"

His nails dug into his palms. Andre had called them just that when he'd come over last year and ranted about his wife's need to visit the club and offer herself to other Doms.

"Get the hell down there!" Drake started to run toward the stairs but had to stop when another wave of dizziness nearly sent him to his knees. "Sam! Help me out, here. I have to get to her."

Sam and one of the bouncers virtually carried Drake down the stairs. He gathered his strength to face Andre and kill him for hurting Madison. His heart lurched as one of the bouncers reached the first of too many private rooms.

* * * * *

Madison bit her tongue until the pain blocked out the biting lashes that never seemed to end. With each one, Andre called her a bitch in heat or a pain slut or a fucking whore. She lost count at thirty. Her manacles were so tight that her hands bled from trying the techniques the escape expert had taught her. No matter how far into her palm she brought her thumb, no matter how hard she pulled and twisted, she couldn't break free.

Something warm dripped down her back. Still, the whip kept coming. The pain lancing her back drove her closer and closer to insanity.

Drake, her mind screamed, even though she knew he couldn't hear her, knew that even if he could, he was in no shape to help her out of this hell. *I can't get free, Drake. I can't.*

She saw him in her mind, standing in the living room and wiping the blood from her hands each time the escape expert tightened her manacles, heard him tell her that if she's in real trouble, then do anything, even break her own bones.

Andre lit another cigarette. A strangled scream ripped through her throat. The side of her breast still burned from the last one he had lit then pressed into her flesh after each drag. The smell of charred flesh mingled with her sweat and the scent of the cigarette. Bile filled her mouth. Gathering what little strength she had left, she bent her wrists the way she had learned and with a roar, shoved until she heard her bones snap. White-hot pain shot up her arms. Keeping her hands in the manacles, she struggled to stay conscious and waited for Andre to finish preparing his cigarette.

It didn't take long. Like the other one, he only smoked it until it bore a long, red-hot ember. He approached her unmarked breast.

"You like pain, whore?" Andre's eyes glittered as he stared at her skin.

Madison yanked her injured hands free and head-butted Andre with all her might then brought up her elbow and slammed it into his neck. He never made a sound as he fell back onto the concrete floor. Sobbing into the duct tape, she frantically tried to unbuckle the manacles imprisoning her ankles, but her hands were useless.

Someone pounded on the door. Muffled yells came from the hall, but she couldn't make out the words. She screamed then tried to rip the tape from her mouth but it was no use. The slightest pressure on her fingers and her hands felt as if a razor-edged knife sliced through her hands and up her arms. Dropping down and crouching at the foot of the crossbar, she held her hands between her breasts and prayed someone would break through the door before Andre came to. He looked dead, but with her luck she had only stunned him.

As if he heard her thoughts, Andre opened his eyes. Madison whimpered and shied away when he rose up on his elbows. Rage twisted his face, making him look like some demon from a horror movie.

"You bitch!" He brought his hand up to his nose then stared at the blood on his fingers. "You broke my fucking nose."

She must have damaged something in his neck. His voice sounded weak, and his eyes watered as he spoke. Madison forced herself to stand. The manacles around her ankles unbalanced her, but she rose onto the balls of her feet. Tensing her muscles, gathering all her pain and anger into an imaginary ball, she awaited his attack.

Andre lunged just as the door burst open. Ignoring the commotion by the door, Madison waited until his body just about reached hers, before she dropped into the position she had when they had played football.

Andre's shins slammed into her shoulders. Using every last ounce of energy she had left, she lifted him and sent him flying over her shoulder. His head hit the concrete floor with a sickening crack.

Someone draped a shirt over her shoulders. The cloth clung to the blood on her back, pulled at the raw flesh.

Someone else unbuckled the manacles around her ankles.

Still trapped in her nightmare, she struggled to see Andre's body. Sure that he would rise again like in every horror movie she had ever seen, she raced for the door.

Terror like she had never experienced still surged through her body. She couldn't take anymore. Not another minute with those eyes glittering with insanity. Not another minute so completely vulnerable. She had to escape before he got back up.

At the door, someone grabbed her. She fought, screaming from the crippling agony in her hands and the searing pain blanketing her back and breast. She kicked, bit and raised her head to slam it into whoever dared try to keep her in this hellish nightmare.

And looked into Drake's eyes just as blackness engulfed her.

Holding Madison's limp body in his arms, Drake sat on the floor. "Someone call 911. Now!"

"You want me to take her up to the office, boss?"

"Nobody touches her. You hear me? Nobody." He scowled at the bartender. "And call me boss one more time and I swear...I swear—" Drake cringed when his voice broke on a sob.

"Sure, you just wait here." Sam patted his shoulder. "You did well. You got us down here in time."

"Did well? In time? Look at her!" Drake held his cheek over her face, careful not to put any pressure on her mangled nose or swollen lips. "That bastard. I'll kill him. I swear, I'll kill him."

"Seems the damsel in distress took care of that," a bouncer crouching over Andre muttered.

"Who's calling me a damsel in distress?" Madison mumbled against his shirt. Lifting her head, she frowned. "I kicked his ass."

Blessed relief washed over Drake. Tears blurred her face, dripped onto her lips. He didn't care who saw him cry or what they thought. He cupped her cheek. "Don't move, Madison. And don't try to talk."

She frowned and licked her lips. "Who took off the tape?"

Recalling his horror when he had peeled away the tape and first caught sight of her mouth, he wanted nothing more than to get up and kick his friend's lifeless body. Instead, he gently touched his fingers to her lips. "Did he punch you in the mouth?"

She shook her head. "Why?"

"Your lips are all swollen. It must be from the tape." She looked so frail so confused. "Maybe an allergic reaction."

She grinned. "You big jerk. I put collagen in them."

"Collagen?" Laughing, relieved that she could still smile, he kissed the bridge of her nose. "Please, tell me this is collagen too."

"Yeah, like I'd ever keep this for three months. Take it off, Drake. My hands are killing me."

One glance at her hands, and the rage once again coiled in the pit his stomach. "I should have known it was him." He picked at the spongy fake bridge of her nose.

"We never suspect the people we love." She raised her hand to her nose then yelped and brought it back to her chest.

"No. I had so many clues." He held up his palm so she could see his scar. "I was his first. Remember?"

"You were kids then, Drake. How could you know?"

"All this time, trying to figure out how the girls left my club without anyone noticing their condition. Sam and I went over it and over it. There are only three exits. The front door, the fire exit and the owner's exit." He glanced up. Sam stood in the doorway. his eyes darting between Drake and the hallway. "To get from here to the front door or fire exit, they would have had to pass through the playroom. Sam would have noticed something. Andre knew about door from my office, but I never even considered him. Not until he hurt you."

Madison kissed his jaw. "He was your best friend, Drake. And married. Wait. Did you just say your club? Your office?" She tensed, drew slightly away.

"Let me ex—"

"You're the new owner." She shoved her elbows into his chest, nearly breaking free of his arms.

"Think, Madison. If word got out that the Vice President of *Exposed* had bought this club, I'd lose half the patrons."

"But you didn't work at the magazine a year ago. Aunt Louisa told me she sold the club last year!"

"Cops are here, boss, ah, sir." Sam called from the door.

Drake adjusted the cloak draped over Madison until only her feet were exposed. "I worked for the *Enquirer* at the time."

"That doesn't explain why you never told me. Why you let me..." Her eyes darted down to the hand resting on her thigh, the hand bearing Andre's mark. "How do I know, how will I ever know if you were involved or not?"

"My God, Madison. You know me. I would never—"

"What? Hit a woman? Whip her?" Her eyes widened and filled with that glazed look of terror he'd seen in their depths right before she'd passed out.

She wriggled out of his arms and stumbled to her feet just as the police surged into the room. The cloak slid down and pooled at her feet. He expected her to cringe or move to cover herself or drop back down into the cover of his arms.

She didn't even blink. She just kept staring at him with condemning eyes. Drake moved to retrieve the cloak. Sam beat him to it and quickly covered her, but not before everyone in the room got a look at the abuse she had suffered at Andre's hands.

The men behind her gasped as they stared at her back. Drake shot to his feet and swallowed the bile rushing up his throat as his gaze fell upon the black, ragged 'D' burnt into the side of her breast.

"Madison," he choked out her name but was too horrified to say anything else.

Her face crumpled just long enough to give him hope but then reformed into the determined one of the woman who had brought him to his knees in the elevator that first day. "I'm going to interview every one of those victims. I'll get dates. So get your alibis ready, *boss*."

He took a step toward her, needing to touch her, yank her back into his arms. "Don't do this, Madison. Don't let this come between us."

Her eyes filled with tears, but her expression hardened. "There never was an 'us', Drake. This was an assignment. Nothing more."

Before he could reply, before he could take her in his arms, capture her lips and expose her lie, she called to one of the cops.

"I'd question the owner if I were you. I think he and his friend here worked together." She stared down at his marked hand. "Get me the hell out of here."

Someone grabbed his arms and yanked them behind his back. The sharp stab of handcuffs cinching his wrists barely registered through the searing burn in his chest as he watched Sam and the cop accompany Madison out of the room.

She stopped just outside the door. He held his breath when she glanced back.

Her gaze swept over the faces of those crowded around him and Andre.

"Where's Rob?"

Chapter Fifteen

☙

Three months later, Madison still couldn't dredge up enough courage to leave her apartment. If not for the help of her family and a decent-sized bank account, her landlord would have kicked her out onto the street. Hugging her knees to her chest, she watched from the couch as her aunt raised the blinds of another window. Squinting into the blinding sunlight, she stopped herself from leaping up and tackling the woman.

"I'm fine, Aunt Louisa. Please, just go home."

"Fine?" Her aunt raised her brow higher than Madison had ever seen it. "Fine? You call sitting all day in a dark room, fine? It's been three months, Madison. Three months!"

"I just need some time alone. I-I'm waiting for…" She hugged her knees tighter and started to rock.

"For what?" Aunt Louisa yanked up the last of the blinds.

"I tried." Tears burned her eyes, cut a hot path down her cheeks. Rocking faster, she pressed her face into her knees and whispered, "I-I can't help it. Every man is him! And if I so much as smell a cigarette…"

She felt the couch sag but didn't dare raise her head and look at her aunt. Lately every face held pity. Her mother and father cried if they so much as glanced at her. Friends avoided looking her in the eyes. Even the therapist her aunt insisted on bringing over every day failed to conceal his pity when he forced her to recount Andre's abuse again and again.

Drake had called constantly the first week then pounded on her door for three more. How could she face him? Trust him? She didn't trust her own brothers anymore. Not realizing how their rage would affect her, they had punched the walls of her hospital room until their knuckles bled and threatened to kill Aunt Louisa, Rob and Drake.

"Drake calls me every morning, every afternoon and every night." Her aunt wrapped her arm around Madison's shoulder. "Why don't you at least talk to him?"

Madison jammed her eyes down onto her knees. "I can't stop thinking about him, Aunt Louisa. I miss him so much it hurts."

"Then—"

"But when I just imagine being with him again, I get so damned scared." Rising from the couch, she strode over to the window, but stopped a few feet away when fears she couldn't understand gripped her mind. "You want to know how sick I am? I dream of being locked in one of those cages I saw in the club."

"Oh, Maddy, he'd never—"

When she felt a hand on her shoulder, she flinched, even though she knew her aunt meant her no harm. Spinning around, she laughed bitterly. "You don't get it. It's not a nightmare. I'm happy. I hold the only key!"

"Oh, Madison." Aunt Louisa reached out, her eyes filled with tears.

With pity.

Again, Madison jerked away. "Don't touch me." A sob ripped at her throat. "I just want to be alone. Why can't you all just leave me alone?" She backed into the wall. "And shut those damn blinds!"

Aunt Louisa took a step toward her, her hands out.

Madison slid down the wall. "Don't."

"Calm down."

"Don't, Aunt Louisa, please, don't touch me."

Someone knocked on her door. Her heart slammed into her ribs.

"Hey, Maddy, open up," her brother Lex called from the hall.

"Don't open it," she begged her aunt.

"It's only Lex, Maddy."

As Aunt Louisa walked to the door, Madison jumped up and ran to the bathroom. Locking the door, she climbed into the tub, swung the shower curtain closed, and huddled into a ball. Rocking, she cringed every time she heard her brother's deep, masculine voice.

* * * * *

"Thank God, you're here. She's been in there since Lex came by this morning." Louisa stood in the doorway, wringing her hands. She backed into the apartment. "I didn't know what to do. Who to call."

Drake couldn't believe she was the same woman who always managed to lure the young and old men at the club. Black mascara trailed down her blotched face. Her lush lips were pursed and white, and her hair looked like she had just walked through a windstorm. The woman looked like she would start screaming any second. Her appearance told him all he needed to know about Madison. His heart pounded in his ears. For months, he waited for a call, a reason to see her. Now after one look at Louisa, it took every once of control to keep himself from charging through the apartment, finding Madison and carrying her home where he could spend the rest of his life begging for her forgiveness.

"I doubt I'll be much help, Louisa. Madison has made it perfectly clear that I'm the last person she wants to see. Maybe we should call her therapist." He followed Louisa down the hall to the bathroom.

"No. Yesterday, he mentioned hospitalizing her, and she nearly tore the place apart." Louisa stared at the bathroom door then whispered. "Just before you came, I heard her chanting something. Then it sounded like she was throwing things around."

"You don't think she'll do anything like..." He couldn't even voice his sudden fear.

Obviously the thought had entered Louisa's mind. She calmly shook her head. "There's nothing in there but some Advil and Midol. I checked last week."

"Still..." Drake went to the door and laid his palm on the wood. "If she really wanted to...Madison?"

"She never goes out, Drake. How could she get something?"

He held his ear to the door. "Madison, open the door, honey." When only silence met his ears, a sliver of dread rippled down his spine. "Come on, baby. Open the door."

He should have heard something, some sign of her moving around in there. Anything. His nails dug into the wood.

"Oh, my God." Louisa ran down the hall.

The image of Madison lying dead on the bathroom floor flashed before his eyes. He slammed his shoulder against the door repeatedly. "Madison, open the goddamned door!"

He couldn't lose her. These past three months had been a living hell. Knowing that she hurt, that she hid away in her apartment and he couldn't get close enough to help had eaten away at him.

His apartment felt barren without her presence. He tossed and turned all night in a bed that did nothing but remind him of what he had lost.

And every time he entered his kitchen, he saw her standing at the stove in nothing but his collar as she tried to cook him breakfast, saw her sitting on his counter and giggling as he smoothed ointment on her burns.

Saw the black "D" Andre had burned into her breast.

When the door finally gave and swung open, he closed his eyes and prayed she would be all right before daring to glance into the room. Empty bottles of Advil, Midol and various cold syrups caught his eye.

"Madison!"

He flung aside the shower curtain. Huddled in the tub, she raised red-rimmed eyes and muttered, "Relax. I only tossed them down the toilet. Go on. Look."

He forced himself not to glance toward the toilet. "You scared the hell out of me."

"Yeah, well, payback's a bitch. Crashing through that door didn't calm my nerves much." Rocking, she hid her face in the hollow between her knees and her chest. "You can go now. You saved the damsel in distress."

Drake stared down at her. "Nobody calls Madison Garrett a damsel in distress."

It broke his heart to see his she-cat so defeated. She started to tremble.

"Is she all right?" Louisa stood in the doorway, a large carving knife in her hand.

"She's—"

"Would you both get the hell out of my apartment?" Madison yelled in a hoarse voice. "Get the fuck out of here!"

While her words sounded like the Madison he knew, her voice sounded more like a child pleading for mercy.

"Go home, Louisa." Drake took the knife from her hands. The woman looked ready to keel over.

"Go easy on her, Drake. She's…" Louisa glanced at the Madison.

"A mess." Drake glared down at Madison. "And it's about time someone told her."

Louisa, a woman who made strong men cry, wrung her hands and backed away. "Just don't hurt her, Drake. You do, and I'll send every bodybuilder I know after you. You hear me?"

He reached into his jeans and wrapped his fingers around the choker he'd carried around since the night of Madison's attack. "Get out."

Louisa looked down at Madison then nodded and left. When he heard the apartment door slam shut, he started picking up the empty bottles and tossing them into the small wastebasket.

"Go away," Madison wailed from the tub.

Ignoring her, he flushed the toilet and watched until the last pill vanished. Turning to the door, he pried the doorknob off with the knife.

"What the hell are you doing?" Madison called from behind. "This is my safe room!"

"The bad guy is dead. Madison Garrett, the woman who could bring any man to his knees, killed him. Remember?"

He left the bathroom and removed the doorknobs from her bedroom door, her closet doors and her office door. When he finished, he carried the kitchen wastebasket and all the doorknobs into the bathroom. Dropping it on the floor beside the tub, he tossed the doorknobs into it, one by one.

Madison's eyes widened. "What the hell did you do?"

"Get up," he ordered, making sure no anger slipped into his voice.

She looked up at him with terrified eyes.

He almost lost it. He loved Madison more than he thought he would ever love anyone and dreaded facing one more day without her but trapped beneath her fear, a she-cat lurked. A she-cat Madison needed to survive. No matter the cost to him or his relationship with her, today he would free that she-cat. Even if it meant losing his sweet slave. Even if it meant losing Madison.

"Either bite my head off or get the hell up." Part of him rejoiced when she obeyed, part of him longed to dig up Andre and rip him apart. "Take off those clothes, they smell."

She picked at a shiny pink scar on her wrist. "You have no right to—"

"I have two days coming to me. You promised me a week and whether you like it or not, I'm finishing my week."

Tears clung to her spiked lashes. "I can't do it, Drake," she whispered. "I-I can't."

"I didn't ask, Madison." Joining her in the tub, he grasped the bottom of her tee shirt. Skimming his hands up her waist, he raised the hem to just below her breasts. Her skin felt like satin beneath his palms. "Arms up, slave."

She didn't even argue. When he unclasped her bra and slid it off her shoulders, she crossed her arms over her breasts and slouched. His heart stuttered.

He hooked her chin with the tip of his finger and forced her to look into his eyes. "If you want to be punished, you don't have to defy me. You only have to ask."

Dropping her hands to her sides, she started to ramble. "Don't bind my hands, Drake. No manacles. No chains. I'll freak. I know I'll freak. I just can't be restrained. Not yet. Not ever."

Still holding her chin and gazing into eyes that darted back and forth, he kissed her forehead. "No restraints, baby. Now take off your pants, or I'll do it for you."

Drake sat on the edge of the tub and turned on the faucet while she undressed. Water splashed over his shoes. It didn't matter. Nothing mattered anymore but Madison. He plugged the drain, took a box of Calgon from a wicker basket on the floor and sprinkled the powder over the rising water.

"Fine. I'll take a bath. But you get out. Please," she pleaded, backing to the far end of the tub.

Out of the corner of his eye, he took in every clue about the past three months. He already knew by the dark rings under her eyes that she barely slept. The outline of her ribs and hipbones told him just how little she had eaten. Red nubs covered her mound and legs. Thick eyebrows topped her eyes.

Clues that he had stayed away too long.

"Sit." Avoiding her eyes, he grabbed a washcloth from the towel rack. An array of bath gels cluttered the corners of the tub. "I'll let you pick the scent of the day."

When she didn't answer, he held up vanilla bean.

"I like the rose," she said, her voice lilting on 'rose' and turning her statement into a question.

He switched gels and squirted some onto the cloth. Rising, he stared down at her a moment. Other than the warm water sloshing under her quivering legs, nothing softened the sharp edges of what she had to face today. "Stay."

He searched her apartment until he found all he needed. Relieved that she had remained in the tub, he lit at least thirty candles and set them up around the small room.

"Turn off the light, Drake," her voice cracked. "Please."

Round, luminous eyes raised to meet his. Flicking the switch, Drake drew in a sharp breath. Surrounded by the amber glow of the flames, she looked like a wounded angel.

"My God, you're beautiful."

"No, Drake. Not anymore," she said in a sad, hushed voice. Shoving further back against the tub, she sniffed. "Not anymore."

What could he say? What could he do? Louisa had told him about the scars on Madison's back. Apparently Madison feared his reaction to the signs of Andre's abuse.

Taking the bowl of rose petals he had gathered from the multitude of floral arrangements littering her house, he scattered them over the rising water. She picked up a white one that landed on her thigh and brought it up to her nose.

Drake took her hand and tossed a pile of the petals onto her palm. "You have a lot of people worried, Madison. I read each card. You're lucky mine were the only ones by a lover."

She snorted. "I have no lovers."

"You have me." He sat on the edge of the tub and took off his shoes.

"Don't even think about it, Drake." Her voice sparked with anger.

Sweet, sweet anger.

Ignoring her, he slowly removed his clothes. She fought, but he managed to squeeze in between the tub and her back. As he lowered himself into the warm water, she pushed her back into him. He felt his heart wrench. She tried so hard to hide the sight of her back from him. Inch by inch her skin kissed his legs, groin, stomach, then slid up his chest. Before he could stop it, a moan slipped free.

"I've missed this," he whispered in her ear.

He nudged her butt forward and dropped his chin on her shoulder when her body tensed and she shoved her back firmly into his chest. "Relax. I won't look. Yet."

She turned her face and stared into his eyes. "I could have you arrested for this, you know. I will. As soon as you leave, I'll call the cops and—"

"Go ahead. I know them all. After a night in jail, we became good friends." He kissed her shoulder. "But then, I have you to thank for that. Don't I?"

She turned away and shook her head. "I didn't really think you were guilty."

"I know. You were scared." Drake tucked her hair behind her ear. "The worse part of it was not being with you."

The water rose, covering her legs. Not waiting for the tub to fill completely, he lifted the washcloth. Silently he lathered her arms. She cringed, flinched and whimpered like an injured puppy. Her breathing hitched when he swirled the cloth over one of her breasts. When he released the cloth and used his hands, her nipples hardened under his palms.

He kissed the crook of her neck, felt her pulse rise under his lips. "I'm not giving up on you, Madison."

Her head lolled to the side.

Nibbling his way up to the sensitive skin under her ear, he whispered, "I'm done staying away and waiting for you to come to your senses. More than chains bind us. So much more."

A soft moan met his ears. He smoothed the lather down her stomach. When he reached the apex of her legs, he stopped. "Open your legs, baby."

Her head shot up. She shook so much the water rippled around her. "What are you going to do?"

"I'm going to take care of my slave." He squirted gel into his hand. "You're obviously not taking care of yourself. As soon as you're clean," he hesitated long enough to make her wonder, "I'm getting some food into you. You're so skinny, you make Giselle look healthy." He closed his eyes and thanked God when she gasped than softly snickered.

"Now open your legs."

When she obeyed without hesitating, he slid his fingers at an excruciatingly slow pace down her labia. Feeling her soft folds and the glance of her clit after so long would have aroused him if her shaking had stopped. Instead, it grew more frenzied and shook him to the core. Her whimpering resumed then turned into a high keening.

"Snap out of it, Madison. This scared little girl act is over."

He hated being so harsh, but the doctors he had spoken to over the months, doctors used to dealing with subs who experienced abuse, were adamant he reinstate himself as her Master. Madison had to remember that her life, her safety and her health rested in firm hands. By maintaining control of himself and her when he wanted to rant and rave and curse the powers who had allowed her to suffer, he assured her that her well-being mattered more to him than his own.

And above all, Drake could show no pity.

He took hold of her wrist and raised her arm, baring the raised 'D' on her breast. She cried out and covered it with her free hand.

"Remove that hand, right now, slave. I won't ask again."

Her hand slid away, but her nails dragged over her skin. Wincing at the scratches she left behind, he leaned under her arm and kissed them, hoping to soothe the pain.

"Thank God, he put my initial." He ran the tip of his tongue over the scar.

"What," she croaked, trying to pull her arm back down.

"It would have cost me a fortune to fix, if he'd put an 'A'."

"You're sick," she spat out, but he detected some amusement in her voice.

Enough, for now.

He nibbled his initial, sucked it into his mouth. Her breathing grew more and more labored. Her arm relaxed.

"This must have hurt like hell."

Madison nodded. "I don't want to talk about it. Okay?"

"Okay." Drake lowered her arm. "According to the coroner, Andre had old cigarette burns covering his butt and scrotum." He waited, but she gave no sign she even heard. "I questioned his family and discovered his father abused him from the time he was four. He never told me, Madison. All those years and he never complained. Not once."

A tear dripped into the water floating around her stomach. "I won't feel sorry for him. I won't."

"No one expects you to."

At least talking kept her mind off his fingers caressing her pussy. Her thighs relaxed, sagged open. Her head rested on his shoulder.

He slid his finger into her moist channel. Wrapping his other arm around her shoulders, he burrowed his face in her hair.

"Did the doctor say if you'll have any other permanent scars? Other than my initial?"

"Not on the outside," she muttered. "He expects the others will fade with time."

"You must be pretty disappointed." He slid another finger in, felt the flesh around it clench.

"What the hell is that supposed to mean?" She tried to pry his hand away.

He burrowed deeper. Tickled her G-spot.

A spark of the old Madison shot him a seething glare before her eyes flared. A low moan broke free of her pursed lips.

"I remember how proudly you showed off the scar near your bellybutton." He traced the fingers of his other hand over the scar from her knifing. "I just meant it's a shame you won't have anything to show off from this."

"I have a damned ugly 'D' on my boob!" She raised her arm and lifted her breast.

"Yeah. That's true. But I doubt you'll be baring your breast to everyone. At least, not without my permission." He cupped her breast, covering his initial.

"I'll decide who I show." She gasped and jutted her hips forward driving his fingers deeper.

Hope. He never realized how good hope felt.

Washing her hair with one hand while he continued to arouse her with the other, he chuckled. "Looks like some kid did it. I could always hire an artist to make my mark prettier. Maybe add a flower or heart?"

Madison shot him a look of disbelief. She opened her mouth then pursed her lips as an orgasm shook her. Feeling her muscles spasm around his fingers, he caught her face in his hand and captured her cries with his mouth. Too soon, she pulled free.

"You're making fun of it? I have to walk around with this the rest of my life. Stop, dammit." She grabbed his wrist and pulled his hand from between her legs.

"What would you rather I do? Lie and say it looks pretty?" Reaching up, he grabbed the showerhead. As he rinsed her hair, he laughed. "Fine. Would it make you happy if I had a large 'M' branded on my chest? I've never been into pain, but for you, I might consider it."

Madison stood up so suddenly, water sloshed out of the tub. "You're a sick man, Drake Williams."

"I must be, to love a she-cat like you. You really are a mess. Look at this." As he stood, he brushed his fingers over the hairs covering her mound.

She jerked away. Losing her balance, she flung her arms around his neck.

He stared into her eyes. "You know the routine."

"Drake, I don't—"

"I should have led a normal life, you know that? Fallen for someone who didn't need me to keep her hair-free. Someone who washed and fed and shaved herself."

"Drake, I won't let you shave me."

"A Master's work is never done. But some say I'm a workaholic." He smiled down at her.

The water in the tub rose precariously close to overflowing. Candles sputtered in puddles of melted wax. The woman who held his heart shook her head and for one brief moment, almost smiled.

Did she realize she had wrapped her arms around his neck? That she hadn't let go? Did it mean less than he thought it did? He kissed her furrowed brow then slid her arms from his neck. "You know the position. Leg up."

Hiding his smirk when she cursed under her breath and placed her foot on the side of the tub, he lifted the menthol shaving cream. When he finished shaving her legs, he laid a towel on the floor. "Get out and assume the position."

She stepped out and slammed her shoulder into him as she sidled past. Somehow, she managed to keep her back concealed. She lay down and lifted her legs. "You'll pay for this, Drake Williams."

"How about this? How about I pay right now? I want you to call me a bastard...no...a fucking bastard while I shave this sweet pussy. Say it with every smear of cream, every glide of the razor."

He slid a dollop of cream over her mound.

When she only stared between her legs at him, he firmly shouted, "Say it!"

"Are you losing it?"

"Fine." Drake spread her legs wide. He smacked her pussy, not too hard, but hard enough to create a slight sting. Then he waited and prayed.

"Fucking bastard," she muttered and turned her head to the side.

Bending down, he kissed away the sting. "I know exactly where your line between pleasure-pain and real pain is, slave. You have my word, I'll never cross it."

He slid the razor over her mound. When she remained silent, he smacked those lips again, this time a little harder.

"Fucking bastard," she mumbled, rolling her eyes.

This time he licked the pain away and swore he felt her flesh quiver. "No matter how naughty you act. I'll never cross it."

By the time he held her legs up to shave her anus, Madison was calling him every name in the book and some he was sure she made up. Sometimes she hesitated, and he reminded her with a soft slap. Sometimes he stopped because her legs struck his arms and chest as she sped along a litany of insults. He knew, by the names and her dazed eyes, that she cursed Andre and not him. He caressed, kissed and licked away every stinging smack, every biting insult.

When he shaved the last hairs off, he took his shirt from the floor and wiped the tears from her face.

"All clean." He rinsed away the last of the cream, patted her dry with a soft towel, then slid his finger down her crease. "Don't move, slave. Time for your reward."

Covering her with his mouth, he suckled her clit and fingered her until she writhed and moved in rhythm with his fingers. Using her own juices, he lubricated her tight virgin ass then gently slid one digit of his thumb in. Groaning, she raised her hips. Keeping two fingers deep in her pussy, he slid his thumb in to the knuckle.

Madison stilled. He gave her a moment to grow accustomed to the feeling while he continued to suckle the swollen nub wrapped in his tongue. When she started to moan, he withdrew his fingers and thumb then thrust them back in slightly. Her hips jerked up off the floor, a silent demand for more. Drake fingered her pussy and ass until she screamed. Her convulsions rocked him. When she finally calmed, he soothed her swollen lips with a cool cloth.

The pain in his cock grew unbearable, but he couldn't give in. He had to prove that this was all about her pleasure, not his. Someday he would tell her that watching her body tremble as he cleaned her, knowing it had nothing to do with fear, pleased him more than he thought possible.

Brushing his knuckles down her pink lips, he watched her wriggle her hips. "Still greedy, I see."

She sat up and scowled at him. "You are so going to jail for this."

Helping her to her feet, he leaned over and kissed each nipple then straightened and grinned. "I'm sure the cops will understand that you didn't mean a full week when you agreed to be my sex slave but if they don't, you can explain. And you can explain why you accepted my collar." He pulled the cat's eye green tourmaline choker out of his pocket. "Turn around. It's time I took my slave home."

She reached out and touched the teardrop diamond then with a gut-wrenching sob, ran past him out of the bathroom.

* * * * *

"Hit me."

Clutching the blanket wrapped around her shoulders, Madison spun around at the sound of Drake's voice. He stood naked in the doorway to her bedroom, the ends of her choker hanging from his clenched fist. Tears tracked down his cheeks, dripped from his jaw. The rage and torment she caused bled from his eyes. Her throat closed.

"Don't," she whispered then jumped back when he approached.

"Here," he held out a knife and stalked her until the backs of her knees hit the mattress. "Shove this in my chest. If killing me will snap you out of this, then do it. Do it because I can't take this anymore, Madison. Tell me what will work. I'll do anything."

"Drake, please, don't do this." She stared down at the knife rather than look into those eyes again.

"Look at me, Goddammit!"

His voice shook with rage, but she just couldn't. "I'm fucked up, Drake. He broke something in me, and I don't know how to fix it."

"Drop that blanket and turn around. I want to look at what that bastard did to your back. Now slave!" His voice cracked.

She stole a peek at his tormented expression through her lashes then spun around. What had she done? Taking a deep breath, she released her hold on the blanket and cringed as it pooled at her feet.

"Oh, dear God, Madi—" His sob ripped through her.

She could almost feel his gaze rake over the pink stripes of various shades crisscrossing her back and buttocks. Each told a tale. Each revealed the fury in the man and the weapon he wielded. She wondered if Drake recognized the signatures left by the cane, bullwhip and chain flogger. If his mind would absorb how many times Andre struck her, how he continued long after she felt her own blood drip down her back.

Another strangled sob met her ears.

"Don't you pity me, Drake Williams. Don't you dare pity me."

She jumped when Drake let out a roar behind her. When she turned, his fingers caught her chin and forced her to look into a face that held no pity, only fury.

He grabbed her hand. "Punch me. Punch me hard and tell me how I failed you. Do it!"

Madison remembered that Drake felt he'd failed his sister in his youth. She cupped his cheek. "You didn't fail me, Drake."

"He manacled you, didn't he?"

When she didn't answer, couldn't answer, he held her hand in a fist and slammed it into his chest. "What did he do, Madison? What did he use first? The cane? The bullwhip?" His face crumpled. "The chain flogger?"

The door she had slammed shut on those memories creaked open and let out the sharp snap of that first strike. Madison flinched. "Why are you doing this to me?"

Drake's hand shook then slammed her fist into his chest again with so much force her fingers hurt. "Where'd he hit you first, Madison?"

"I don't know! You're hurting my hand, Drake. I just got the casts off."

"That was a month ago, Madison. A month! Now it's time to get whatever you've wrapped yourself in off."

Grabbing her, he shoved her fist into his chest again. "Think. That first one. Think or I'll put you over my lap and remind you."

"I can't! I won't!" She punched him and struggled to break free, but he wouldn't let go. Memories crashed down upon her head, rage churned in her stomach.

"Tell me! Where'd he hit you?" He grabbed her shoulders and forced her to sit on the bed.

She wrenched free. "You want to know what your poor little abused friend did first? He lit a cigarette, Drake. And while he burned your initial into me—yours!—he called me Drake's bitch in heat and Drake's pain slut and Drake's whore who'd spread her legs for any stranger. He burned those names into my soul!"

"No, Madison. You don't believe that."

"And then, when he was all done, he told me what he'd burnt into me. *Your* brand. So no man would ever touch Drake's whore again." Her voice shook with anger. "My Master's mark."

Drake dropped to his knees and buried his face in her lap.

His breath warmed her as his muffled voice broke her heart. "I'm so sorry, Madison. I should have protected you from him. Come back to me, Madison. I can't make it without you." He rubbed his damp cheek against her skin. "Give me another chance to prove I can protect you."

The setting sun peeked through the alley of the buildings across the street. She stared into the blinding light and felt it wash over her as she sank her hands into Drake's thick hair. A horn blared outside. Drake's fingers dug into her thighs.

Closing her eyes, she revisited that night. The pain, the humiliation. Her triumph over a man who had never let *his* wounds heal.

She slid off the bed and gathered Drake in her arms. Kissing away the tears that somehow touched the woman she had lost that night, she started to laugh. "If you want some wimp who needs protection, you're with the wrong woman."

Cupping her face in his hands, Drake gazed into her eyes.

"Are you listening, Master D? I got hurt because *I* screwed up, not you."

"I still should have stopped you. Or been there."

"You once told me I couldn't bring a man to his knees if I was in chains. Remember?"

While his eyes still replenished each tear that fell, he smirked. "I recall saying something like that."

"I killed a man while still shackled, Drake." She dragged in a deep breath and felt a rush of power remembering how she had taken Andre down. "I used the football trick you taught me and hit the bastard way below the belt, just like you told me to. So, in a way, you *were* there. In a way, you did save me."

His lips brushed hers, the briefest kiss. He sat back on his heels and pulled her hips toward him until she straddled his thighs. "Fine, she-cat, protect yourself. But if you need help, you come to me."

"So, you still want me, Master? Big, ugly 'D' and all?" She held his gaze as she rose up and positioned herself over his erect cock.

"I'll always want you, my sweet slave. Always." His eyes shone with such intense passion, she felt it melt the ice that had run through her veins these past months.

"This slave may buck a little at getting tied up." A shudder ran through her body as she lowered herself onto his cock. His heat burned her, branded her more than any scar ever could. "And it might take me a while...a long while to remember how good my Master made me feel when he punished me."

"It could take years of re-training," he whispered as he planted butterfly kisses on her cheeks. "But you will remember, slave." Her nose. "And one day." Her eyes. "You will beg for the sweet pain only I can offer."

He slid his hands under her butt and lifted. She cried out in abject need when she felt his hard cock slide out. As he carried her to the bed, she wriggled and struggled to take him back in, to fill the aching void he had left behind.

Drake laid her down on her bed and stared at her splayed legs. She watched him reach down, felt him graze her slick folds with his finger. Watched that finger slip between *his* lips. The sight of his eyes flaring and his cock jerking inflamed her.

When his body finally covered hers, she wriggled her hips until she felt the thick head of his cock nudge between her slick lips. She raised her hips in one swift motion and took him in.

The choker, warm where it had nestled in his hand, cold where it had draped free, meandered over her shoulder. "And you *will* remember not to take the pleasure of my cock without my permission."

He bumped his cock deeper, reminding her of her offense. His expression hardened. His rock hard body covered hers and pinned her to the bed.

"Hands over your head, slave."

The sudden change in his voice shocked her into complying before her mind could wrap around his intent. She gasped when she felt him imprison her wrists in one hand. Her throat closed. Her heart pounded.

"Drake, I…"

"Hush, my sweet slave. Trust me."

He worked quickly and efficiently, encircling then fastening the choker around her wrists, reminding her how easily Andre had imprisoned her.

Closing one hand over her wrists, Drake murmured, "Remember what's holding you, Madison. My collar. Your collar. Do not break it. Do you understand why you…"

Madison didn't hear the rest of his question over the roar of her blood pounding in her ears. The first few words told her all she needed to know. Feeling more vulnerable than she ever had before, she closed her throat on a scream.

The man she had brought to tears vanished. The Master who would always dwell in Drake reappeared. Realizing she had broken a cardinal rule, one that wrought severe punishment, she struggled for freedom. Drake's grip on her wrists tightened. The choker dug into her skin.

Words she had not spoken for months tumbled freely from her lips. "Yes, Master. Forgive me, Master."

He snagged her lower lip. Fire seared her veins, cold sweat drenched her body. The pressure of his teeth increased subtly. Tensing with fear and anticipation, she whimpered and sent a silent plea with her eyes.

While the fingers of his free hand caressed her neck and tears still shimmered over the midnight blue orbs holding her gaze, the determination in Drake's eyes denied her any mercy. When he released her lip, she sighed and watched as he trailed kisses down her neck and over the swells of her breast.

"You will remember everything, my sweet slave. Even your manners."

"Yes, Master," she breathed.

What she had done, taking his cock without his permission, taking before he could give, warranted a lashing. She had made that mistake once, and the punishment had been severe. So severe, she had nearly fainted from the orgasms it wrought. This punishment had not even hurt.

Remembering her lessons that a Master punishes to better his slave and the slave must always thank him for such a gift, she added, "Thank you, Master."

"That's my baby. But you speak too soon."

Wondering what he meant, she arched her back when moist heat enveloped her nipple then jerked when his teeth took painful possession. Although she had felt those teeth sink deeper countless times before and enjoyed the sweet pain, her cries rent the air. She tossed from side to side, trying to dislodge him, but he held on and his teeth clamped down even harder.

The scrape of his tongue over her tortured bud broke through the haze of pain. Pleasure joined hands with pain. Blessed molten heat seared her sex.

No longer struggling for freedom, she absorbed the exquisite, sweet punishment. Another sharp nip and the pressure of her choker cinching around her wrists when he tightened his grip reminded her of her place.

"Thank you, Master. Thank you."

He released her tender peak and slammed his cock into her as he kissed his way to her other breast. This time the pain sliced through her with delicious speed and hurtled her toward the crest of a climax. She needed no reminder. Only her Master's words could send her over it.

When his teeth scraped free, relief and Drake's husky voice soothed her. "One day, my sweet slave, you'll welcome the fire fanning out over your swollen lips as I whip that fine ass. You'll slip your hands into my manacles and take what you deserve."

She didn't realize he had released her wrists until she felt his hands cup her face. His mouth crushed hers in a ravenous kiss. He drove his tongue in and tasted every corner like a starved man. His every breath filled her lungs. She felt his fingertips trace where their lips met, felt his palms glide down her neck, over her shoulders, her breasts, hips then back up to hold her face to his.

Madison kissed him back, raising her head and meeting him with equal force.

The lingering sting of her nipples, the bruising power of each thrust of his hips and the relentless pressure of his lips crushing hers swamped her with his hunger, his need, his desperation to reclaim her. Tears flowed from her eyes down her temples. His dripped onto her face and slid between their lips.

The emotions encompassing them magnified every electric charge of pleasure, every precious shudder that ran from his body through hers.

Never had it felt like this. They were both so out of control, so animalistic yet intimate and tender.

When she thought she would disgrace herself and come without permission, he tore his mouth free and tilted her face up. His eyes warned her to hold on. She ground her teeth and met his gaze with fierce determination.

He rammed into her and stilled.

"Come for me, my love," he ordered, his voice filled with awe.

At his command, she shattered, fine crystal hitting a brick wall, the shards of her being showering her, shredding her control. Losing touch with everything but Drake falling apart with her, she absorbed his deafening roar, felt surge after surge of his burning seed flood her womb.

Tender kisses fluttering over her face greeted her return to reality. She felt Drake's hands unwind the choker from her wrists.

Her moisture seeped down her thigh but the lingering tingle around her wrists resurrected the memory of Andre's abuse, the memory that still lurked in the dark recesses of her mind.

"What if I can't get past the fear, Drake? What if I never wear your chains?" A sob tore through her throat at the thought of never again feeling their possessive tugs, of losing Drake. "You'll take another, more willing slave. I know you will."

"Never. You are the Master of my heart. No one but you, Madison" With the choker draped over his open palm, he gazed down at her with eyes that told more than words ever could. Still he said them. "I love you, Madison, with or without your chains. So? Do I get my sweet slave back? Forever?"

Tilting her head, she offered him her neck. Her heart. Her soul.

About the Author

୨୦

Multi-published author Doreen Orsini is highly acclaimed by reviewers and fans for suspense that captivates them from the first page until the last, for haunting descriptions that bring her books to life, and for intense, in-your-face erotic scenes that make readers do the "Orsini Cross Legs & Squeeze". Between books, she entertains the members of her Yahoo fan group with her comic, kinky "Breaking News" posts about Orsini Fans Gone Wild.

Determined to shock, awe, and bring teas to her reader' eyes, Doreen pens dark erotic contemporary and paranormal tales that break the traditional rules of romance. She writes constantly, losing herself in the worlds she creates and crying as she writes tragic scenes for the characters she sees as living, breathing people who eventually tell her where the story will lead and end.

When not writing or enjoying her time with her family, Doreen spends most of her time interacting and forming friendships with her readers.

Doreen welcomes comments from readers. You can find her website and email address on her author bio page at www.ellorascave.com.

Tell Us What You Think

We appreciate hearing reader opinions about our books. You can email us at Comments@EllorasCave.com.

Why an electronic book?

We live in the Information Age—an exciting time in the history of human civilization, in which technology rules supreme and continues to progress in leaps and bounds every minute of every day. For a multitude of reasons, more and more avid literary fans are opting to purchase e-books instead of paper books. The question from those not yet initiated into the world of electronic reading is simply: *Why?*

1. *Price.* An electronic title at Ellora's Cave Publishing and Cerridwen Press runs anywhere from 40% to 75% less than the cover price of the exact same title in paperback format. Why? Basic mathematics and cost. It is less expensive to publish an e-book (no paper and printing, no warehousing and shipping) than it is to publish a paperback, so the savings are passed along to the consumer.
2. *Space.* Running out of room in your house for your books? That is one worry you will never have with electronic books. For a low one-time cost, you can purchase a handheld device specifically designed for e-reading. Many e-readers have large, convenient screens for viewing. Better yet, hundreds of titles can be stored within your new library—on a single microchip. There are a variety of e-readers from different manufacturers. You can also read e-books on your PC or laptop computer. (Please note that Ellora's Cave does not endorse any specific brands.

You can check our websites at www.ellorascave.com or www.cerridwenpress.com for information we make available to new consumers.)

3. ***Mobility.*** Because your new e-library consists of only a microchip within a small, easily transportable e-reader, your entire cache of books can be taken with you wherever you go.

4. ***Personal Viewing Preferences.*** Are the words you are currently reading too small? Too large? Too… ANNOYING? Paperback books cannot be modified according to personal preferences, but e-books can.

5. ***Instant Gratification.*** Is it the middle of the night and all the bookstores near you are closed? Are you tired of waiting days, sometimes weeks, for bookstores to ship the novels you bought? Ellora's Cave Publishing sells instantaneous downloads twenty-four hours a day, seven days a week, every day of the year. Our webstore is never closed. Our e-book delivery system is 100% automated, meaning your order is filled as soon as you pay for it.

Those are a few of the top reasons why electronic books are replacing paperbacks for many avid readers.

As always, Ellora's Cave and Cerridwen Press welcome your questions and comments. We invite you to email us at Comments@ellorascave.com or write to us directly at Ellora's Cave Publishing Inc., 1056 Home Avenue, Akron, OH 44310-3502.

Cerridwen, the Celtic Goddess of wisdom, was the muse who brought inspiration to storytellers and those in the creative arts. Cerridwen Press encompasses the best and most innovative stories in all genres of today's fiction. Visit our site and discover the newest titles by talented authors who still get inspired - much like the ancient storytellers did, once upon a time.

Cerridwen Press
www.cerridwenpress.com

Discover for yourself why readers can't get enough of the multiple award-winning publisher Ellora's Cave.

Whether you prefer e-books or paperbacks, be sure to visit EC on the web at www.ellorascave.com

for an erotic reading experience that will leave you breathless.

CPSIA information can be obtained at www.ICGtesting.com
Printed in the USA
LVOW061935160413

329452LV00001B/203/P